Escape to the Little French Café

BOOKS BY KAREN CLARKE

Escape to the Little French Café

Karen Clarke

Bookouture

Published by Bookouture in 2019

An imprint of StoryFire Ltd.

Carmelite House
50 Victoria Embankment
London EC4Y 0DZ

www.bookouture.com

Copyright © Karen Clarke, 2019

ISBN: 978-1-78681-798-3
eBook ISBN: 978-1-78681-797-6

This book is a work of fiction. Names, characters, businesses,
organizations, places and events other than those clearly in the
public domain, are either the product of the author's imagination
or are used fictitiously. Any resemblance to actual persons, living or
dead, events or locales is entirely coincidental.

For my daughter Amy, with love

Chapter One

'What are you doing?'

'Nothing much.' Before I could slam my laptop shut, Charlie was at the table, looming over my shoulder.

'Swimming micro pigs?'

I reluctantly paused the YouTube clip I'd been watching. 'They're so cute,' I said. 'Look at their little trotters in the water!'

'You do know those piglets grow into enormous porkers that the owners don't want and abandon?'

'You're such a killjoy.'

'I suppose it's better than those pet adoption websites you keep looking at, even though you know you can't have a dog.'

I discreetly closed the page of pooches I'd been browsing earlier – why couldn't Dad be allergic to leaves or grass instead of animal fur? – and switched back to the document I was meant to be working on. 'I suppose I could write a feature about the abandoned pigs.'

'It's been done.' Charlie sat opposite, his grin as bright and sunny as the weather outside. 'How do you think I knew about their plight?'

'Because you're a know-all?'

'Unfair.' He flapped a hand in front of his eyes as if to quell tears, then rested his elbows on the table. 'If that were true, I'd know why you're still working for that boring paper instead of, say, *Paris Match.*'

'*Paris Match* is too much like *Hello!* magazine,' I argued, which wasn't really the point. 'It's not the right fit for me.' The truth was, when I'd started writing for *The Expats' Guide to Living and Working in France*, I hadn't envisaged I'd still be doing it a year later. Admittedly, my contribution had proved quite popular, once I'd started injecting some personality into my column (*From experience, driving at 130 mph on a French autoroute is going to get you in trouble. Remember, speed signs are in kilometres, not miles. And DON'T DRIVE ON THE LEFT!*) but my real dream was to work for a famous magazine, where I'd have my own desk, attend meetings and interview A-list stars – specifically *Magnifique*, the country's bestselling glossy, owned by editor-in-chief, Nicolas Juilliard, and published in several languages.

'Hey, I've got a good headline.' Charlie made popping motions with his fingers. '*Why I while away my days in Île de Ré's most popular café, by Natalie Bright.*'

'What's with the hands?'

'It's your name in lights.'

'That's only for Broadway stars.'

'You know what I mean.' Charlie grinned. 'Anyway, a feature like that could easily be made into a Broadway show.'

'A show about me escaping my father's mid-life crisis while pretending I'm not having a quarter-life one of my own?' I managed a chuckle. 'I don't think so, Charlie. Plus, I've written about your café enough already.'

'Not that we need the publicity,' he said, eyeing the bustling interior, and the tables outside on the pavement. It was true that the Café Belle Vie was busy all year round, partly due to its picturesque location, but mostly because of the warm welcome and homely atmosphere, and the delicious cakes and pastries baked by Charlie's mum, Dolly. I'd put on half a stone since arriving on the island and discovering the café, a five-minute walk away from where Dad lived.

'Shouldn't *you* be working?' I grumbled, peering at the counter, where Dolly was stacking a display of buttery croissants while glancing surreptitiously at us from beneath her neat, blonde fringe. 'She sent you over, didn't she?'

'I don't need an excuse to come and chat to my bestie.'

'Don't say bestie, you're not a fourteen-year-old girl.'

'OK, my *best friend*, then.'

Despite the buzz of chat and clatter of mismatched china, Dolly seemed to freeze, as if she'd overheard, even though we were four tables away. She couldn't understand why Charlie and I weren't a couple and was baffled as to why it was taking us so long to realise we were perfect for each other – like the plot of a Nicholas Sparks movie.

It was true that Charlie and I had clicked the day I entered the café and blearily requested caffeine and something sugary to eat. Seeming to read my mood, he'd instructed me to sit exactly where I was now ('It has the best view of the harbour') before bringing over a bowl-sized mug of milky coffee and the lightest, tastiest pair of *pains au chocolat* to ever grace my taste buds.

'How did you know I'd want two?' I'd asked, making light work of them while he sat opposite – exactly where he was now – watching with smiling eyes. It should have been creepy, but felt oddly natural, which I'd put down to him being a fellow Brit, but was actually to do with him being so at ease with himself.

'No one can just eat one,' he'd said, with great authority. 'And you looked like you hadn't had breakfast.'

It was true, I hadn't, and once introductions had been made, I'd found myself telling him about how I'd lost my job in London when

the magazine I'd worked for had folded, and that my long-term relationship had crumbled not long afterwards, so I'd decided to come to
Chamillon on the Île de Ré to live with my dad while I worked out
what to do next.

It turned out that Charlie and I had grown up not far from each
other in Buckinghamshire; that we both had birthdays in January (at
thirty-three, he was two years older) and parents who were no longer
together, and we'd come to France with broken hearts, looking for a
change – Charlie to help his mum run the café she'd bought six years
earlier, and me to… well, I was still figuring that out.

Since that day, we'd had many conversations at this table. We'd
played card games during Charlie's breaks (I told myself I was
entitled to a break even though I was barely working), had dinner at
each other's homes and had even travelled to England together the
previous Christmas to visit family and friends. I'd seen him sleeping,
purse-lipped and double-chinned; he'd seen me snotty with a cold. He
knew that Matt, my boyfriend of four years, had traded me in for an
ex-girlfriend he'd 'reconnected' with and was due to marry her, and I
knew that Charlie's long-term girlfriend Emma had cheated on him
with his cousin Ben, causing a family rift – though the relationship
hadn't lasted. But whatever mysterious alchemy made two people
fall in love, it hadn't happened for us. On paper, Charlie was perfect;
tall and broad-shouldered, with lively brown eyes and wavy, blond
hair just the right side of messy, and I apparently fitted his preferred
aesthetic: short and curvy, with naturally curly hair the colour of a
pint of bitter ('the reddish-brown type') and blue eyes that sometimes
looked grey. We enjoyed cycling along the many paths that connected
all ten villages and hamlets on the Île de Ré and knew each other's
deepest, darkest fears (Charlie: swallowing his own tongue, and being

swept away by a hurricane, me: being chased through a forest by a clown; falling out of an aeroplane; dying alone and being eaten by rats. 'At least if you're dead, you won't know you're being eaten by rats,' Charlie had reasoned.)

We'd tried a kiss once, last New Year's Eve, at my best friend Jools's party, which I'd dragged him to back home – to prove I actually *had* a friend – carried away by the countdown to midnight, too much alcohol and the snogging couples around us – but after a few open-eyed, close-lipped seconds (I was drunkenly aware it should have been the other way round) we'd sprung apart, struck by the wrongness of it.

'No offence, but nothing's happening.' Charlie's hand had circled the air around his groin and he'd looked so baffled, I'd burst into helpless laughter.

'Me neither,' I replied and we'd hugged, relieved to have got it out of the way, before reverting to our usual state – much to Dolly's disappointment. I was certain she'd been expecting a ring on my finger by the time we returned to France.

She was currently pouring an espresso for Gérard, an elderly man with a shock of white hair, who came in every day with his stripy-sweater-wearing Scottie dog, Hamish. Gérard had been married to a Scotswoman, hence the breed of dog and Scottish name, and his eyes lit up whenever Dolly stopped to chat with him.

The locals were treated like extended family at the Café Belle Vie, and for the last three years, Dolly had opened on Christmas Day and cooked enough food for anyone who wanted to drop by, which had inspired me to write a column for *Expats* about the importance of community spaces for bringing people together and helping to alleviate loneliness.

Charlie was trying to peer at my screen while I resisted the urge to pick Hamish up and run away with him. Sometimes, he came over and lay by my feet while I was pretending to work, and I pretended he was mine. 'What are you writing?'

'I was trying to think of something interesting for this week's column for *Expats* but, honestly? Writing about French tax laws isn't exactly firing my creative juices.'

'Let's have a look.' He gave me a supportive smile, which I appreciated, considering he must be fed up of hearing me moaning. If it wasn't my dad's current dating disasters, it was my stalled career, or the fact that my skin wouldn't tan. He swivelled my laptop around and narrowed his eyes at the screen. '*If you want to know the tax laws in France, why don't you Google it?*' He lifted his eyebrows. 'Really?'

'I agree it needs some work.'

'I thought you were still pitching ideas to *Magnifique*.' He said it with an exaggerated accent, though we both spoke passable French. I'd had a gift for it at school and would practise on holidays with my parents, while Charlie had picked up the language since moving to the island, nearly four years ago.

'I keep trying, but it's disheartening when Monsieur Juilliard rejects everything.'

'I don't know why, it's not as if you're not experienced,' Charlie said, loyally.

'Yes, but not at writing the sort of stuff he's interested in. He doesn't want to read about a woman who had an affair with the undertaker who buried her mother, and that they liked to do it in the morgue.'

Chatter, the magazine I'd worked for in London, had specialised in the kind of readers' true-life stories that were designed to mildly horrify. My job had involved interviewing said reader with a photographer in tow, then writing down and fleshing out the (often scanty) details. The story would then have to be verified and the 'other person' offered the chance to tell their side – which they usually declined. It hadn't exactly been thought-provoking, but I liked to think I'd handled the stories sensitively. Jackie, my editor, had liked me and would sometimes let me write a piece about the latest talking points making (minor) news – *Should toddlers be allowed a mobile phone?* or *Why are so many young women opting for Botox?*

The trouble was, more people were getting their gossip and news online and sales of weekly magazines had drastically dropped, so it wasn't exactly a shock when *Chatter* finally went under. Subsequent attempts to find work in an overcrowded yet diminishing market had failed and I was far from ready to retire and write my memoirs – unlike my dad, who was making notes for a book about his time in the police force called *It's Not Like CSI!*, which I'd rashly promised to help find a publisher for.

'He didn't like your idea of interviewing stars alongside their closest friend or a family member for a more honest portrayal?' said Charlie, referring to my latest proposal for *Magnifique*.

I shook my head. 'Even when I explained it wouldn't be like the writing I've done in the past. No *my boyfriend asked me to move in with him and his wife*, or *my dog was possessed, so we had him exorcised.*'

Charlie smirked. 'They took him for a walk?'

'You know what I meant.'

'Did you make that last one up?'

'No! The owner really believed her Labradoodle was inhabited by an evil spirit. She showed us before-and-after videos and I had to admit, he *did* seem like a different dog.'

Charlie shook his head in mock despair. 'Well, I can see why Nicolas Juilliard wouldn't want his upmarket magazine sullied by tales like that.'

'I'm not offering tales like that, that's the point, but he won't even give me a chance.' I peered hopefully into my empty mug, as if it might have magically refilled itself. 'And why would he, when he has Fleur Dupont writing all the best stuff?'

'Ah, the gorgeous Fleur.' Charlie pressed a hand to his heart, as if he knew her well, though all he'd seen were the photos I'd shown him online. She *was* stunning though, with smouldering eyes behind thick-rimmed glasses, full lips and sleek black hair. Since writing an award-winning interview with a famous but reclusive novelist, she'd appeared on television culture shows, and even been interviewed herself in *Grazia* and *Elle*. I deeply admired that she'd worked her way up from an unpaid internship to becoming Nicolas Juilliard's second-in-command with single-minded determination ('Yes, I have amazing talent, but so do lots of people. Persistence is key to success.') and was sure I could learn a lot from her, if I could only get my foot in the door.

'Maybe you need to set your sights a bit lower,' Charlie suggested, but it was an old conversation, and *Magnifique* was the only magazine worth writing for, in my opinion. With its mix of global news, politics, intelligent opinion pieces, star interviews and sprinkling of high-end fashion, it was bucking the trend and raking in good sales. The key factor (I'd done my research) was not making its content available online right away, as some of its competitors did, which removed the incentive to buy the magazine. 'You could try for an internship at the magazine.'

'I don't want to work for nothing, Charlie.'

'How about staying freelance? Surely there are more opportunities?'

'Too much competition, not paid enough, plus, I want a regular job in an actual office, with colleagues and a salary,' I said, stabbing the table with my finger to make my point.

'Or you could write a novel.'

But Charlie knew I wasn't interested in fiction. Even as a child, I used to 'interview' my parents and grandparents, my friends and teachers at school, painstakingly recording their answers in little notebooks. Later, I'd write down my thoughts and opinions about anything and everything – snippets I'd read or heard on the news, or the plight of old people in care after visiting my grandma in her nursing home and being shocked by how fast her mental health had declined. That piece had been published in our local paper and I'd caught the bug after that. Real life had proved more fascinating than anything I could make up, and somehow getting my thoughts down in words had helped make sense of it all. Although, it wasn't remotely helping with my current predicament. It wasn't so much that I *needed* a big salary, thanks to money from the sale of the house I'd shared with Matt sitting in my account – which was just as well, as my column didn't pay a lot – but I was desperate to move my writing up to the next level. The next few levels, actually. I wanted to have my own byline like Fleur Dupont. Then I'd know I'd made it. And maybe I would get my own place if I had regular money coming in. It wasn't much fun living with Dad in his current incarnation as a would-be Romeo.

As if on cue, my phone whistled, alerting me to a text.

'I expect that'll be Marty,' said Charlie, pushing his chair back as old Madame Bisset entered the café with a twinkle in her faded blue eyes. She lived in the village with her daughter and came in most days to show us the latest photos of Delphine, her spoilt and extremely fluffy Persian cat. 'Another dating emergency?'

It was. I groaned as I read Dad's message. *Think I've nailed my new image. What do you think?* With great reluctance, I opened the attached photo, my eyes widening so far they were in danger of popping out. 'It's definitely an emergency.' I flashed the picture at Charlie and watched him recoil.

'Christ.' His voice sounded strangulated. 'I think you'd better go.'

Chapter Two

Despite fleeing from the café, I found myself walking slowly back to the house, reluctant to face the vision of Dad now gracing the gallery of pictures on my phone, reflecting instead on how well I'd settled somewhere so different from where I'd been raised. It still made me smile, recalling the sense of excitement and new beginnings I'd felt on the drive from La Rochelle airport with Dad, across the curving two-mile bridge to the Île de Ré. I'd been lucky enough to spend several summers here growing up, thanks to a colleague of Dad's owning a property he'd rented out cheaply to family and friends. We'd never have afforded it otherwise. The island – situated on the south-west coast of France – had long been a go-to destination for rich Parisians and A-listers (we'd once spotted Audrey Tautou buying morning baguettes at the market) and we'd fallen in love with the island and its villages, with their narrow streets and cycle paths, pretty harbours and long, white sandy beaches. Now I was back, I couldn't imagine living anywhere else, though it was good to know I could visit Mum any time I wanted, at my childhood home in England.

As I entered the whitewashed house on the rue des Forages, the living room sprang warmly into focus. It wasn't so different to the one back home, perhaps due to a lack of imagination on Dad's part, with two deep armchairs in front of the fireplace and a sofa in soft blue fabric, lined with bouncy cushions. Deep shelves supported Dad's books – mostly Stephen King and tomes about World War II – as well as framed family photos, including one of me aged seven, dangling from the branch of an oak tree in our garden like a capuchin monkey. A collection of pens bequeathed by my grandfather were neatly arranged on the oak mantelpiece, above which hung Dad's favourite painting: a couple on the Orient Express, drinking champagne in a velvet-upholstered bar. He'd planned to take Mum to Verona on the replica train, and it made me sad to think this would never happen now.

I closed the door and turned at the sound of footsteps on the stairs, my mouth falling open at the sight that appeared in front of me. It was so much worse than the photo. 'Dad, what the... what are you *wearing*?'

He jumped the last two steps and did a slow twirl as I stared, torn between hiccupping laughter and waves of affectionate despair. 'What do you think?' he said, as I fought to keep a straight face. 'I've been looking for tips online. I hadn't realised my style was what they call "dad dressing".' He scraped quote marks with his fingertips. 'Thought it was time to ring the changes and see what happens.'

'But you *are* a dad.' I held melodramatic fingers to my forehead. 'Dads are *supposed* to dress like dads.'

'You have to admit, I've been stuck in a rut, style-wise.' He nodded to where his usual 'Dad' attire of short-sleeved shirt, blue jeans and leather jacket was strewn across the sofa, though I was touched to see his black boots – similar to the ones he'd worn in the police force – stood neatly side by side, the leather gleaming softly. Retired five years, he still hadn't lost the habit of polishing his outdoor footwear. 'I thought I'd go for a younger vibe,' he said.

I frowned. Dad had never said 'vibe' before. Or taken much notice of what he was wearing, beyond asking if I thought he looked presentable before setting forth on another of his doomed dates. 'Is… is this why you've trimmed your beard?' I decided to focus on the least shocking part of his appearance.

'Do you like it?' He fondled the layer of grey-speckled bristle on his chin, which on its own was an improvement on his previous untamed fuzz. 'I found a blog that gives style advice,' he said. 'The look I'm going for is: beard, quiff, slogan T-shirt, statement jacket and designer trainers.' He was clearly quoting whichever terrible style blog he'd stumbled across.

'And did this advice include *dyeing* your, er, quiff?'

'Well, not specifically.' Looking a little uncertain, he gingerly fingered the mud-coloured pelt on his head. Instead of sweeping back from his forehead as usual, his hair was gelled to a swirly heap at the front, horribly reminiscent of the poo emoji on my phone. 'I thought it added a youthful touch, but I've left my beard grey so it doesn't look as if I'm trying too hard.'

'R-i-i-i-ight,' I said, edging further into the room, half-wishing I'd stayed in the café so I didn't have to deal with whatever was happening. 'But your grey hair suited you, Dad. It was quite, you know, distinguished.' I plundered my brain, searching for the right words. 'That shade of brown looks a tiny bit harsh, even with your tan.'

'It'll wash out, it's not permanent.' *Thank God.* 'I just thought I'd be adventurous and give it a go.' He struck a pose as he flapped the edges of a silky gold bomber jacket lavishly embroidered with peacocks that Mum would have loved. It was closer to her size too, straining around Dad's arms, and I wondered what she would say if she could see him now. Probably, *Are you going to a fancy-dress party?* 'What do you think of the T-shirt?'

Blinking, I dragged my gaze away from the beady-eyed birds. 'It's very *pink*,' I said, though I was more perturbed by the words emblazoned across the front: *Lady wanted enquire within.* 'Do you think that's the right message to be putting out?' I placed my laptop bag on the dining table, noticing that its surface was cluttered with crumpled packages from various clothing outlets. He'd obviously had an online shopping spree – and possibly some sort of breakdown.

'It's vintage,' Dad said, as if that excused the slogan. 'And, let's face it, I'm doing all this to attract a lady, so the message couldn't be better.'

'Oh, *Dad.*' My gaze dropped lower, to a pair of indecently tight leather trousers. I desperately hoped he hadn't stepped outside the house in them.

'They're really comfy,' he said, doing a jig to demonstrate ease of movement.

My vision dissolved. 'I don't think the ladies want to see the outline of your, er…' Unable to conjure a suitable word I let the sentence die, spotting the leopard-print trainers encasing his feet.

'They're designer.' He hoisted a foot in the air, as if a closer look might convince me he hadn't taken leave of his senses. 'Apparently, that rapper wore them, the one married to the singer with lots of hair.'

'Beyoncé?'

'Maybe,' he said, vaguely. Dad's musical tastes were firmly stuck in the seventies – The Clash and Roxy Music were particular favourites, and he had a soft spot for Cher. *Particularly that song where she's on a battleship in her stockings*, I'd overheard him say to Uncle Steven one Christmas, and they'd fallen into a brief but reverent silence.

'But, Dad, you always said people should only wear trainers if they're going running.'

'Don't you like them?' He stood, hands on hips, looking like an ageing hip-hop singer as he studied his feet. 'They feel a bit tight, mind you.'

My diplomacy skills were fading fast. 'Is that a friendship bracelet?'

'This?' He admired his wrist, which was bound by a braided leather strap. 'Do you think it's a bit much?'

Where to begin? 'At least you're not wearing a back-to-front base-ball—' I stopped, noticing a distinctive shape poking from under one of the discarded packages. 'Really, Dad? You've bought a *baseball* cap?'

'Actually, they're called snapbacks.' He snatched up the hat and squashed it on his head, but his quiff was too big and the peak reared up at the front. 'I thought I'd get plain navy, so it looks smart.' He tried to jam it down. 'And I'd never wear it the wrong way round, it would look ridiculous.'

My throat tightened at the sight of him in his… *get-up* was the only word I could muster. 'You look like a security guard who's lost his uniform and raided a teenager's wardrobe in the dark.' I decided it was best to be honest, the way Dad preferred. There was no way I could allow my father – a former, highly respected police officer – to go anywhere near the public dressed like this. 'I'm sorry, Dad, but it's just not you.'

'That's the whole point, Natalie.' He yanked the hat off and his quiff sprang back to life. 'I'm not getting anywhere being myself.'

'You mean with the ladies?'

'Of *course* I mean with the ladies.'

I wanted to say it had nothing to do with his clothes and everything to do with the type of ladies he was targeting – the sort who were wrong for him. Too young, too old… too French, in most cases. Dad still hadn't got to grips with the language and could barely ask for directions, never mind hold a fluent conversation with someone who didn't speak English.

'You have looked in the mirror?' I said, instead.

'Obviously.' He jettisoned the hat onto the table and removed his jacket with a dejected shrug. 'I did wonder whether I looked like a bit of a clown,' he said. 'But the blog's a good one, Natalie. It's won an award, so I assumed the chap who wrote it knew what he was on about.'

'Which blog?' I crossed to his laptop, discarded on the sofa on top of his jeans.

'He used to be a style editor for that *HQ* magazine.'

'It's *GQ*, Dad.' I looked at him as I cleared a space and sat down. 'Are you sure?'

'See for yourself.'

As he leant down to shake the laptop from its slumber, I caught of a whiff of aftershave strong enough to repel an army of wasps. 'Christ, what's that smell?'

'It's called Purple Seduction.' Dad straightened, rubbing his neck self-consciously. 'It's a signature scent, whatever that is,' he said. 'It made me sneeze twelve times in a row.'

Laughter rose, even as my eyes watered. 'Surely that was a sign you shouldn't be wearing it,' I said. 'Honestly, Dad, what are you like?' I scanned the article as he eased himself beside me, leather trousers creaking.

I stifled a giggle as I read the first two paragraphs.

'What's so funny?' Dad craned his neck.

'You've got it the opposite way round.' I jabbed the screen. 'You've read it wrong, see? This is how *not* to dress if you're over a certain age and want to look cool.' It actually said *how not to look like a twat over fifty*, but I couldn't bring myself to say it out loud.

'*What?*' Dad grabbed his reading glasses off the side-table and leaned over to read, while I tried not to choke on laughter and Purple Seduction.

'These are the tips you *should* have been reading, look.' I scrolled down and indicated a bullet-pointed list of sensible outfits, alongside a photo of a handsome, fifty-something man, wearing black jeans and a plain white T-shirt under a leather jacket. 'This is pretty much what you already wear,' I said. 'He's even got grey hair, like you.' I gave Dad's collapsing quiff a sideways look. 'I mean, maybe your jeans could be darker, and you could use a few new shirts, but otherwise you look fine as you are.'

'God, I'm such an idiot.' He sat back with an air of defeat and I tried to concentrate on his face, with its familiar laughter lines around twinkling, kind blue eyes, and not the unnatural-looking thatch on top of his head. It had never been that shade, even before he'd gone grey. It had been the same reddish-brown as mine, and pretty much the same style when he was younger, but not as curly. Mum used to say she'd envied his hair, as hers was thin and mousey if she didn't colour it (usually blonde, though once she'd tried to dye it black but it went patchy and looked like Alsatian fur).

'You're not an idiot.' I shut the laptop and patted his knee, relieved there was a simple explanation for his 'new' look. 'You're just trying a bit too hard.'

'But maybe some women go for this look.' As he tugged at the hem of his T-shirt the zip of his leather trousers flew apart and he yanked a cushion over to protect his modesty. 'I bet Mick Jagger doesn't have this problem,' he muttered.

'That's because he's Mick Jagger.' I slipped my cardigan off. Bright sunshine flowed through the windows, warming the cream stone walls and parquet floor; a reminder that summer wasn't far away. 'Most women would run a mile if you turned up looking like that.'

He huffed out a dejected sigh, and not for the first time I tried to reconcile this version of Marty Bright with the one who'd been in the police force for thirty years, dealing with things most people would never have to, and the father who'd guided me through childhood with gentle encouragement. *Unflappable* was the word most often used to describe my dad, whether at work or at home. He'd barely even batted an eyelid when Mum suggested they should separate three years ago, agreeing with her that it was time they had a fresh start.

It had been on the cards for a while. With Dad working crazy hours over the years, it hadn't come as a massive surprise that my parents had drifted apart and had little in common but me once he'd retired. Mum had become increasingly wrapped up in fundraising for the charity shop she managed, while Dad enjoyed long fishing trips with his police buddies at weekends. Even so, I'd cried for an alarmingly long time when they finally broke the news and was still convinced they should have fought harder to save their long, and mostly happy relationship, instead of being so... *polite* about it. No prolonged shouting matches, brittle silences, or laying the blame at each other's feet – more a sad acceptance by both parties; though *I'd* felt Mum's disappointment that Dad didn't object, even if he hadn't. He'd simply moved in with Uncle Steven for a while, before dipping into his pension fund to buy the house on Île de Ré, which he'd snapped up for a bargain price as the owner had wanted a quick sale. He'd always planned to retire here, based on those happy holiday memories of us at Saint-Clément-des-Baleines, where Mum and I used to climb the two hundred and fifty-seven steps in the lighthouse to look at the view, while Dad fished for lobster in the bay. Unfortunately, Mum had never been keen on his retirement plan ('Holidays and home aren't the same, Marty.') which, in my eyes, had been the leading cause of them going their separate ways. Dad hadn't even tried to persuade her, telling me she 'had every right to live her life in whatever way made her happy'. (Mum had said the exact same thing about Dad.)

Used to dealing with people from all walks of life, he'd settled in well, claiming to enjoy the quiet pace of the island outside the holiday season. I'd worried that he'd miss his job and his colleagues, but the one time I'd visited before moving over, he'd had visitors, and I'd had to stay at the little guest-house next door. His ex-colleagues and friends were delighted to have somewhere to escape to, and although Dad loved hearing news from home, I believed him when he said he didn't miss his job. Most officers who'd been in the force as long as Dad were burnt out by the age of fifty. They'd seen too much, been swamped by paperwork and hampered by government cutbacks.

'I got out at the right time,' he was fond of saying, and I knew he meant it. He seemed content to fill his days fishing, reading, socialising at the local bar, and making notes for his book about the day-to-day reality of front-line policing in Britain.

It was only when Mum started seeing a life coach called Gareth late last year and 'making over' her life – which Dad took to mean dating again – that he'd announced, shiny-eyed over dinner one night, that he thought he might be ready for a new relationship.

My insides had gripped at the thought. It wasn't that I thought either of my parents should be single for the rest of their lives, but they hadn't seemed interested in meeting anyone new. They hadn't even got divorced, and still wore their wedding rings ('because it was easier') but I supposed that wouldn't be the case for very much longer.

Unfortunately, Dad was so far out of his comfort zone, he was on another planet. Having not dated for decades, he hadn't a clue how to go about it – until I'd jokingly mentioned he should sign up to a dating website. He'd barely been off it since, like a boy in a sweetshop, unable to believe he had access to all the goodies on offer, even if he didn't know what to do with them. Also – though I only acknowledged it to myself in the dead of night – his enthusiasm for putting himself out there had brought home my own determinedly single status since splitting from Matt, and how little desire I had to do anything about it.

'What about all this stuff?' Dad gave his trousers a disconsolate prod. 'I paid for first-class delivery.'

'Send it all back.' I indicated the heaps of packaging. 'I'll help, if you like.'

'Listen, I'm sorry I dragged you away from your work.' Rising, he swiped up his jeans and looked at them fondly. 'Have you had any luck with that magazine?'

'Not yet,' I said lightly, trying to give the impression that it was only a matter of time before Nicolas Juilliard begged me to write something for *Magnifique*. 'I did my piece for *Expats* though,' I fibbed. 'And a magazine in the UK is doing a series about women who've uprooted to a different country, so I've put something together for that.' I didn't mention they'd already turned me down, saying, '*We're looking for somewhere more exotic or unusual, necessitating a total culture change – like giving it all up to marry an African tribesman!*'

Crossing the channel to live with my dad was hardly exotic or unusual – though the culture change was real. I'd never eaten so many *pains au chocolat* in my life.

'Anything else?'

How to explain that I mostly read other people's writing online, retweeting posts by new writers that caught my eye, occasionally linking in editors I thought might be interested, and that I sometimes updated my blog 'Notes from a French Island' for my own amusement. 'Um, not much,' I said.

'Why don't you interview that famous actor?' Dad picked up his comb and bent his knees to check his reflection in the mirror by the door. 'He's going to be shooting scenes from his new movie around here.'

'Actor?'

'Marie, next door, she was telling me about it earlier,' he said. 'You know her friend Jeanne is a cleaner at L'Hôtel des Toiras in Saint-Martin? Apparently, the whole place has been booked for a week by the film crew and leading actors.'

'You know, you really should ask Marie out on a date,' I said, momentarily distracted. Marie Girard was the owner of the guest-house next door; a petite, softly-spoken woman, around the same age as Dad. She'd clearly taken a shine to her kind-eyed English neighbour, but Dad had once seen her knitting, and decided she wasn't 'lively' enough for him – despite me explaining that knitting was the new yoga. (He'd declared he wasn't a fan of that either, since Mum had taken it up.) 'There's definitely more to Marie than a pair of knitting needles,' I said. 'I'm sure she's got loads of stories to tell.'

'Yes, like the one about the famous actor staying on the island.' He spoke with rare impatience, wincing as he attempted to tug the comb through his quiff. 'You've met him before, so you might get first refusal for that interview.'

The bomber jacket I'd just picked up slipped through my fingers to the floor. 'I haven't met any famous actors,' I said. 'Not on a personal level, anyway.'

'You have met this one.' He caught my gaze in the mirror. 'It's Jay Merino.'

Chapter Three

I hurried back to talk to Charlie, slowing as I approached the café to appreciate the tall, whitewashed building, its wisteria-coloured shutters framing the upstairs windows, vines entwined around the wrought-iron balcony. On the bistro-style tables below, stripy red-and-white parasols offered shade from the sun, which glinted off the golden letters on the window, spelling out 'Café Belle Vie', the glass mirroring the glitter of the marina – as well as my rosy-cheeked, bright-eyed reflection.

Dolly was clearing a gingham-clothed table outside, despite Stefan, the young waiter, hovering nearby with a tray and a hopeful smile. Dolly was terrible at delegating, and almost had to be bribed to take a break. 'Can't keep away?' She smiled as I crossed the cobbled road, her acorn-brown eyes sparkling with pleasure. It was flattering to be greeted so effusively whenever I showed up, even though I was destined to disappoint her. 'He's out the back,' she said. 'You look like you've got good news.' Her eyes dipped to my stomach, as if I was about to announce I was pregnant with Charlie's baby.

'It's all the pastry I've been eating.' I smoothed a hand over my loose-fitting top. 'I really should cut back.'

'Rubbish.' She assessed me with obvious approval. 'Men prefer a well-upholstered woman, don't they, Frank?' She turned to a man at the next table, and he put down his coffee cup and held out a broad, tanned hand.

'I have eyes for no one but you, Dolly,' he said with an adoring smile.

She gave a satisfied chuckle and squeezed his fingers and I tried, for the umpteenth time, to picture the woman Charlie had told me used to work as a marketing manager for a tech company before his dad left, when she'd overhauled her life, buying the Café Belle Vie to indulge a love of baking inherited from her French grandmother. We'd wondered for a while whether it would be weird if Dolly and Dad got together, but then she'd fallen for Frank, a retired widower from England, who'd frequented the café on holiday the previous summer, and now rented a cottage in the village.

'But you are very beautiful,' he said to me, his Labrador-brown eyes barely leaving Dolly's.

'Bumps in all the right places,' she agreed, flapping Frank playfully with her cloth.

'I'll take that as a compliment,' I said, slipping past her with a smile and through the coffee-scented café, mouthing hello to the staff as I entered the busy kitchen, which smelt deliciously of almonds. My mouth watered, and I tried not to look at the tray of crisp but gooey *financiers* fresh from the oven as I stepped through the open door into a flower-filled courtyard. Charlie was standing in a pool of sunlight, gripping a coffee cup and chatting to Giselle, the café's newest recruit. A tall, whippet-thin blonde, she was everything I wasn't – including, ten years younger and in the grip of a serious crush. As usual, Charlie seemed oblivious to her subtle flirting; the way her fingers brushed his arm as she spoke, and how she watched intently as he drank from his cup, her smoke-grey eyes never leaving his face. I caught the tail end of a joke about a spaceman and a monkey, and Giselle gave a burst of laughter and lightly slapped his hand. '*Tu es tellement drôle*, Charlie,' she said. 'He eez funny,' she translated for me, though I'd understood perfectly well.

'Hilarious,' I agreed, as Charlie spun round, his eyes crinkling into a smile.

'Hey, how did it go with Marty?' He dug his free hand in his jeans pocket, forcing Giselle's fingers to fall from his arm. 'Tell me he's not intending to go out in those leather trousers, Natalie, you could see the outline of his—'

'He's not,' I said quickly, flashing a look at Giselle's frozen expression. '*Bonjour*,' I offered in a friendly fashion. Her grasp of English was poor, and I could tell she didn't like it when Charlie and I lapsed into our native tongue. It was clear, to me at least, that I represented some sort of threat, and I hadn't the heart to tell her – even if my language skills had been up to the complexities – that Charlie wasn't the settling down type and the best she could hope for was a fling. Although, maybe that was all she wanted. Giselle had been clear from the start about her life goal, which was to eventually move to Paris and become an actress – as if it was that simple. 'Can I have a word?' I said to Charlie, when Giselle didn't respond.

'You can have as many as you want.'

He didn't seem to hear Giselle's soft tut, or notice the sweeping stare she gave me, which openly mocked my sandals, cropped jeans and swishy, owl-patterned top, which were no match for her casual elegance. She oozed style, in plain black skinny trousers that emphasised her long legs, and a simple white T-shirt that hugged her tiny breasts. Even her bistro apron looked chic, double-tied around her narrow waist, and she moved like a ballerina in plain black pumps.

'In private,' I said, when she showed no signs of moving. '*En privé, s'il vous plaît.*'

Removing her gaze, she threw Charlie a regretful smile and stalked back into the café with a toss of her long, sleek ponytail, and a seductive sway of her (non-existent) hips.

'OK, what really happened?' Charlie placed his empty cup on the picnic-style table we sat around during the warm evenings last summer, when Dolly had kept the café open to cook suppers for tourists, and Frank had insisted on helping with the washing-up as they got to know each other better. 'Was that a wig your dad was wearing in his selfie?' He indicated one of the benches, but I was too fired up to sit down.

'Never mind that,' I said. 'You'll never guess who's staying on the island.'

'Paddington Bear?'

I tutted. 'He's not real.'

Charlie gave a theatrical gasp and quivered his chin. 'How could you be so cruel?'

'Charlie!' I was too excited to laugh. 'I'm being serious.'

Crossing his arms, he assumed the expression of a mathematician. 'Your mother?'

'I've already told you, she's at a yoga retreat in Yorkshire.' Mum's programme of self-improvement since meeting Gareth included going long-distance running with a couple of friends ('It's wonderful, Natalie, we burn up so many calories, we've started going for pizza and ice cream afterwards.') and he'd convinced her that learning yogic breathing would help her run a marathon, as well as improving her flexibility.

'Is this person male or female?'

'Male.'

Charlie narrowed his eyes. 'It's not your ex?'

Now it was my turn to gasp. 'I'd hardly be excited if *he* turned up,' I said. 'And why would he, now he's about to get married?' For once, the thought of Matt's upcoming nuptials barely made a ripple on my subconscious. Living across the Channel had more than its share of advantages, and knowing I'd never run into him was one of them.

'Good point.' Charlie tilted his head, squinting as the sun lanced into his eyes. 'You do look excited,' he acknowledged. 'Is it someone famous?'

My stomach gave an odd little lurch. 'Yes.'

'Wow.' His brow creased. 'Well, it can't be a politician,' he said. 'Or Donald Trump.'

'Ha, ha,' I pretend-laughed, holding my ribs. 'He's an actor.'

'Donald Trump?'

'Charlie!'

'You mean, there's a famous actor on the island?' He looked around, as if one might be about to crash through the little red gate set into the wall surrounding the courtyard. 'Have I seen anything he's been in?'

'Yep.' I nodded slowly, waiting for the penny to drop.

'Wait, I've got it.' He waggled a finger, eyes sparking with enthusiasm as he caught my mood. 'Is it Jason Bourne?'

'For God's sake, Charlie!'

'Sorry, I meant the actor who plays him.'

'No, it's not Matt Damon.' Charlie's mouth turned down. 'Great.' I chucked my bag on the table. 'Now you're going to be disappointed whatever I say.'

'I won't be, I promise.' He made a show of recovering, squaring his shoulders and rubbing his hands together. 'Only make it quick, my lunch break's almost over.'

I pressed my lips together, then burst out, 'It's Jay Merino!'

Charlie looked at me as though I'd turned into a unicorn. 'Jay Merino?' His mouth dropped open. 'You mean the one who plays Max Weaver in *Maximum Force*?'

'Unless you know any other actors called Jay Merino?' I felt as if I'd said Jay Merino too many times.

Charlie shook his head. 'I love those terrible films,' he said, sounding slightly dazed – just as Dad had, after he'd dropped his bombshell and I'd grabbed my bag and said I had to go.

'Go where?' he'd called, his hair moving in different directions as he followed me to the door. 'Can I at least keep the underpants?' he'd shouted, as I raced out of the house. 'They're David Beckham's and cost a bloody fortune.'

'I heard they'd started shooting the third film somewhere in Europe.' Charlie's eyes were twice their usual size. 'Max is finally going to find the gang who killed his wife and son.'

'I'm guessing that's why they're here,' I said. 'He's going to be doing some scenes around the island. Marie next door told Dad about it.'

'Could she be wrong?'

'I don't think so.' I rolled up the sleeves of my top. The courtyard was a sun trap, and I was in danger of overheating. 'It's too random for her to have misunderstood, and Marie's friend is a cleaner at the hotel where the crew are staying.'

'But surely we'd have heard rumours?'

'Not necessarily, if they're keeping things under wraps,' I said. 'Jay Merino hates publicity. He's practically reclusive when he's not filming.' Saying his name was acting like a tripwire on my heart, which was beating much faster than it normally did when I was standing still.

'Hang on a minute.' Charlie stiffened. I could practically see the cogs turning, dredging up a conversation we'd had on Dad's sofa, over a year ago, in front of *Maximum Force 1: The Beginning*, which had just come onto Netflix. 'Isn't Jay Merino your "before they were famous"?'

He snapped his fingers, eyes popping wide again. 'You bloody well know him!'

I nodded as though my head was on a spring. 'Well remembered, Charlie Croft.'

'He lived on the rough estate near where you lived.'

'That's where he was born, he didn't live there,' I corrected, remembering the blue wash of police lights outside the rundown apartment blocks and houses, visible from my bedroom window.

'Didn't his brother crash your best friend Gemma's brother's eighteenth birthday party with some mates and try to sell them drugs?'

'He did.'

'And your friend called the police and your dad turned up?'

'Not just my dad, but yes.' I was impressed by his powers of recall. 'I thought you were nodding off when I told you all this.'

'Of course I wasn't.' Charlie sounded sheepish. 'I was just jealous that your claim to fame was so much better than mine.'

'What, that your friend's dad once bought Paul McCartney's mum a beer?'

He grimaced. 'Yes, but I did pull up at some traffic lights next to Mr Bean.'

'You mean Rowan Atkinson?'

'*Any*way,' said Charlie. 'Wasn't Max Weaver's mum an alcoholic?'

'Jay Merino,' I amended. 'You definitely had your eyes shut when I told you that.'

'I can watch TV through my eyelids.' he said. 'It's my special skill.'

'I can't believe you've remembered all this.'

'I hadn't until just now,' he said, tapping his temple. 'It's all flooding back.'

It was flooding back to me too – how Jay's brother and his mates had fled before the police turned up, and I'd escaped outside to find Jay on a swing-set at the bottom of Gemma's garden, the tip of a cigarette glowing orange in the gathering darkness. I still wasn't sure what had made me sit on the swing beside him instead of running away. I knew my father wouldn't have approved for a start, and I already had an on-off boyfriend called Henry, who played the cello and wanted to join the Philharmonic Orchestra (he never did, as far as I knew).

Jay was a couple of years older than me, and despite his brooding air and unrefined accent he'd been polite and, for some reason – maybe because I was a stranger (and a girl) or it was late and getting dark, which made it easier to talk – we'd fallen into conversation. He'd told me about his broken family; his useless Italian dad, who'd walked out on him and his baby brother when he was three, and his mother who'd turned to drink, and how he'd tried to look after her, only for social services to get involved when she went out one weekend and left them alone in the house with no food. He and his brother had been in and out of foster care for years, but he was visiting his mother that weekend and had got roped into coming to the party with his brother, mostly to keep an eye on him as he was going off the rails – again.

'I can't wait to get away from 'ere,' he'd said, expertly blowing smoke rings in the air, tracing their progress with long-lashed eyes. 'I'm gonna make something of myself.'

'Good for you.' My prim and proper tone had brought a tingle of heat to my cheeks, and I'd hoped he couldn't tell. The sky had dipped from navy to black, the only light from the house behind us where heavy drum-and-bass music had resumed. 'I'm going to be a writer.'

I'd caught the flash of his eyes as he turned to study me. 'Novels?'

'Newspapers or magazines.'

'Like, reporting?'

I'd already decided I didn't want to be a hard-hitting journalist – I didn't have the stomach for it. 'More like articles, I think, and I'd love to interview famous people one day.' I'd wished it hadn't sounded so childish. There was something about Jay that made me want to sound as grown-up and sure of myself as he did. 'Get to know the real them.'

He'd carried on looking at me – as though really seeing me – and the air around us had stilled. I'd thought how good-looking he'd be if he cut his long, unruly dark hair, got rid of his moustache and wore some nicer clothes, and wondered what I would do if he kissed me. 'Well, when I'm famous, you can interview me.'

'Promise?' I'd become unusually skittish, suddenly fixated on his lips.

'Promise.' As he tossed his cigarette onto the grass and ground out the butt with his boot, the swing twisted towards me. Our knees had brushed, and I'd felt a frisson of excitement. 'I reckon you'll be a natural,' he said, holding my gaze – almost as if he'd felt a frisson too. 'You're a good listener.'

I'd felt short of breath as we swung together in silence for a while, close enough that our knuckles gently grazed, and when he stood up, I'd got unsteadily to my feet and let him take my hand. His fingers had felt warm around mine, and when he dipped his head, I'd thought, *oh my God, he's actually going to kiss me* and I kissed him back, feeling as if my body had lost its bones. I hadn't even minded the tang of cigarettes, or his moustache, which had felt soft against my skin, but he'd pulled away too soon. Rubbing a hand round his jaw, he'd cast his eyes to the ground as I struggled to catch my breath and said gruffly, 'I shouldn't have done that, I'm sorry.'

Before I'd managed to stupidly squeak out, 'It's fine, don't worry,' he'd gone, the swing moving in his wake as though vacated by a ghost. I hadn't expected to see him again, but our encounter had felt somehow pivotal. I'd dreamed about him for the next two nights, and knew I couldn't keep seeing Henry, who still hadn't made up his mind whether he really wanted a girlfriend, and whose exploratory kissing I now realised did nothing for me. I'd cited a heavy workload as an excuse to break up for good, and found myself later defending Jay to Dad, when he'd warned me to stay away from the Merino brothers, relaying some of the conversation I'd had with him in Gemma's back garden. I'd replayed our encounter numerous times in my head, and even wrote an article about first kisses, which had been published in a magazine called *Young Woman*. But with nothing to sustain the fire he'd ignited, the flame had gradually flickered and died, and life had swept me along in its tide. I'd barely given Jay a thought for the next ten years, until his first film came out.

'Come on.' Charlie was sitting down now, and gestured for me to do the same. I didn't argue, the adrenaline that had powered me for the past half-hour subsiding. I'd never mentioned the kiss to Charlie, or anyone else for that matter – some hard-to-define instinct had held me back, even as I'd relayed to him how I'd met Jay Merino in my friend's back garden when I was seventeen. 'Let's have a drink,' he said as Giselle returned, her gaze bouncing between us.

'I thought your lunch break was over.'

'It's just been extended.' He grinned. 'Two coffees, please, Giselle.'

'*Bien sûr.*' She forced a smile that wouldn't have fooled anyone, apart from Charlie, and I almost felt sorry for her. It wasn't that he was insensitive to women's feelings, more that he refused to acknowledge their existence, especially if they were romantic. Unfortunately, his insouciance inspired determination, and Giselle was giving it her best shot. 'Tart?' she queried, eyes skimming my thighs – they looked bigger when I was sitting down – before flashing her white teeth at Charlie.

'Natalie's not a tart.' He winked at me. 'She's the classiest woman I know.'

Giselle's stare could have frozen the sun.

'Just coffee, thanks.'

'She's got it in for you,' said Charlie as we watched her flounce away, her hands clenched into fists.

'You know she fancies the pants off you.'

'She's friendly,' he said, with massive understatement.

'She's more than friendly, Charlie.'

'Can I help it if she can't resist my charms?' He made a seducer's face, quirking an eyebrow and making his eyes suggestive.

'You can tell her you don't like her that way.'

'And ruin her life?'

'Charlie!'

He inspected me closely and nodded. 'OK, I hear you. I promise I'll tell her I'm not looking for a girlfriend, but I can't be responsible for her actions, and I can't exactly stop talking to her altogether.'

'As long as it's talking, not flirting.'

'Sounds like a song title.'

'Charlie, I'm being serious,' I said. 'It's not fair to lead her on if you don't fancy her back. Plus, you're kind of her boss.

'I get it.' He muttered *spoilsport* under his breath. 'I'm kidding,' he said, when I opened my mouth to protest. 'Honestly, I do.' He propped his chin on his hand, eyes dancing. 'So… Jay Merino.'

'I know.' Excitement bounded back. 'Dad thinks I should interview him.' He'd clearly forgotten that long-ago warning – as had I, until now.

'I was going to suggest that myself,' said Charlie, leaning back and clasping his hands across his stomach. 'He's bound to be receptive if he knows you.'

'Not necessarily, and he doesn't *know* me.'

'Didn't he practically invite you to interview him once he became famous?'

Heat ran over my face. 'Yes, but remember I told you I tried, after he appeared in that breakthrough film about zombie gangsters, and got turned down.'

It had stung a little, at the time. My heart had leapt when his name cropped up in one of the tabloids in a feature about the boy with the troubled background making waves in Hollywood, and I'd realised it was *that* Jay Merino. (Not that there were many – I'd checked. There were three, and one of those was a leading brand of knitwear.)

Jackie, my editor at *Chatter*, had been thrilled (if sceptical) to learn of my tenuous connection with him, and keen to land an interview with the up-and-coming star, but he was already proving adept at avoiding the press and all attempts to contact him had been shot down in flames. He simply didn't 'do' interviews.

'We could run a piece anyway,' Jackie had pressed. 'You must know stuff about him.' But it would have felt seedy, somehow. His dad had already surfaced, talking about wanting to reconnect with his son, then it came out that Jay's brother was in prison and an ex-girlfriend sold a story, claiming Jay had dumped her when he started filming, and went on to describe how good he was in bed – 'he really knows how to pleasure a lady' – and when pictures emerged of him with a famous but troubled singer, his fate as a 'bad boy' was sealed. He'd never tried to dispute his reputation, and gradually stories had stopped appearing – and so had he, except on screen.

'It would be amazing to get an interview with him in *Magnifique*,' I murmured, jumping when Giselle returned with our coffee. Some of the liquid slopped out when she banged my cup down, but Charlie got a chocolate-topped *madeleine* with his espresso.

'He might be more approachable now his career is established.' Charlie pushed his plate across to me when Giselle had gone. 'You could get him to open up, tell his side of things and show he's human, instead of the scowling, monosyllabic Neanderthal the papers make him out to be.'

As Charlie gurned and swung his arms to demonstrate, something was stirring in my stomach. Probably the *madeleine* I'd just whipped off Charlie's plate and eaten in two swift bites. I imagined going to the hotel, Jay inviting me to his room – or perhaps for a meal in the restaurant – where he'd spill the beans about his rise to stardom over a glass or two of champagne. And then I imagined Nicolas Juilliard's face when I submitted my exclusive, sensitively written interview; how he'd beg me to come and work for him; how I'd suddenly be in demand. Other reclusive stars (I couldn't think of any offhand) would be lining up to talk to me. 'I'll only talk to Natalie Bright,' Kate Moss would say (Kate Moss was pretty reclusive). 'That piece she did with Jay Merino was just so... so *moving*.' Jackie, now working for bestselling *Gossip* in the UK, would be kicking herself for not taking me there with her – not that I'd have wanted to go. My friend Jools had worked there before joining *Chatter*, and had told me some terrible truths about working as a Z-list celebrity interviewer.

'Why don't you email Nicolas Juilliard again?' Charlie's voice jolted me out of my rapidly spiralling fantasy. 'Don't take no for an answer this time.'

'I'll do better than that.' Resolve flowed through me as I pushed back my chair and stood. 'I'm going to call him.'

Chapter Four

After promising Charlie I'd keep him updated, I managed to avoid bumping into Dolly by leaving through the courtyard gate and making my way down a narrow, winding path that led to the beach. Walking barefoot along the soft, pale sand to the gentle lapping of waves in the background, I worked up a pitch in my head I was certain Nicolas Juilliard wouldn't be able to resist, then rang his Paris office in a state of anticipation, only to be told by a bored-sounding assistant that Monsieur Juilliard was walking his dog.

From everything I'd read, I knew Nicolas had a French bulldog called Babette that he doted on, which I'd thought boded well for his character – he was reportedly close to his mother too (but not in a Norman Bates way) – until he'd started rejecting all my proposals. Normally, I'd send my ideas to a features editor, but Nicolas was known for being hands-on and welcomed direct submissions, claiming to have a psychic sense for a feature that would double the magazine's readership. It was no secret in the industry that Fleur Dupont wanted his job when he retired, and he'd openly laid down a challenge – bring him an exclusive that would triple circulation, and the job was hers. Maybe an exclusive with Jay Merino would bag me a job there too.

'Could you please ask him to call me?' I asked in my very best French. 'I have someone in mind for an interview that I think he'll want to hear about.'

'Who?'

Reverting to English I said, 'I'd rather not say at this stage.'

'Can't you put it in an email?'

'I'd prefer to speak to him in person.' I was attempting to create some intrigue, though I suspected she'd probably heard it all before.

'And you are…?'

When I said my name, I was certain I heard a sigh, and wondered for a horrible moment whether I might be the subject of office gossip.

Oh, it's that silly English woman who worked for that awful magazine in the UK, and now thinks she's good enough to write for Magnifique*!*

'You will ask him to call me, won't you?' I said, after reeling off my number and asking her to read it back, which she did in perfect English, as if to prove her grasp of language was way better than mine (which it was). 'I promise he won't regret it.'

'That's quite a promise, Miss Bright,' she said dryly. 'I'll be sure to convey the very grave importance of your message to Monsieur Juilliard.'

Definitely taking the mickey. 'Thank you,' I said, injecting a smile into my voice to show I wasn't offended. 'If he wants to check out my writing, I have a weekly column in *The Expats' Guide to Living and Working in France*.'

'I believe 'e is familiar with your work.'

'Really?'

'*Non.*'

Rude. 'The office is in La Rochelle,' I pressed on. 'The magazine is really popular.' Talk about sounding needy. 'He might even know the editor, Sandy Greenwood.'

'I'm sure 'e does, Miss Bright. All the magazine editors in France, they know each other very well.'

'Really?'

'*Non.*' She hung up.

I supposed it was unlikely. Sandy, who I'd met a couple of times at her home office, was a brisk, no-nonsense Liverpudlian with short, side-parted hair and a penchant for Hawaiian shirts, who'd moved to La Rochelle with her husband and toddler twins twenty years ago, and had started the paper to connect with other expats on the back of a former stint as editor at *The Sun* newspaper. *Expats* had grown to the point where everyone who'd ever migrated to France subscribed, but although she'd done a good job with keeping the website updated, she had little interest in any other form of social media, preferring the increasingly old-fashioned medium of print and paper. The idea that Sandy might move in the same circles as Nicolas Juilliard was almost laughable, but even so, it was rude of his assistant to hang up on me. I stuck my tongue out at my phone, which drew some funny looks from a couple on the cycling path by the beach.

As I slipped my feet back into my trainers and retraced my steps to the marina, I wondered whether my message would even get through. Maybe I should have been more specific, but I didn't want Fleur Dupont getting wind that Jay was on the island (if she didn't already know). Although he fiercely guarded his privacy, Fleur was notorious for drawing out the most reluctant of prey; some more infamous than famous. She'd actually coaxed a murder confession from a man who'd been freed from jail, a year after a well-known television documentary had 'proved' his innocence. It was surprising, giving her status, that she hadn't managed to interview Jay before. She must have tried. His films had grossed millions at the box office, and his air of mystery, coupled with the looks he'd grown into since our brief encounter, had made him number one on every journalist's wish list. So, as much as I admired Fleur's writing, if I wanted even half the career she had, I had to use whatever means were at my disposal to get there, which meant getting to Jay before she did.

As I reached la rue des Forages, I noticed Marie unloading groceries from the basket of her bike, her small frame almost buckling under the weight. Her face lit up as I approached, and I wondered afresh why Dad didn't ask her out. She must have been a beauty when she was younger and was still very attractive. There was barely any grey in her thick, dark hair, always styled in a neat chignon, and her soulful eyes were large and dark. It was a shame she looked sad when she wasn't smiling, but that could be her natural, resting expression. (Mine was anxious.) I'd often wondered about her past, but she didn't like to talk about it. I knew she'd been married and divorced, had never had children, and she'd been running her home as a guest-house for several years. Her visitors tended to return time after time, and she considered some of them friends. She loved to cook traditional, rustic food, which Dad and I had benefitted from, especially during the winter when business was less brisk. She kept trying to improve Dad's French, finding his efforts hilarious, and in her spare time she enjoyed knitting – hardly a crime, but this was the hobby that had (unfairly) put an end to any romantic notions Dad might have had about her.

'*Bonjour*, Natalie.' She propped her bike against the wall, and pulled her keys from the pocket of her flower-patterned skirt. 'You are liking this weather?'

I smiled. Marie knew all about the British fascination with the climate and always made a point of asking. 'It's beautiful,' I said, taking in the terracotta-topped roofs, baked orange by the sun, the whitewashed walls, and the weathered shutters painted in maritime colours, complemented by the island's trademark hollyhocks, spilling in splashes of pink along the house fronts. 'You have visitors?'

'Tomorrow,' she said, picking up her canvas shopping bag and hooking it over her arm. 'My Americans, Larry and Barbara, are coming back, so I've been to the market for ingredients. They love my *bœuf bourguignon*.'

'Lucky them.' I loved that Marie cooked from scratch. Hardly anyone I'd encountered since moving to the island ate the sort of processed food I'd mostly lived on in England, apart from when I'd eaten at Mum and Dad's. I was always too tired after work to cook and Matt hadn't been much use in the kitchen either, preferring to eat takeaways whenever possible. 'Um… my dad mentioned there's a famous actor staying in Saint-Martin.' I tried to say it casually, aware that I was breaking a confidence, but couldn't disguise my interest.

Marie's eyes widened. 'It is supposed to be a secret.' She glanced over my shoulder, her gentle face creased with worry, as if someone might be about to rush up and arrest her. 'My good friend, Jeanne, she is very excited, but they had to sign the non-disclosure agreements to stop them talking about it.' It clearly hadn't worked as Jeanne had immediately told Marie. 'She has a big squash on him.'

'Crush,' I said with a smile. 'I won't mention it to anyone.' I was aware as I spoke that it wasn't strictly true. I'd already told Charlie and was planning to tell Nicolas Juilliard, but that was different – it wasn't idle gossip, it was to do with work – and I hadn't known it was such a big secret. Though I couldn't help thinking it was a bit precious of Jay to be sneaking around like this; forcing people to sign confidentiality agreements, not to mention it being pointless. He could hardly shoot scenes for his film without the public realising what was going on, and once they clocked what was happening and recognised him, he'd have reporters on his back day and night. They'd soon find out where he was staying.

'Actors, they like to come here,' said Marie, with a hint of pride. It was true that the island – known as the French Hamptons – tended to attract the rich and famous due to its sunny climate and exclusive vibe, and it wasn't unusual to hear that Johnny Depp, or a member of the royal family, was visiting.

'It's just, I used to sort of know him,' I said, to divert her from being worried. 'He was born not far from where I grew up.' I briefly allowed my mind to drift back to that night on the swings, and wondered how many times, during my childhood, Jay Merino might have been less than half a mile away from me, perhaps playing in his garden, as I had been in mine (mostly up and down the oak tree with Gemma, hoping to meet Moonface from our favourite Enid Blyton books), then remembered that even if Jay Merino had had a garden, it was doubtful he'd have been playing in it.

'Where you lived with Marty?' Marie's face softened as her gaze flipped to the adjoining house, and I bit back the urge to say, *Of course with Marty, he's my dad*, knowing it was just an excuse to say his name.

'With Marty, and my mother,' I said, amused that she was more interested in Dad than in Jay Merino. 'I mean, I didn't know him well. Jay Merino, I mean, not my dad—'

'Would you and your *papa* like to come for dinner tonight?' I could tell she'd been waiting for a reason to ask. 'I need to practise the *bourguignon* for my guests.' It was a blatant lie. She'd cooked the dish so many times, she could probably do it in her sleep, but she seemed to enjoy our company, and I doubted Dad would be able to resist the invitation. My cooking skills were basic at best, and Dad's eager attempts at French cuisine were getting harder to stomach. When I told Mum he'd made steak tartare, but cooked to resemble leather, she'd laughed heartily and said, 'Now you know why I was in charge of the kitchen.'

'I'll ask him,' I said. 'Around seven?'

Marie nodded, a smile brightening her eyes. 'I will look forward to it.' With a gracious nod, she let herself into her house and shut the door just as Dad opened ours.

'Where did you go rushing off to?' he said. Thankfully, he'd washed his hair, and although it hadn't quite returned to its normal hue, it no longer resembled a cowpat.

'I needed to have a think about what you said.' I stepped past him into the living room, pleased to see most of the clothes he'd been wearing earlier were neatly parcelled up, ready to be returned, and the bottle of Purple Seduction – shaped to look like a man's shoulders and gym-honed chest – relegated to a pile of recycling. 'And to tell Charlie.'

'Of *course* you had to tell Charlie.'

Unlike Dolly, Dad had accepted my friendship with Charlie for what it was, despite him once saying it was a shame that Matt hadn't been more like Charlie, because if he had, we'd still be together. He hadn't liked Matt much, because as far as Dad was concerned the chip on his shoulder had been obvious from the start (though, sadly, not to me). Matt had thought me too good for him, because I'd been to university where I'd written for the student magazine, and landed a job in London, whereas he did manual work, rarely read a book and played football on Sundays. Of course it hadn't bothered me. I'd met him on a visit home, where he'd been sorting out the garden because

Mum and Dad were too busy at the time to keep on top of it. I'd made him some coffee and got chatting, and quickly fell for his sexy smile, strong hands and funny anecdotes, and the way he'd transformed the overgrown tangle, filling it with meadow flowers, delphiniums, stocks and roses, talking me through what they were with touching enthusiasm. I'd loved having the anchor of a serious boyfriend at last, glad to move out of my flat-share with Jools and into a tiny new-build house in Chesham that Matt and I had poured our savings into. I'd even enjoyed commuting to work every day like a proper grown-up, returning home each evening to snuggle on the sofa with a ready meal or takeaway, in front of a boxset with Matt. But he'd never really liked me working in London and had gradually reconnected with his single life, staying out late, drinking too much and playing endlessly on his X-box, to the extent that I grew used to seeing him weaving about in the light of the TV screen, playing *Call of Duty*. On one of his nights out, he'd bumped into the girlfriend before me, a nail technician called Steph, who I remembered him saying used to get emotional about babies on television, and he'd told me he was 'in love' – just not with me.

'So, what did Charlie think?' asked Dad, pulling me back to the moment.

'The same as you,' I said. 'That I should try and arrange an interview with Jay.'

'Of course you should.' Dad scoured the street, as though for spies, before closing the door.

'What are you doing?'

'Seeing if my taxi's coming.' He glanced at the watch that Mum had bought him for his fiftieth birthday, and I noticed he was wearing his leather jacket and boots and smelt of his usual shower gel (rather than Purple Seduction). 'Should be here any minute.'

'Taxi?'

His gaze dipped away from mine. 'I might be meeting a lady.'

'A lady?'

'In La Rochelle.'

A tiny sigh escaped. 'Is that what all the dressing up was about?'

He nodded, a cloud of worry passing over his face. 'She might be a bit younger than me.'

'Why do you keep saying *might*?' I said. 'Either you're meeting a lady, or you're not, and she's younger than you, or she isn't.'

'I'm definitely meeting a lady.'

I crossed to the chair by the window and sat down, trying not to look like I was interrogating him. 'How much younger than you?'

'Not much,' he said quickly.

'Younger than me?'

'Thirty-nine?'

'Are you asking or telling me?'

'OK, she's thirty-nine.'

I rubbed between my eyebrows where a headache was brewing. 'Does she know you're sixty?'

'Yes, but I said I looked young for my age.'

'Did you use that photo I told you not to?'

He scratched his chin. 'It wasn't taken *that* long ago.'

'It was taken before you went grey.' I eyed his hair. '*That's* why you dyed it.'

'I didn't want to disappoint her.'

'You wouldn't have, if you'd been honest.' Sometimes, I wished I could delete the whole internet. 'Once you're face-to-face it'll be obvious you've fibbed.'

'Oh, Christ.' He collapsed onto the arm of the sofa and smoothed a hand over his neatly swept-back hair. 'Do you think I should call and tell her this isn't my natural colour?' His eyes flooded with worry.

'Best leave it now,' I said. His shirt was half-unbuttoned, revealing a gold chain nestling among his chest hairs, and the sight made me want to simultaneously hug him and replace the shirt with a woolly, high-necked sweater. 'She'll be so bowled over by your personality, she probably won't even notice.'

He brightened. 'I've been working on that.' He pulled a piece of paper from his jacket pocket. 'I printed out a list of questions to ask in French.'

'I thought you were going to stick to speaking English after last time.' I recalled his despondent face as he'd recounted how, after dinner with a woman who'd travelled from Paris to meet him, he'd said, *Je suis plein*, thinking it meant *I'm full* and not *I'm pregnant* and ended the evening (and the chance of another date) by telling her he was sexually aroused, instead of keen to meet again. 'Or you could use a translation app on your phone.'

'That's not very romantic,' he said, as though asking for a condom instead of jam with his croissant was (another misunderstanding that had led to his companion walking away from their afternoon tea date without a backwards glance). 'I've copied these questions off a website and checked the pronunciation, so I can't go wrong.'

Watching him mouth the words, typed in extra-large font – he wouldn't want to put on his reading glasses – I was about to protest, when I heard the honk of a car horn outside. Dad shot to his feet. 'That'll be my taxi,' he said unnecessarily.

'Where are you meeting?'

'Ars en Ré,' he said, naming a nearby village. 'I could have cycled, but didn't want to get sweaty, and it didn't seem worth getting the car out.'

'Marie's invited us for dinner at seven.'

'You'll have to go on your own, if I get lucky.'

'That's gross, Dad.'

I waved him off, hoping the lady would be kind to him, and wondered if this was how it had been for my parents when I'd started dating. If so, it sucked, though I hadn't given them much to worry about, thinking back. No pregnancy scares, or even a badly broken heart to contend with, before I met Matt. After breaking up with Henry, I'd had a couple of boyfriends, but I'd been the one to end things, not keen enough on either of them to give up my independence.

Sighing, I decided I might as well make a cup of tea and headed into the sun-filled kitchen, my favourite room in the house. Dad had painted the ceiling beams a cheery red, in contrast to the plain white walls, and the wooden worktops and open shelving – crammed with jars, tins, packets and mismatched crockery – gave it a cosy feel. A lot like his parents' kitchen, I'd realised, the first time I saw it. There was even a photo of Nan and Grandpa Bright on the windowsill, keeping a smiling eye on everything. They wouldn't have approved of Dad being here without Mum. They'd thought the world of her though. Sadly, Mum's mum, in her foggy-minded dotage, had reverted to her initial conclusion about Dad: that all police officers were corrupt.

Dad's notepad lay open next to the fruit bowl and I smiled as I read his latest list of contrasts between real life and TV policing, which he'd titled *Facts VS Myth.*

Crimes are rarely solved in an hour

Real police don't jump from moving cars

Female detectives rarely wear tight trousers and high heels

Officers don't beat confessions out of suspects.

Banishing a half-formed plan to grind out a few sentences for *Expats*, I decided instead to make a start on writing up Dad's list in a more book-like format, perhaps in a chatty style: *It's funny how on television, a crime will often be solved in between commercial breaks, which in most cases is actually less than an hour.* But I had only just filled the kettle when my phone began its old-fashioned ringtone.

'Hello?'

'Mademoiselle Bright?' It was a man with a voice that brought to mind late nights in smoky jazz clubs, though I'd never been to a late-night, smoky jazz club in my life.

'*Oui?*'

'Nicolas Juilliard,' he said, his French accent comically sexy. 'I believe you have a very important proposal you wish to discuss.'

Chapter Five

'Monsieur Juilliard, thank you so much for calling me back,' I gushed
in French, clattering the kettle onto the worktop. 'It's so good to finally
speak to you, um... in person.' I stumbled with the phrasing, certain
I'd said *with our voices* instead of *in person*, and repeated the sentence
in English, as I knew he was bilingual.

'*Mon plaisir*, Mademoiselle.'

'Please, call me Natalie.'

'Natalee.' I'd heard my name spoken many times, but never like
that – as though we'd just tumbled into bed together. Heat flooded my
face and I was glad he couldn't see me. 'Blushing idiot' was never a good
look. 'I'm guessing it is about ze actor 'oo is staying in Saint-Martin.'

I almost dropped my phone. 'How... how did you know?' I realised
at once how naïve I must sound. Of course a man in his position would
have his ear to the ground, or sources who would pass him information.

'I've known for some while 'e was going to be filming over 'ere.' His
deep voice was laced with amusement. 'We 'ave wished to interview
Jay Merino for a very long time.'

'But you never have.'

'*Non.*' He sounded regretful. 'But it ees a perfect opportunity now
'e is in the country. We 'ave been in contact with 'is people and 'e is
thinking 'e might be 'appy to talk to us, finally.'

Damn, damn, damn. 'Have you already set up a meeting?'

'*Non*, but 'e requested to see some of our work a leetle while ago and 'as now expressed an interest in meeting Fleur Dupont.' Again, I was glad he couldn't see me as I slapped my forehead and mouthed a very bad word. Of *course* if Jay Merino was going to grant anyone an interview it would be a veteran profile writer like Fleur. Beautiful, award-winning Fleur, in her geek-chic glasses, who'd once been photographed lounging on a shell-shaped inflatable in a swimming pool with Brad Pitt while he talked about his marriages. The interview had been reproduced around the world.

'What's her angle going to be?' I was being wildly over-optimistic, but there was an outside chance that Jay might still refuse to talk to her.

'Angle?'

'He won't talk about his private life.' I said it with as much conviction as I could summon. 'Not even to Fleur Dupont.'

His laugh was warm and gravelly. 'And yet, he'll talk to you? An unknown, 'oo once wrote about a man being attacked by a magpie on 'is way to work, and a lady going to 'ospital because she ate so many spicy foods her stomach exploded.' I didn't really believe he'd check out the links I'd sent him, and now I wished he hadn't.

'I'm good with people.' I had a childish urge to win him over. 'I'm a good listener.' *Wasn't that what Jay Merino once told me?*

'These people, they approach *you* with their story,' he said, pleasantly. 'You do not 'ave to draw them out, Natalee. I know 'ow it works. My friend's son, 'e worked for one of those magazines in London.' His tone implied exactly what he thought of *those* magazines, and I wondered why he hadn't already hung up when it was clear from his throaty chuckle he was simply indulging me. Why he'd rung me at all, if Fleur was on the case. Perhaps he was having a laugh at my expense, and wanted to share the exchange with her when he got off the phone. That was if she wasn't interviewing the Dalai Lama, or Beyoncé.

'I write a column too.' I was aware how lame it sounded. A column hardly qualified me to interview an A-list actor.

'Yes, it's that leetle magazine for foreigners living in our country.' He paused. 'I 'ave seen it.'

'Really?' Maybe he'd read the piece I'd devoted to food, all about the places where you could find the best bread and cheeses in the area, tied in with an amusing anecdote about struggling to do up the zip of my jeans after living in France for three months. I linked my columns to my blog, and that one had trended on Twitter for about three seconds.

'Your writing ees very *capable*,' said Nicolas, not unkindly, but it still felt like a slap. *Capable* was one of those words like *pleasant*, or *nice*. It meant *not noteworthy*. 'At *Magnifique* we demand a very high standard of writing, and a…' I heard the clicking of fingers as he presumably sought the right words. 'A certain *je ne sais quoi*.'

Naturally. 'I'm British, like Jay Merino.' I cringed, recalling the people that Fleur had interviewed. Probably only a handful had been French. One had been a notoriously media-shy Russian astronaut, and rumour had it that Fleur had learnt to speak Russian ahead of their meeting. 'What I mean is, he may be more likely to speak to a fellow countryman. Or woman.' I ground the heel of my hand into my eye, wishing I was as *capable* at the spoken word as I was at the written one. It was my writing that had won me a permanent job at *Chatter*, where I'd been on a work placement, after filling in when one of the staff writers went on maternity leave, and I hadn't got as far as having an interview since leaving. It was probably just as well. I was clearly rubbish at selling myself.

'I think you need a better *angle* than sharing a place of birth with Jay Merino.'

My cheeks fired up again. 'Well, as it happens, I have one.'

'Oh?'

I hesitated, anxiety fluttering in my throat. I doubted that Jay would remember an encounter I was attaching too much significance to – plus, my previous requests for an interview had been turned down – but I had a hunch that if I could wangle a face-to-face meeting, he might just agree to honour the promise he'd made to me all those years ago.

'I know him,' I said, concentrating on keeping my voice steady. 'We were practically neighbours growing up.' *Liar, liar, pants on fire.*

There was a pause at the end of the line. I imagined Nicolas running a hand through his attractively greying dark hair and slow-blinking his heavy-lidded eyes. (I'd seen photos of him, where he was referred to as 'charismatic' and 'France's sexiest man over fifty'.) 'You *know* Jay Merino?'

'From a long time ago.' At least that much was true.

'Yet you 'ave never interviewed him.'

'No, but only because I've never had the opportunity before.'

'How so?'

'We, er… we lost touch.'

'But surely 'e would 'ave granted you an interview if you'd made contact wiz 'im?' Nicolas persisted. 'If you know 'im "from a long time ago"?'

It was clear from his implied quote marks that he didn't believe a word. 'Actually, I ran into him, here on the island.' I bit my lip, imagining Dad's disapproval. He'd always encouraged me to be truthful, whatever the consequences. I'd never been a hustler, like some of the people at *Gossip* that Jools had told me about, who'd have sold their own grandmothers to get access to a celebrity. It was why I'd preferred 'real-life' writing back then, even if the people I'd talked to had never been near a red carpet in their lives.

'You ran into 'im?'

'Yes, and we got chatting, and when I told him what I did for a living, he offered me an exclusive.'

'Why did you not say this straight away?'

Because I just made it up. 'I… I suppose I—'

'You didn't want to give away that 'e was out running,' Nicolas interrupted, and I realised he'd misunderstood (I doubted Jay Merino went running; he might be seen). ''E would not want this to be widely known,' he said, as if he didn't quite believe it either. His voice thickened with curiosity. 'You are quite the dark 'orse, Natalee. 'Ave you offered this anywhere else?'

'No, no, it's been my dream to write for your magazine since I moved to France,' I said. I could tell he was the sort of boss who commanded adoration and loyalty from his staff, and probably got it. 'I'd love to work for you full-time,' I rushed on. 'I could come for an interview, if you like.'

'We 'ave a good team 'ere, Natalee,' he said, kindly. 'I do not need new writers.'

'But…'

'You 'ave no skill at this.'

My spirits drooped. He was right. Interviewing someone of Jay's calibre was way beyond my experience level and yet… I knew I could do it, given a chance. 'Then why did you even bother calling me back?'

'I'm intrigued by you, Natalee. I 'ave read all your emails,' he said. 'You are very, *persistent*. And passionate.' He sounded mildly amused. 'I wanted to 'ear your voice.'

'So why not give me a chance?' I ignored the last bit, which sounded like something a lover would say.

'Like I say, we are in talks with Jay Merino.'

On impulse, I said, 'OK, well, I'm going to interview him anyway, and I'm sure other editors won't be so picky about my lack of experience. In fact, I'm certain they'll pay top dollar…' *Top dollar? Who was I?* '… for an interview written by someone who knew the actor before he was famous.' It was a wild gamble, considering I'd yet to speak to Jay, but if Nicolas believed I really knew him, he might just give me a shot.

'I admire your tenacity, Natalee.' His tone ripened into admiration. 'I think I would like us to meet.'

My heart jumped into my throat. 'Meet?' *Too squeaky.* 'At your office?' I was going to Paris! I would book a ticket online, and then—

'I would not expect you to come all zis way.' I felt a blast of disappointment. 'La Rochelle, tomorrow evening at seven.' He named a Michelin-starred restaurant I knew only by reputation. 'Bring me proof that you know this man, Natalee, and I'll consider your proposal.'

I couldn't settle after Nicolas had hung up. I kept rushing to the windows, staring first at the empty street, then at the stone-walled garden at the back of the house, before dashing through the living room and up to my bedroom, where I sat on the chair by the wardrobe, before jumping up and racing back downstairs.

My breathing was heavy, my heart beating too fast again. How was I supposed to get proof I knew Jay Merino at such short notice? Or, at all? I could hardly call his hotel and ask to speak to him directly. *Could I?*

I rooted my phone from my bag, found the number of the hotel and tapped it in, but hung up before it rang. No one was supposed to know he was there, for a start. Reception were hardly going to put me through, and I had no chance of getting past his manager, or security detail (I'd read that in the early days, he'd employed a bodyguard after a stalking incident) even if I said I was a good friend – which I wasn't.

Maybe it would be better to turn up in person. I could watch the hotel and wait for a sighting, then contrive running into him, just as I'd told Nicolas I already had. Maybe seeing me would trigger a memory from that historic evening. I didn't look that much different these days, even if he did. Just to be sure, I checked out one of the photos of him online – the promotional shots for his previous films. He wore his dark hair cropped close to his skull, which made his cheekbones stand out, and his jaw – which I hadn't remembered as being so defined – was bristly with stubble. His narrowed eyes looked almost black as they glared into the camera, and his expression was fierce – like a man on a mission to kill. (The bad guys responsible for the death of his wife and son, which was the over-arching theme of the franchise. There seemed to have been an awful lot of people involved, the reasons as yet unclear.) He was dangling out of a helicopter in the shot, so unlikely to be smiling, but I couldn't picture him grinning in a friendly fashion. In every picture, most of them stills from film-shoots, he was either blank-faced or scowling, and in one – a grainy shot, taken with a long lens – his mouth was wide, almost filling his whole face, as if he was roaring.

I shuddered. He no longer resembled the young man with the gentle voice I'd spoken to in my friend's garden. He looked like the sort of person I wouldn't want to get on the wrong side of. He'd clearly been toughened by his troubled, early life and subsequent rise to fame, as well as his struggle to stay out of the spotlight. What did he do when he wasn't filming? Did he have a girlfriend? Nothing had been reported in the press since his appearance with the tormented singer, but he'd no doubt learned his lesson after that and made sure to either stay single, or only date women who were happy to stay out of the limelight. Perhaps he made *them* sign non-disclosure agreements, too.

I twizzled the ends of my hair and paced some more, trying to focus my energy. I would cycle over to Saint-Martin early the following morning and try to catch him before he started filming. I had no idea of his itinerary and he didn't have a publicist that I knew of, so there was no point trying to find out where he'd be. The only thing I could be sure of was that he'd have to leave the hotel at some point, and when he did, I'd be there. *Unless he came out in disguise and I didn't recognise him.* And what if it was all a massive red herring and he wasn't staying at the hotel at all, even though Marie had said the rooms had been booked by the film company for the week? Or, what if they'd already gone out filming by the time I turned up, and didn't return until it was too late to meet Nicolas with proof? What if I *did* bump into Jay and he didn't recognise me, or he did and told me to get lost, or had me arrested?

My brain felt like it was melting and when my phone rang, I screamed.

'Mum, you made me jump.' I wished she hadn't insisted we use our cameras so she could see me whenever she called – which was invariably as I was about to get in or out of bed, or jump in the shower, or have something to eat, so I always looked vaguely irritable. 'I didn't realise you were going to call today.'

'I didn't realise I had to make an appointment to call my daughter,' she said benignly. Like Dad, her temper was rarely ruffled, to the point where I used to prod her sometimes to try and get a reaction. 'Are you working?'

Mum always said this when she called, as if she might have interrupted a particularly tricky writing project, and while I appreciated her unshakeable belief that I was a prodigy, my guilt that I was barely working at all made me unusually tetchy. 'No, Mum, I'm not working right now, as you can see.'

I swung the phone around, so she could scan the room. She loved to see the house when she called – I'd had to do a video tour for her when I moved in, and she always asked to see what room I was in. Dad's bedroom, as it turned out. I didn't even remember coming in.

'What's that on the bed?' Mum's face loomed close to the screen, bringing what she called her 'life-lines' into view. In spite of them, she was ageing well. Her blue eyes were as bright and inquisitive as ever, her mouth always verging on a smile, while her newly styled platinum bob gave her a touch of the Helen Mirrens. 'Isn't that our old duvet cover?'

I glanced at the bed, surprised. 'I think it is,' I said, wondering why I hadn't recognised the duck-egg blue cover before. It clashed with the orange and yellow striped curtains, crimson lampshade and brown furry rug, but Dad always put it straight back on after washing.

'That's so sweet.' Mum sounded delighted. 'Let me have a proper look around.'

Sighing, I passed my phone over the room, lingering on the photo Dad kept on the nightstand by the bed of Mum, doing the can-can with her sister Harriet at a Christmas party in the nineties, caught mid-kick, her face bright with laughter. She hadn't visited the house since Dad moved in, though I knew she must be dying to. She'd said it wouldn't be fair to intrude on his new life, inserting her personality into his home when he was trying to make a fresh start, and although I knew Dad would have loved her to come, offering an open invitation, he hadn't pushed her when she turned him down. Sometimes, I wanted to bang their heads together.

'Where is he?' she said.

I pulled the phone from the view through the window, of pale blue sky above rooftops, to see her eyes ranging around as if Dad might leap out from behind the oak chest of drawers.

'He's... out,' I said, recalling her reaction when I'd mentioned Marie's wonderful suppers, and how we sometimes ate at hers. I might as well have told her that Dad was getting remarried. She'd wanted a full description of Marie – I'd drawn the line at sending a photo – and a rundown of what we'd talked about, and had finally drawn the conclusion that Dad must be desperate for company because he 'didn't even like brunettes'.

'Out?' Her tone was casual, but her eyes demanded a response. 'Who with?'

'A friend?' I hadn't meant it to come out as a question.

'What sort of friend?'

'Mmm... not a friend, exactly. She's—'

'She?' Mum's eyes lasered through screen. 'Why do you look like that?'

'Like what?' I glanced at the corner of the screen. I looked like I normally did; maybe a touch more flushed, and my curls more springy than usual and perhaps my eyes were too bright, but otherwise totally myself.

'Like you did as a child, trying to stay awake on Christmas Eve.'

'I look like an overtired toddler?'

'It always ended in tears.'

'Yes, because I didn't understand why I wasn't allowed to stay up and stroke Rudolph.' I'd never been interested in seeing Santa, only his reindeer. 'I still don't.'

Ignoring my attempt at humour, Mum said, 'Is your dad meeting a woman?'

I caught sight of my exaggerated wince and knew the game was up. 'He thinks he might be ready for a new relationship.'

Mum appeared to have dropped the phone. There was a view of grass, her favourite glittery trainers and a five-bar gate.

'Mum?'

Her face reappeared, a smile fixed in place. 'Sorry about that.' She gave herself a little shake. 'I thought he was happy on his own, that's all.'

'What about you and Gareth?'

'Gareth?' As her head jerked back, I spotted a horse looking over a fence.

'Where are you?'

'I came out for a run,' she said. 'And there's nothing going on between Gareth and me. He's my life coach, nothing more.'

'But you're at a yoga retreat with him, and you talk about him a lot.'

'Oh, Natalie, that doesn't mean we're… *sexual*.'

'Oh God, Mum.' I shook away an image of her clasped to Gareth's hairy chest. I knew it was hairy because I'd met him at Mum's last Christmas, when he'd bought her a badly wrapped book called *The Power of Breathing* (as though she might have forgotten how), and his beard had met the hair poking above his collar. 'But you said he was handsome.'

'Your friend Charlie is handsome, and you talk about him all the time, but he's not your boyfriend, is he?'

She had me there. 'How's it going at the retreat, anyway?'

'Oh, it's got a bit tedious.' She tilted the phone so her face dipped into shadow. 'All that breathing and navel-gazing and chanting.'

'Chanting?'

'It makes me want to laugh,' she said. 'And everyone takes it so seriously.'

'It's not just you and Gareth?'

'Of course not, there are ten other people here.'

'Ah.' Maybe they really were just friends.

'It's not as relaxing as I expected.' She sounded unusually impatient. Mum had run her charity shop for years, handling a constant flow of volunteers, and was the most patient person I knew. 'It's making me think too much.'

'But you like thinking.'

'It's making me angry.'

I felt a ping of alarm. 'Sounds like you should leave.'

Her face bounced back into view, stippled with sunlight. It was an hour earlier over there, still mid-afternoon. 'Do you know what?' she said. 'I think I might.'

I was starting to feel bad now for mentioning Dad's date. Although their split had been amicable, my parents had been married for over thirty years and it must be hard for them to contemplate the other with a new partner. I didn't like it either, but I was their daughter. I preferred them as a unit, but sooner or later a step-parent might be on the cards, a thought that gave me childish shivers. 'I don't think it's serious,' I said. 'Dad and this woman, I mean.' I headed down to the kitchen. I was parched, and still hadn't had my cup of tea. Jay Merino bobbed into my head, but I determinedly pushed him aside. 'He's been on a few dates, but none of them—'

'He's *dating*?' Mum's voice bordered on shrill.

I paused, hand outstretched to the kettle. 'Isn't that what I said?'

'No, you didn't.' The screen went muffled and black, as if she'd pressed the phone to her chest. I half expected to hear her heartbeat. 'Do you know,' Mum's face reappeared, pink patches on her cheeks. 'Your dad once said to me, "Claire, wherever you are, that's where I want to be."'

'Dad said that?' I was impressed. The most romantic thing Matt had ever said was, 'I'm glad you're not like my mother.' (She had no filter and would say things like, 'You're not fat, Natalie, just short.')

'Well, it was in a film, but he said afterwards that he felt the same way about me.'

'That's so lovely.' My eyes had gone prickly.

'Anyway, how's work?'

It took me a second to switch gear. 'Good, good,' I said, my stock answer. 'I've got an exciting assignment coming up.' A thrill of anticipation was immediately followed by a nosedive of dread. 'I can't talk about it just yet.'

'Intriguing,' Mum said warmly. 'I can't wait to hear all about it.' She looked at her watch. 'I suppose I'd better get back.' She sounded cheerful again, like her normal self. 'I'm definitely leaving this place,' she said. 'I can't stand another day of eating oatmeal. And why do they call it oatmeal instead of porridge? What's wrong with calling it porridge?'

'Not American enough, I guess.'

'Anyway, say hi to your dad for me.'

'I will.' Though I wished she'd say it herself. 'Say hi to Gareth from me.'

'He's practically stuck in a downward dog all day.' I assumed she was referring to a yoga pose. 'He's so flexible, he can turn his head round like an owl.'

The call ended with giggles, but as soon as Mum rang off my thoughts returned to Jay, and even two cups of tea, followed by Dad's early return (his date had been 'money-obsessed and too tall') and dinner with Marie, couldn't distract from the task that lay ahead.

Chapter Six

I'd got out of the habit of rising early since moving in with Dad – which I'd treated as an extended holiday, until it sank in that real life had to resume – but the following morning, I was up and dressed by seven. I'd barely slept, going over my half-baked plan and failing to come up with anything better, as well as wondering what I should wear for my meeting with Nicolas Juilliard, but in spite of a band of tension across my chest, I felt wired and alert.

Once I'd showered and dressed and written a note for Dad, telling him not to bother making me tea (a habit I was trying to get him to break by escaping to the café as soon as I rolled out of bed), I snuck out the back door. I rejected taking the car – it was only three miles to Saint-Martin and a lovely morning – and cycled down to Café Belle Vie, my hair already escaping the clips I'd stuck in to restrain it.

I knew Charlie would be up as the café opened early and sure enough, he was cleaning the windows inside with cheerful concentration. When he saw me, he did a comedy double-take and came out, rubbing his eyes with his knuckles.

'Very funny,' I said, dismounting awkwardly. I still hadn't mastered the art of getting gracefully off a bike; I had fallen off more times than I could count the first time I'd joined Charlie on a tour of the island, having got out of the habit of cycling.

'What's happened?' He tucked his cloth into the belt of his jeans. 'Has your house burnt down?'

'You just can't stop being hilarious, can you?' I said. 'I've got plans.'

'Proper plans, that don't involve looking at dogs in tuxedos online?'

'You know I don't like seeing dogs dressed up, it's undignified.'

'You don't mind seeing Hamish in his stripy top,' he said, as Gérard strolled up to the café, the little dog tucked neatly under his arm. I thrust my bike at Charlie so I could stroke the dog's black furry head, while Gérard looked on indulgently. Hamish adored being petted, and had only tried to bite me once, when I forgot he was under the table and stood on his tail.

'Hamish is different,' I said, once Gérard had escaped. 'He suits knitwear.'

Charlie smirked, indecently bright-eyed for the time of day. He was the sort of person who sprang out of bed in the mornings, ready for anything. 'I take it your call to Nicol*arse* went well?'

'Don't be rude.' I filled him in and he listened with an avid expression, while a steady stream of people flowed past, into the café.

'So now you need to talk to Jay Merino?'

'Shush.' I looked around, noting several customers at a table nearby and Stefan taking their order. 'Don't broadcast his name.'

'The French aren't like us,' he said, folding his arms. 'They're used to celebrities around here. I doubt anyone will bother to turn up to watch filming, especially if it hasn't been made public.'

'I bet they will, and anyway, it's half-term in the UK, so there'll be plenty of visitors from over there.'

'I wish I could come and watch.' Charlie adopted a *Maximum Force* style pose, flicking up his shirt collar and moodily staring down the barrel of his finger-gun.

'Maybe Dolly will let you have some time off.' Even as I said it, I knew this was something I wanted to do on my own.

'Not today,' he said. 'She's having her hair done once she's finished the breakfast rush.' Still in character, he trousered his pretend gun, speaking with a brow-furrowed gravitas that made me giggle. 'And Giselle's not in, she's got a dentist's appointment this morning.'

'Well, maybe it's best if you don't come,' I said. 'It might ruin the mystery to watch him being touched up between takes.'

'Touched up?'

I gave him a hard stare. 'His make-up.'

He pulled a face. 'I don't want to think about Max Weaver in foundation.'

'You mean,' I lowered my voice, 'Jay Merino.'

'Same thing.'

Dolly emerged, fair hair tucked beneath a mustard-coloured scarf, carrying a tray of coffee and a plate of bread and pastries. 'You're here bright and early.' Her twinkling eyes flicked from Charlie to me and back, as if trying to bind us together. 'I've brought you both some breakfast.'

'I've already eaten,' said Charlie, helping himself to a hunk of buttered baguette. 'I'll just have a tiny snack.'

For once, I wasn't tempted, my stomach rolling with a mix of adrenaline and nerves. 'I can't stay,' I told Dolly. 'I've got somewhere to be.'

A knowing smile curled her lips. 'And yet, you came here first,' she said. 'Your home from home.'

'Well, it was kind of on my way.'

Charlie ate his snack and rolled his eyes.

'Oh?' Dolly's neatly trimmed eyebrows rose. 'Where are you going?'

'Just to Saint-Martin.' I hoped she wouldn't ask why.

'Why?' She drew her head back. 'What's in Saint-Martin at this hour?'

She made it sound like the middle of the night. 'I just fancy the exercise.'

'There's an actor staying there.' Charlie spoke at the same time, seeming not to notice me signalling 'shut up' with my eyes. 'Natalie's hoping to interview him. What?' he said when I tutted. 'Mum's the soul of discretion. She won't say anything.'

'I've better things to do than gossip,' she agreed, waving to Gérard, who was settling himself at a window table with his newspaper, Hamish by his feet. 'Maybe you could interview this actor in the café?'

I smiled at such an unlikely scenario. 'I haven't even spoken to him yet,' I admitted. 'That's why I'm going over there. I want to catch him before he starts filming.'

'Him?' Her grip on the tray tightened, betraying her interest. 'Anyone I know?'

'I'm afraid I can't say.'

She pursed her lips then nodded, eyeing the café again as a regular group of early-morning runners gathered inside for their usual order of coffee and muffins. Later, there'd be the school mums, lingering over sweet pastries and lattes, and Dolly's book group would assemble this afternoon to sample her 'special of the day' (and maybe talk about books) and I knew they were more important to her than some actor she'd never met. 'OK,' she said briskly. 'Mum's the word.'

'Get a selfie with him.' Charlie brushed crumbs off the front of his shirt. 'That's all the proof you need.'

It sounded straightforward enough, yet the thought of Jay Merino agreeing to a picture – even if I managed to meet him – was impossible to visualise. 'I'll try,' I said, adjusting the straps of my rucksack before clambering back on my bike. 'I'd better go.'

'Why do you need proof?' Dolly passed the tray to Charlie, her eyes scanning my face for clues. 'You're not planning to blackmail him, are you?'

I gave a nervous laugh. 'Of course not. Why would you even think that?'

'I can't think why else you'd need *proof*.'

'It's a long story, Mum.' Charlie took a gulp from one of the coffee cups on the tray. 'We'll tell you about it one day.'

'Just remember, Natalie, you'll never do better than this one.' Dolly showcased her son with a game-show sweep of her hands while he closed his eyes in despair, and I cycled away smiling, his cry of *good luck* ringing in my ears.

By the time I reached Saint-Martin-de Ré, I'd been overtaken by a family of five – three of them under eight – and felt sweaty and out of breath. Normally, I couldn't fail to be charmed by the unspoilt beauty of the capital village; the dramatic, star-shaped fortifications surrounding the old resort; the gleaming yachts and speedboats crammed in the marina; the seafood market, and the cafés and restaurants that filled up in summer when most of Paris seemed to descend on the island. But I barely took in my surroundings today, except to note it was much quieter than when we'd last visited, on Dad's birthday in March, when we'd eaten scallops at La Salicorne and Dolly told Dad he was a 'catch' (I'd thought at the time she might have her eye on him) and Charlie had insisted on speaking French all evening. Instead, I focused on finding the hotel, which wasn't difficult as it overlooked the harbour, sunshine dusting the stone with golden light.

I pedalled along the quayside, past shops, boutiques, a *boulangerie* – where a tantalising smell of baking bread drifted out – and the newsagent's, until I reached the front of the hotel, which I'd once recommended as 'a place to stay' in my column (I never had, though I'd been to look around it). It wasn't a large building, more classy than flashy, despite a flag-studded turret and its name in discreet gold lettering above the entrance. It contained twenty rooms and suites, all individually decorated and named after historical characters, and I wondered which one Jay Merino was staying in, and whether the secret girlfriend I'd spent the night convincing myself he must have was staying with him. They were probably just waking after a night of heavy passion, hair rumpled (in her case; Jay didn't have enough), clothes carelessly tossed on the floor, debating whether they had time for another session, while the baddie who'd been sent to kill him prepared to abseil through the window... I'd pulled the scene from his last movie and mentally shook myself.

I extracted a bottle of water from my rucksack and took a long swig, eyes skimming the shuttered windows as if Jay might suddenly appear. If he did, I'd look suspicious hanging about, gawping at the hotel as if it were a spaceship, so I cycled round the corner and across the road, noticing some barricading up at the end – even in such an unspoiled place, roadworks were sometimes necessary – and propped my bike against the harbour wall, making sure I locked the chain. I didn't fancy the long walk back to Chamillon if it got stolen. There were several parked cars nearby, alongside a couple of big white lorries taking up most of the space, and a handful of people were clustered outside the Office de Tourism, as if waiting for it to open.

I rearranged my hair, wondering whether I should leave it loose, but it felt too heavy around my shoulders, so I wrangled it back up, then rummaged in my rucksack and swiped my lips with A Hint of Raspberry so at least they matched my cheeks – exercise didn't do my colouring any favours. I'd settled for wearing a plain, scoop-necked top with my vintage jeans, and a pair of ancient trainers, figuring if I was supposed to 'bump' into Jay, I wouldn't be in a show-stopper dress and heels on an ordinary weekday morning. Not that I wore show-stopping dresses these days. I had one, bought for a media event in London – which Matt had refused to attend as 'everyone would look down on him' – but hadn't brought it to France.

I took out my bag, with phone, pen and notepad inside, and flung it across my body, feeling faintly silly now I was here. I needed a better plan than aimlessly wandering about, hoping to catch sight of Jay, but couldn't think of one. It was no good going into the hotel and demanding to speak to him, or inventing a reason to get him to talk to me – even if I could think of one that didn't involve pretending to be his long-lost sister. Journalists had no doubt tried every trick in the book in the past and failed, so there was no reason to think he'd be willing to engage with me.

As the group of tourists moved away, I fell into step behind them as they walked towards the hotel, excitement mounting when the door swung open and a tall man emerged, in baseball hat and shades. It could be Jay's bodyguard, going to fetch him a newspaper (though I couldn't imagine why).

He was walking purposefully in the direction of the *boulangerie* I'd passed earlier, and as the group in front of me followed him, I did too, hoping one of them wouldn't swing round and ask me what I was doing. Maybe if I could speak to the bodyguard, I could ask him to pass Jay a message. Tell him he'd made me a promise a long time ago and I was here to make sure he kept it. *Too menacing.* I was someone from his past, wanting to catch up. *Still too menacing.* I was the girl on the swing he'd kissed and run away from, after talking about escaping his life and making something of himself. Better, but Jay Merino wasn't about revisiting his past, so he was unlikely to be swayed.

I decided to wing it, and waited while the man paused by the bakery and peered inside as if looking for someone, or something, pretending to check my phone as a couple of the tourists paused too, chatting together in French. One of them gave me a suspicious look and said something to her companion and I quickly looked through the window of the bakery, pretending to admire a row of plump eclairs. My hands were clammy, my heart was racing, and I'd probably chewed all my lipstick off, but I knew this might be my only chance to get to speak to Jay. I had to give it a try, even if it meant losing dignity. I'd plead, if I had to.

When the man turned and started walking back the way he'd come, I waited for a moment, before moving after him. One of the tourists called after me, and someone else – a woman – shouted something I didn't catch. Not daring to look back (had they guessed I was pursuing him?), I picked up my pace, heat fizzing in my cheeks. I'd vaguely planned to stop him when he reached the hotel, but to my surprise, he walked past and down the Quai de la Poithevinière, where I'd parked my bike, and kept going. He gave off an air of watchfulness, as if, in spite of his casual clothes – black T-shirt and jeans and a nondescript bomber jacket – he was on the lookout for danger (or strange women following him). He was obviously security, but why wasn't he back at the hotel, keeping an eye on Jay?

As I sped up, determined to talk to him before I lost my nerve, I became aware of more shouting – *lots* of shouting, coming from all directions. Swinging round, I caught a glimpse of a man in spectacles windmilling his arms, but the man in front didn't turn. He was wearing earphones, so probably hadn't heard and as I hurried to catch up, he looked at his watch, as if he had somewhere to be.

'Oi!' The bellowed word behind me was followed by another, extremely rude one beginning with 'c'. I gasped and half-turned, in time to see a crop-haired woman in a metal-studded jacket peel away from the wall of the restaurant opposite. She strode towards the man, one arm outstretched, and I realised with a lurch of horror that she was holding a gun – an *actual* gun, not a finger-one – and pointing it straight at him.

Instinctively, I hurled myself forwards with a warning cry that came from the depths of my lungs. There was barely time to register the man's open-mouthed shock as he swivelled to face me, before I barrelled into him and knocked him flat.

As I lay on top of him, legs straddling his waist, my face pressed into his shoulder, I had a horrible vision of Dad being asked to identify my bullet-riddled body in a back-street mortuary, and a white-faced Charlie murmuring that he should have insisted on coming to Saint-Martin with me.

I twisted my head and saw a pair of heavy biker boots planted on the cobbles. 'Please don't shoot,' I said, my voice constricted by the difficult angle (and fear). 'Whatever's going on here, we can talk about it.'

'What the hell are you doing?' More feet joined the boots – a male pair in leather loafers – and then we were surrounded by feet. I could hear footsteps and shouting, and the ragged breathing of the man lying beneath me. I prayed that some of the feet belonged to the police.

The man was moving now, muttering something about his collarbone being broken, and then I was being lifted by forceful hands and the man was sitting up, reaching for his shades and hat, which must have flown off on impact. The second his eyes met mine, I realised.

The man whose life I'd just saved was Jay Merino.

Chapter Seven

'You!' I stared, as if I'd never seen a human being before, trying to wriggle free of the strong hands gripping my upper arms. I couldn't believe Jay Merino was out and about, wandering around in public. 'I… I thought you were a bodyguard,' I stuttered. He was oddly familiar close up, and not just because I'd seen his films, or spent a couple of minutes lying on top of him. And it wasn't his close-cropped hair, or the band of stubble obscuring his lower face, which hadn't been there the last time we'd spoken. *It was his eyes.* Even tightened with suspicion, they were the same suede brown I must have committed to memory all those years ago, the lashes long and dark beneath thick brows. 'Are you OK?' I said, wondering why he wasn't getting up. Probably in shock.

'Who *are* you?' The man holding me had a hard-edged London accent and gave me a little shake. 'And what the hell do you think you're doing?'

'Excuse *me*!' I finally pulled free and spun round to face my captor, rubbing the skin on my arms where his fingers had pressed. 'I just saved his life, in case you hadn't noticed.' Glancing around, I saw to my astonishment that among the assembled crowd was the gun-toting woman, her weapon dangling loosely by her side. Unbelievably, she was smirking.

Confusion sizzled through me. 'Has anyone called the police?'

'Not yet,' said the man, who was obviously the real bodyguard. He was big and menacing, biceps bulging from the sleeves of a fitted black T-shirt, a ring pushed through his eyebrow. A massive biker beard counterbalanced his baldness. 'Do you want to explain what that little display was all about?'

'She was going to *shoot* him!' I pointed at the grinning woman – who looked familiar now I thought about it – and I saw a couple more people smiling and shaking their heads. 'Why isn't anyone taking this seriously?'

'She clearly didn't get the memo.' The woman spoke in a honeyed American drawl at odds with her outfit and gun. 'We're filming, honey, and you just ruined the take.'

My ears buzzed. 'What did you say?'

She jerked her head and I swivelled slowly and let my gaze travel over everything I'd missed; the tourists – obviously, extras – a man by the restaurant holding a camera, another with a boom that I hadn't even spotted as I'd kept my gaze narrow, focused on following the man I'd thought was Jay Merino's bodyguard. And the man who'd shouted and waved at me was presumably the director, warning me to shift out of shot. '*Cut!*' That was the word he'd bellowed. *Probably.* He'd joined Biker Beard and was furiously glaring up at him. 'Where the eff were you?' he ground out. 'You're supposed to be security.'

'I needed the toilet,' Biker Beard muttered, shooting me a blood-curdling look. 'I didn't see her until it was too late.'

The director rubbed the groove between his eyebrows and I had the impression he was silently counting to ten. He pushed his glasses up into his white hair, and trained his gaze on me. 'You've really effed things up,' he said. 'What the hell were you thinking?'

I fought a surge of nausea. I hadn't saved Jay's life. I'd wandered into his film and humiliated myself.

'Oh God.' I turned to Jay, a hand pressed to my mouth. He'd finally risen and was regarding me with such intensity, I automatically took a step back. 'I'm sorry,' I whispered through my fingers. 'I'm such an idiot. I didn't realise, I thought...'

'You're English.' It was the first time he'd spoken clearly and I realised his voice was the same as I remembered – slightly more cultured, but closer to his original accent than the gravelly half-Irish twang that belonged to his character, Max Weaver.

'Y... yes.' My hand dropped. 'I live in Chamillon with my father. I came here on my bike.' *Could I sound any weirder?* 'You know everything is protected here? The entire town is a UNESCO World Heritage site.' *Apparently, I could.* 'I didn't realise you were filming,' I rattled on. 'I honestly thought that woman was going to kill you.' I realised now she was Susie Houlihan, who played Nova, a recurring villain in *Maximum Force*, who never quite managed to carry out her assassination because she was secretly in love with Max Weaver.

'And you thought you'd save me?'

'It was instinct.' My face felt scorched. Charlie would have a field day with this. I wasn't even sure I could tell him. 'I saw the gun and panicked, it was pure adrenaline.' There was a mumble of voices around us, but I couldn't tell whether they sounded sympathetic or pissed off. 'I really am sorry.'

'It's all right, Brian.' His gaze had flicked over my shoulder. 'Can we take a break?'

The director sprang to Jay's side, throwing me a filthy look. He was shorter than Jay by about six inches, his stomach straining the buttons on his faded shirt. 'We need to wrap this scene by midday,' he said, flipping his glasses back over his eyes so they looked magnified. 'You know we're on a tight schedule.'

'Ten minutes, Brian.' Jay's tone was pleasant, but defied argument.

Brian's shoulders slumped. 'Fine, ten minutes.' He shoved past, making a throat-cutting gesture that I hoped wasn't meant for me. 'Somebody had better go and fetch me a coffee.'

'Simon will get one for you.'

I realised Jay had directed the words to his bodyguard – who should surely be called Popeye or Gunner – and risked a glance to see him glaring at me with open hostility. Even his tattooed bicep-serpent looked angry. 'You want one?'

I jumped. 'Er, no, I'm good, thank you.'

As the group dispersed, grumbling among themselves, I understood why the street had been quieter than usual and barricaded at one end, and why there'd been big lorries in the parking area. There'd obviously been a notice of filming for locals, with only the restaurant and bakery owners in their usual posts. 'I really can't apologise enough,' I said to Jay. 'I feel like I've ruined everything.'

'I normally manage a scene in one take, two at the most.' He pulled on his baseball cap, which suited him a lot better than the one that Dad had tried on. 'They can afford the occasional interruption.'

It was kind of him to phrase it that way, but I knew I'd derailed a tightly planned itinerary, and from his furrow-browed stare and defensive posture, I guessed Jay was being polite. 'Listen, I know I shouldn't have been following you—'

'Your hair,' he interrupted, angling a gaze at my head, and I remembered with a pulse of embarrassment that I'd had it cut short before the party and Gemma's brother had nicknamed me Bubblehead. 'Have we met before?'

'Actually, we have.' I scraped a handful of curls behind my ear. My clip had sprung out when I launched myself at Jay along with his earphones.

'About fifteen years ago, at a friend's house. Her brother had a party and *your* brother…' I stopped. His expression had transformed from wary to delighted surprise, a smile spreading over his face that was like the sun chasing away a raincloud.

'I remember.' He stepped closer, wagging his shades at me. 'You wanted to be a writer.'

My breath caught. 'You *do* remember.'

'Of *course*.' His eyes skimmed my face, as though matching it to a memory. 'Our conversation that night was the first I'd ever had with a girl as nice as you.'

'Really?' I tucked my chin in, ridiculously pleased. 'I find that hard to believe.'

'Why?' He cocked his head. 'Remember, I was nobody back then, and you were…' His smile crept back. 'You were lovely.' *Oh my God.* 'You kissed me,' he said with a full-blown, eye-crinkling smile.

Blood rushed to my head so quickly, I felt faint. 'You kissed *me*, actually.'

'OK, we kissed each other.'

A bolt of incredulous laughter shot out of my mouth. 'I can't believe you remember,' I said. 'You must have kissed…' I waved a hand. 'I don't know, thousands of women since then.'

'You always remember your first kiss.'

'That was *never* your first kiss.'

'The first that made an impact.'

'So much so, you ran away.'

'Yeah. Well, I was young and stupid,' he said with mild embarrassment. 'I had big plans and a girlfriend wasn't one of them.'

'That's OK.' I still felt as if I'd stood up too quickly, even though I hadn't moved. This wasn't a conversation I'd imagined having, even in my wildest dreams. 'I had big plans, too.'

'So, *are* you a writer?'

'Actually, I am.' This was going *so* much better than I'd planned. Apart from leaping on him out of the blue, and interrupting filming. 'I worked for a magazine in London and now I'm… working over here.'

He grimaced, and rapped his forehead with a knuckle. 'This is going to sound awful, but the one thing I can't remember is your name.'

'I'm not sure I ever told you.'

He grinned. *Jay Merino was grinning.* There was nothing remotely feral or scary, or even starry, about him. He looked… *normal.* OK, not going-to-work-in-an-office or on a building-site normal, but nothing like his screen persona either, or the man in the photos I'd looked at online. 'That explains it then,' he said.

'It's Natalie Bright.'

'Great name.'

'So is yours.' *Lame.*

'Things might have been easier if I'd changed it,' he said. 'But it was the name I was born with, so I decided to stick with it.'

'Even if you'd changed it, someone would have recognised you.' I was still having trouble believing I was having a *tête-à-tête* with Jay Merino on a deserted street in France, the sound of boat masts clinking in the harbour. 'You can't hide for long when you're famous.'

'More's the pity.' His eyebrows wrinkled. 'So, were you stalking me, Natalie Bright?'

'No!' The word burst out, startling a passing gull. 'Well, I was, but not in the way you think. I mean, I didn't know it was you, but I was hoping it was someone who might be able to persuade you to talk to me.'

'Hang on.' He looked around, as if there might be a real assassin taking aim at him. 'How did you know we were here, when everyone signed NDAs?'

'DNAs?'

'NDAs. Non-disclosure agreements.'

'Oh, right. Sorry.' I chewed my lip. 'I don't want to get anyone into trouble,' I said. 'I promise I'm the only one who knows you're here, apart from my dad and a very good friend of mine. Two friends, if you count the person who told my dad, but they're very discreet and it won't go any further.' Keen to erase the faint crease of worry that had settled on his forehead, I said, 'Do you remember the promise you made that night?'

He scrunched his eyes, as if looking into the past. 'That you could interview me when I was famous?'

I suppressed a squeal of excitement. 'I tried, after you did that zombie film, but you turned me down.'

His eyebrows jerked. 'I did?'

'Well, your agent regretfully informed me you didn't give interviews.'

He nodded slowly. 'I decided early on I wasn't going down that route, but if I'd known it was you…' The way he said it, with a crooked smile, made my heart leap into my throat. It was utterly astonishing how pleased he seemed to see me, even though I'd knocked him over and made his director angry – unless he was acting, but a gut feeling told me he wasn't. 'I suppose I do owe you, seeing as you just saved my life.'

'Well, now you mention it.' I dipped my head in a coquettish manner.

He gave a boisterous laugh. 'That was pretty impressive, by the way.'

Oh wow, Jay Merino was so *nice*. 'Why, thank you.' I curtsied, hoping I wasn't pushing my luck, and was rewarded with another short laugh. 'What about your collarbone?'

'It's an old injury, from a stunt I did a few years ago.' He rotated one shoulder, and massaged it with his other hand. 'It flares up now and again, particularly when I'm leapt on by eager females, which is why I have a stunt double now.'

'I read somewhere that you bribed him to pretend to be you.'

'Not true, like most things you've probably read about me.'

'That you wanted a hot tub installed by your trailer?'

'*Definitely* not true.'

'You gave up smoking?' I recalled the glow of his cigarette the night we met.

'That *is* true,' he said, his smile suggesting that he was remembering it too. 'I never really enjoyed it.'

It felt like we were flirting, but I was so out of practise it was hard to tell. Then again, he was the one who'd brought up our bygone kiss.

'I'm glad I didn't break anything,' I said.

'It does hurt a bit.' He gave a clownish wince.

'God, I'm so sorry.'

'Don't be.' His eyes softened. 'To be honest, this is the most fun I've had in ages.'

'You should get out more.' Now we were both laughing, as if I was the funniest person on the planet, and I prayed if this *was* a dream, I wouldn't wake up for at least the next two years. 'I can't believe I've just been filmed, jumping on top of you.'

'Don't worry, it won't be used.' Jay pushed a hand into the pocket of his bomber jacket. 'And mobile phones are banned, for this morning at least, so you don't need to worry that anyone else filmed you, either.'

I hadn't been, until then. 'What about him?' I pointed to the restaurant owner, fiddling with his table umbrellas, clearly agog at the unexpected drama that had unfolded in front of him. 'Or the woman in the bakery?'

'They wouldn't dare.' He pulled a fierce Max Weaver face, that wasn't half as intimidating as it looked onscreen – or maybe it was just that now I knew he wasn't intimidating at all. 'They're being paid for their time and wouldn't want to risk being cut out of the film, or sued, by posting something online.'

'I don't suppose my scene will stay?'

'I'm afraid not.' He slipped into character, his face transforming. 'Nobody puts Max Weaver down.'

'Except, I did.'

He smiled that smile again. 'Yes, you did.'

I shivered. Not with cold – the sun was warm, heating the top of my head – but with a mix of giddy excitement and… something hard to pin down.

'I should let you get on,' I said, following the line of his gaze.

The director was holding a cardboard coffee cup, talking to the cameraman, while Jay's bodyguard Simon stood nearby, his burning gaze fixed on me. Maybe he wasn't convinced that I wasn't a stalker, after all, and he must be fuming that he'd got into trouble for not spotting me sooner.

'Don't worry about him.' Jay must have read my mind. 'Simon's just doing his job – or at least, he should have been.' His mouth did a rueful twist. 'You wouldn't believe the lengths people go to get close to me, and I'm not being big-headed when I say that.'

'Reporters?'

'And a woman convinced I'd asked her to marry me. But mostly reporters.'

'Maybe it's your own fault,' I said. 'If you gave them what they wanted, they might leave you alone.' His expression darkened and I regretted my impulsive comment. 'It's just that there's all this mystery around you, which makes people crazy. You won't even do publicity for your films.'

'I don't have to.' His voice remained steady, but with a slight edge. 'It hasn't done the franchise any harm. If anything, it's better this way. The public can't confuse me with Max Weaver.'

'But they think you *are* him.'

'And that's a bad thing?'

'He's a violent, vigilante womaniser.'

Jay sighed. 'He's not *real*.'

'Some people think you're just playing yourself.' I'd heard the comment on a late-night review show, once. 'If you gave an interview, you could control the narrative.'

He passed a hand over his jaw, his gaze brightening. 'Funnily enough, I had been thinking of talking to someone from a magazine here. There's a writer who's been persistent, and from what I've read, she's good.'

'Fleur Dupont?'

He nodded. 'You probably know her.'

I nearly smiled at the idea of Fleur and me, hanging out together, but my insides were a mass of nerves again. 'She *is* good,' I said, as firmly as I could. 'She's probably the best, but she doesn't know you or where you've come from, like I do. I know it's a bit of a cheek, Jay, but would you consider talking to me for the magazine instead?'

His eyebrows lifted. 'You work there too?'

'Um, no, I'm sort of freelance at the moment, but I've got a meeting with the editor-in-chief this evening, and if I can prove I know you, he's agreed to consider letting me do the interview, if you say yes. It's my shot at a permanent job, you see. I'll get my own byline, a desk and… everything.'

Jay was frowning. 'You've spoken to him about me?'

'I know that sounds bad, but once I knew you were here—'

'It's OK, it's fine,' he cut in, rather tersely, and I knew that if I'd been anyone else, he'd have walked away by now. 'So, you came here to get proof that you know me?'

'Well, and to talk to you, really.' I twisted the strap of my bag, which had somehow survived me flinging myself at Jay. 'Obviously, if you don't want me to interview you, I can just go away, and you can pretend this didn't happen.' I felt suddenly sick, and wished we could have carried on flirting – or whatever it was. 'I'm sorry, I know this is the last thing you need, and considering I've just ruined your scene and you haven't set eyes on me for years, you don't owe me anything.'

'It's just hard for me to trust anyone, especially in the media,' he said, unsmiling, no doubt recalling the spurious stories that had appeared in the press, during his early career.

'But it's not like we've never met.' A flashback to our kiss shot into my head, sending fresh heat to my face. 'And you would have the final say.' *He hadn't said no.* 'Nothing would be published that you didn't completely approve of.'

His gaze stayed on me for what seemed like ages, and I tried to convey all the sincerity I felt and hoped he wasn't disappointed that I'd been following him with an interview in mind. 'I suppose I *did* make a promise.' His mouth was curving into a smile once more. 'And I am a man of my word.'

I stared. 'You mean, you'll do it?'

'Jay, we must get a move on.' The director was back, looking as if he'd like to vaporise me. 'We've got that motorboat scene at two. We're wasting time here.'

Jay nodded. 'If I do, you have to promise that in return, you'll tell me what you've been up to since the last time we met.'

'What?' The director looked momentarily confused, until he realised that Jay was talking to me.

'Of… of course,' I said eagerly, nearly crossing my heart. 'Anything. Though I'm not very exciting.' My heart was beating wildly. 'Really, not very interesting at all.'

'I'll be the judge of that.' His smile wasn't quite as strong as it had been and, for a second, I wished I could turn back time and not mention the magazine. 'Come to the hotel in the morning, around ten,' he said. 'We can have a chat in my room.' He slid his shades back on so I couldn't see his eyes – only my reflection in the lenses. I looked every bit as unkempt, big-haired and dumbstruck as I'd feared. 'Give me your phone,' he instructed, holding out his palm.

'Sorry?'

'You said you needed proof.'

'Oh! Right.'

The director huffed and muttered while I fished around in my bag, heart pumping so hard, my chest could barely contain it. 'Shall I…?' I fumbled with the password and opened the camera, flipping the screen so my face appeared, bleached out by the sun.

'I've never done this before.' Jay was beside me now, so close I could discreetly sniff him. He smelt minty, like herbal tea, laced with a hint of warm skin. 'You're my first,' he said.

Another deep blush crept up my face. 'I'm honoured.'

He wrapped a strong arm around my shoulders, sending such a strong wave of electricity down my spine it was a struggle to stand upright. Susie Houlihan and most of the extras had drifted back and were watching, some of them open-mouthed, as if they'd entered a parallel universe where nothing was as it seemed. Which was exactly how I felt.

'Smile!' Bending his knees, Jay pushed up his shades, tilted his head towards mine and made a sideways V-sign with his fingers. 'Cheesy enough?'

'Perfect.' With a shaky hand, I held the phone high, unsure what to do with my face, and snapped a picture and then another for luck. 'I promise I won't post it anywhere.'

'I hope not.' Turning, he looked right into my startled-rabbit eyes. 'I hope I can trust you, Natalie Bright.'

Chapter Eight

'I cannot believe you're going to interview the mighty Max Weaver.'

'It's Jay Merino, and neither can I,' I said, through a mouthful of quiche.

'Or that you didn't hang around to watch him escape the lovely Nova's latest assassination attempt.'

'I didn't dare, you should have seen the director's face.' I shuddered, recalling Brian's glacial stare as he'd guided Jay away, making it clear he was nowhere near as forgiving. 'He hates me,' I added. 'And, I think if beheading still existed, the bodyguard would be in big trouble.'

'Simon,' said Charlie with a chuckle. 'You'd think he'd have a tougher name, like Chopper.'

'He's still a human being,' I argued, even though I'd thought the same thing. And I wasn't entirely sure about the 'human' part.

'This photo's adorable.'

'Give it here.' I tried to snatch my phone off Charlie, but he drew it closer to his face. 'It's definitely Jay,' I said. 'Can't you tell?'

'I'm talking about *your* face.'

'Oh God, I know.' I put down my fork and pushed my plate to one side. As soon as I'd got back to the café, Charlie had taken his lunch break and served up some food, knowing I'd be starving. 'I look deranged.'

'Did you know you were pulling that face?'

'I was smiling,' I protested. 'Just a bit too much.'

'You look happy, but scared.'

'That's pretty much how I felt.'

'The way the sun's on you but not him makes it look like you've added him in.'

'Oh no, do you think so?' The last thing I needed was Nicolas Juilliard thinking I'd faked a picture with Jay Merino.

'Actually, this one's not too bad.'

He thrust the phone under my nose and I saw that I'd angled my head a bit closer to Jay's in the second shot, so my face wasn't as overexposed. An involuntary smile pulled at my mouth. 'He wasn't at *all* what I expected.'

'So you've said.' Charlie looked at me. 'You like him,' he said, sounding slightly awestruck. It was a long time since I'd liked a man in a way that made my pulse race. Even Charlie's closest friend Ryan from England, who – according to Charlie – no woman could resist, had failed to ignite anything but mild interest when I'd met him over Christmas.

I opened my mouth to argue, but just seeing Jay's face on my phone had affected my breathing. 'He was *really* nice.'

'Considering you floored him.' Charlie's eyes glowed with amusement. I hadn't been able to resist telling him after all, and had had to wait five minutes for him to stop laughing. 'Honestly, Nat, that's a story in itself. Your readers at *Expats* will love it.'

With a guilty pang, I realised I still hadn't finished my column. Or started it. 'I'm not writing about that,' I said. 'I've still got to convince Nicolas Juilliard to let me do this interview.'

'Oh, I don't think you'll have a problem now Max has agreed.'

'Jay, not Max.'

Charlie slid my phone across the table. 'I've changed your ringtone to the theme from *Maximum Force*,' he said and I tutted. 'Anyway, you're two of the things Juilliard likes, from what I've read.'

'And what might those be, Charles?'

'Attractive, and a bit of a challenge.'

Giselle had materialised at the table next to ours, her shoulders stiffening when Charlie said *attractive*. He threw her a sunny grin and her face melted into a smile.

'Still leading her on?' I said.

'I can smile at her, can't I?'

'Not if it's giving her the impression you're in love with her.'

'If I wanted her to think that, I'd smile like this.' Charlie tilted his head and arranged his features into a sugary beam that made me dissolve into giggles.

'That's terrifying, but oddly cute.' Giselle threw me a dead-eyed look that made me wince. Madame Bisset, who'd been trying to engage Giselle in conversation, shrank back as though she'd had a glimpse of hell.

'So, what's the plan with Max?' Charlie waited while I resumed eating and finished my quiche, which was too delicious to ignore, though I'd sworn I was too hyped-up to eat when Charlie brought it over.

'You mean Jay,' I said. 'He's invited me to his hotel tomorrow morning.'

'Oi-oi!'

'Charlie, stop it.' I looked around, but no one was remotely interested. Dolly, her hair freshly trimmed and styled into waves, wasn't even looking our way for once, absorbed in conversation with one of her regulars,

Monsieur Moreau. He'd once been a famous violinist, and now came to the café to plan his music lessons (and get out from under his wife's feet). For a moment, it struck me as odd that peoples' lives were carrying on as normal, when my own felt like it had shifted. I was full of crackling adrenaline and there was a storm of butterflies in my stomach at the thought of meeting Nicolas later on. 'I have to work out what to ask Jay,' I said. 'I can't go in without a plan or it'll end up being a mess.'

'Maybe he doesn't want to *talk*.' Charlie licked his lips in a lascivious fashion and made revolting kissy sounds.

'Stop it,' I said, an image of Jay's full lips sliding into my head. 'I expect he could have any woman he wanted, and he probably has a girlfriend tucked away.'

'But you said yourself, he seemed really pleased to see you.'

'He did, but probably in the way you'd be pleased to see your kid sister if you hadn't clapped eyes on her in a long time.'

'If I had a kid sister, I don't think I'd be taking selfies and inviting her to my hotel room for a chat.'

'That's exactly the sort of thing you'd do with a kid sister you hadn't clapped eyes on for years,' I said. 'And you haven't got a kid sister, so it's irrelevant.'

'Point taken.' Charlie wiped his mouth with a paper napkin. 'He could be having a thing with his assassin, Nova.'

'Susie Houlihan.'

'Doesn't that sort of thing happen on location?'

'I wouldn't know, I've never been in a film,' I said. 'And neither have you, but good to know that's how you'd be behaving.'

'Come on, Nat, I was making a point, that's all.' He stood up, preparing to get back to work and let Stefan have his lunch break. 'But if they're both free and single, why not?'

'I just don't think he'd be that unprofessional,' I said, with a surprising amount of confidence given that I'd just spoken to Jay for the first time in years and had no idea how he behaved on-set.

'I'm sure you're right,' said Charlie, as I banished a vision of Jay and Susie Houlihan thrashing around on his (or her) duvet. 'And you'll be fine when you get there.' He had a touching amount of confidence in me, considering I'd never interviewed a bona fide A-lister before. 'Get your meeting with Juilliard out of the way and you're good to go.'

Luckily, Dad was out when I got back to the house. I'd exhausted myself telling Charlie about meeting Jay, and wasn't sure I had the energy to go over it again – plus, I was worried about too many people knowing. Dad was completely trustworthy, but if he mentioned something to Marie in passing and she told her friend Jeanne… well, I had no idea what would happen, if anything, but I'd hate to get anyone in trouble.

I ran upstairs, desperate for a shower. Hearing voices drifting up, I looked out of my bedroom window to see Dad in the garden next door with Marie, and a couple who must be Larry and Barbara, her returning American guests. They were sitting around a table with tall glasses of something refreshing, and were laughing at something Dad had said. I felt a pang of pride. He was so good at getting along with people and putting them at ease – it was just a shame it didn't extend to his dates. He tried so hard, he always got it wrong.

I pushed open the window to let in some air and heard him say, 'You don't see officers on television cleaning human poo out of a police cell,' followed by gales of laughter.

I shook my head, smiling. It had long been annoying to watch a police drama with Dad, due to his tendency to pick up on the smallest inaccuracy, despite my protests that it was meant to be entertaining and no one would watch if it was all about paperwork and drunks being sick on their shoes.

'You're a blast, Marty,' said Larry. Marie nodded in agreement, her eyes fastened on Dad, and I wondered whether I should set them up on a date. Get Marie round on the pretext of cooking for her for a change and then leave them to it.

Refreshed by a shower, with a few hours to spare, I tried to focus on writing my column for *Expats*, but couldn't stop going over the morning's events, cringing as I relived the way I'd felled Jay, like a rugby player. It didn't say much for my powers of observation that I hadn't clocked it was him, or that I'd failed to notice all the signs of filming taking place. In danger of convincing myself he'd only been nice because I'd put myself in harm's way to 'save' him, I found myself typing *How Not to Impress an Actor on Location* and writing up what had happened, leaving out Jay's name and the exact location, and embellishing my role for comedic effect. Not that it needed much embellishment being pretty ridiculous as it was.

Let's just say, I didn't hang around to ask for his autograph, I finished, before adding a sidebar of regulations around filming in France, plus details on becoming an extra (which was unglamorous and poorly paid, according to my online research) and emailed it to Sandy before I could change my mind. It was better than a piece about tax laws.

Nerves stirred in my chest as I searched my wardrobe for something suitable to wear to a Michelin-starred restaurant in La Rochelle. The occasion demanded more than my usual going-out jeans and a top designed to minimise my boobs. I might not be allowed in if I wasn't dressed up and wished now I'd thought to buy something in Saint-Martin – or that I hadn't left my show-stopper dress in Mum's wardrobe back home.

After trying on and discarding several items, I remembered Marie had lent me a dress to wear for Dad's birthday meal, and bolted next door to ask if I could borrow it again.

'Of course!' she said, when I'd apologised for dragging her away from her guests. 'I will fetch it for you.'

I wouldn't have dreamt of raiding Mum's wardrobe. Her idea of dressing up was a purple mohair sweater over boot-cut jeans with sequinned pockets (Mum loved a sequin detail) and a pair of high-heeled boots, but Marie's innate sense of style meant her outfits spanned the age barrier, and although she was a size smaller, the dress I'd worn before was very forgiving.

'You are meeting a nice man?' she enquired, a smile playing over her face as she handed me the dress.

'I don't know about nice,' I said, laughing too heartily. 'But he's definitely a man.'

'A man?' Dad bobbed up behind her in the doorway, eyebrows raised. 'Is it—?'

'Just a man, an ordinary man, no one special at all,' I sang, causing Marie to jerk back and a hand to fly to her throat.

'It's a very nice outfit for someone not that special,' Dad persisted, eyeing the dress over Marie's shoulder. 'You're sure it's not—'

'No one you know, no one you know!' I blasted.

'Well, who then?' He looked baffled, completely missing my flashing eye signals, warning him not to mention Jay Merino.

'Leave her alone,' chided Marie, turning to place a slender hand on his arm. 'She doesn't want to tempt fate.'

'Oh no, it's not that.' I didn't want her getting the wrong idea. 'Actually, I'm meeting a magazine publisher.' Why the hell hadn't I said that in the first place? 'I've pitched an idea, and he's interested.'

'Oh!' Dad's eyes grew big. 'Is it an interview with—?'

'No, no, no, no, NO!' I held up my palm in exasperation. '*Not* an interview, not at all!' So much for him being a police officer. How could he not detect that I wanted him to *shut the hell up*? 'It's… it's top secret at the moment. I'm afraid I can't talk about it.'

'Blimey, Natalie, no need to get worked up.' He looked at Marie as if for support, and taking control, she shook her head kindly.

'Natalie does not want an inquisition from her father, Marty. You must let her go and do what she has to do, and she will tell you about it in good time, yes?'

I wanted to hug her. 'Exactly,' I said. 'I'll tell you about it later, Dad, OK?'

Again, I tried to message him with my eyes.

'Are you feeling all right, love?' he said. 'You shouldn't be meeting anyone if you've got one of your heads coming on.'

He was referring to the occasional migraines I'd suffered on and off since my teens, though I hadn't had one since moving to the island. 'I haven't got one of my heads,' I assured him, leaning in to kiss his cheek. 'I'll see you in a couple of hours.'

'Have fun,' said Marie, and I thought what a nice couple they made, standing together on the doorstep, waving me off.

Chapter Nine

When we reached La Rochelle, I instructed the driver to drop me a little way down the street, out of view of the restaurant, in case Nicolas Juilliard happened to be watching from the window. Unlikely, but I didn't want him to see me scrambling out of the car, trying not to flash my knickers.

I paused to check my carefully applied make-up in a compact mirror I hardly ever used. I'd initially tried a 'barely-there' look, which had given the impression I was recovering from a bout of food poisoning, so I'd added a swipe of cherry-red lipstick, but that had brought to mind the scary clown from *It*. In the end, I'd settled for some Caramel Nude lipgloss, and eyeliner with a flick, and hoped that by combining it with the silky black knee-length dress I'd borrowed from Marie, I was channelling Audrey Tautou. If Audrey were twenty pounds heavier with a perm. Although I'd managed to tame my curls into glossy waves, I expected them to rebel before the evening was out.

As I stepped through the door of the restaurant – famed for its sea views as well as its gourmet food – I told myself this wasn't the first time I'd been to a nice restaurant to meet a man, but the truth was, I'd never been to a restaurant quite this nice, to meet a man with as much power as Nicolas Juilliard. The fact that there was a lot riding on this meeting – I was assuming he'd come from Paris especially – only heightened my nerves.

'Ah, Mademoiselle Bright!'

To my surprise, Nicolas was already there, rising from a table and waving me over, before the maître d' had even noticed my presence, and I wondered how he'd recognised me. Trying to give the impression I'd been there before, I forged a path between linen-draped tables, heels sinking into the navy carpet, glad to note that at least I didn't look out of place among the scattering of well-dressed diners. 'It's lovely to meet you at last, Monsieur Juilliard.'

'Nicolas, please,' he said, ignoring my outstretched hand in favour of a robust kiss on each cheek, his masculine scent almost overwhelmingly sensual. 'The pleasure eez all mine.' Hands on my shoulders, his gaze danced over my face, down Marie's dress to my pointy-toe shoes and back again. Though I'd normally bristle at being appraised like something delicious being served on a platter (judging by his expression), I had to admit to being a tiny bit flattered – plus, I was doing the same to him, just in a subtler way.

Nicolas Juilliard *oozed* charisma, as if it was coded in his DNA. He was an imposing figure, tall and solid, his hooded eyes an unusually deep shade of brown, his grey-streaked hair and sideburns neatly groomed. His light-coloured suit looked expensive, but he wore it carelessly. I could easily picture him reclining on a sofa, brandy glass in one hand, cigarette in the other, instructing a pretty woman to remove her stockings. Luckily, I wasn't wearing stockings – if I had been, they might have fallen down of their own accord.

'Your picture does not do you justice,' he said, with a puzzled frown. He must have been referring to the one that came up in a Google search from my time working at *Chatter* – a headshot that made me look twenty years older – or the one on my blog, where my nose dominated my face. I rarely photograph well.

'It's very kind of you to meet me,' I said, determined to maintain a businesslike air in the face of his probing gaze. I quickly sat on one of the thickly padded chairs around the table before he had time to pull one out for me. While I wasn't averse to gentlemanly behaviour, from the way his eyes had roved over me when I arrived, I had the sense that with Nicolas there would be strings attached. In his world, #MeToo and the 'Time's Up' campaign probably hadn't registered, and I wasn't the sort to trade sexual favours for a job. Even one I wanted very badly.

Out of the corner of my eye, I noticed a small animal sitting on the chair beside Nicolas, curling its lip at me. He'd brought his little white bulldog, Babette, and while I longed to scoop her up and kiss her crumpled face, she was growling at me in a very unladylike fashion.

'Shake hands,' Nicolas instructed, and Babette held up a delicate paw with what looked like great reluctance.

Charmed, in spite of myself, I leaned over and took her soft foot in my hand and bobbed it up and down. 'She's gorgeous,' I said, even though her ears were flattened to her head with hatred.

'She's very protective,' said Nicolas fondly, as Babette snapped at my fingers with pointy incisors. 'My little lion.'

I snatched my hand away, feeling ridiculously hurt. She could take a few lessons from Hamish the Scottie at the café – he'd never snap at me like that.

'You know,' said Nicolas thoughtfully, smoothing his white shirt front as he sat opposite, eyes still scoping my features. 'You 'ave a look of a young Hedy Lamarr. She was a beautiful film star many years ago.'

'I've heard of her,' I said, thrilled in spite of myself. I'd been compared to an Irish Water Spaniel once – or at least, my hair had – but never a glamorous actress from the 1940s.

'She was not satisfied with the film world, she was an inventor,' Nicolas continued, his gravelly voice and French accent hard to resist. 'She was an early pioneer of wireless communications, after helping to develop a secret communications system for ze US Navy.' He shook his head in awe. 'A remarkable woman.'

'I didn't know that.' I was impressed by his knowledge and passion. Maybe I'd misjudged him after all.

'She had ze first ever orgasm on screen.'

Maybe not. 'Really?' I returned his lazy smile with a brief twist of my mouth. Babette was watching me with bulging eyes, as if she knew the effect her master was having and was pleased. 'Well, if you've finished with the sex talk, perhaps we can get to business.'

He threw back his head and gave a belly laugh that drew attention from the people around us. 'I knew I'd like you, Natalee,' he said, beckoning a hovering waiter, who was eyeing the dog with thinly masked disapproval. 'What do you think of the restaurant?'

'It's amazing.' I gratefully turned my attention to the modern décor; the marine-blue colours, clever wall art, and curvy ceiling panels designed to reflect the shape of the waves washing onto the beach in front of the glass wall. The sun was setting over the ocean, filling the room with the sort of peachy light that flattered complexions and glanced off glass and cutlery, the whole effect like a film set. 'It's my first visit,' I said, forgetting I was meant to be playing it cool. 'I love it.'

Nicolas gave a gratified grin, his slightly imperfect teeth only adding to his attractiveness. 'I know ze chef,' he said, which explained why Babette had been allowed in. He plucked the menu from the waiter's hand. 'Ze man, 'e is a genius.' Nicolas bunched his fingertips and kissed them. 'We try ze oysters?' He arched an eyebrow, clearly alluding to their aphrodisiac properties, and I tried not to roll my eyes.

'I'm allergic,' I fibbed. Dad had once encouraged Mum and me to try them on holiday, but Mum had fretted about ingesting flesh-eating bacteria, and I'd retched until my eyes felt like they were bleeding – and that was just at the sight of them.

'In zat case, we will 'ave ze monkfish.' Nicolas handed back the menu.

'Do I get a say?'

'Trust me, Natalee, you will not regret it.'

I decided not to argue. I wouldn't have known what to order, and wasn't sure I'd be able to eat anyway. My stomach was swarming with nerves.

'Champagne?'

'I prefer white wine,' I admitted.

He chuckled. 'I think you are very 'onest, Natalee. I like that.' Babette let out a yelp as though jealous, while he ordered something in rapid-fire French. The waiter gave an obsequious nod and vanished. 'Now, please tell me 'ow you know Jay Merino.'

Startled by the switch in tone, I hitched my chair closer to the table to buy a few seconds' thinking time. I didn't want to lie any more, especially after being complimented for my honesty, so opened my bag and took out my phone, deciding to get to the point. 'You asked for proof and I've brought it,' I said, scrolling to the photos I'd taken, grinning automatically at the sight of Jay's smiling face. Despite viewing the pictures several times, I still had trouble believing he was there, on my phone. 'I was with him this morning,' I said. No need to mention the circumstances. 'We had a chat before he started filming and he confirmed he'd like me to interview him exclusively for the magazine.' Nicolas took my phone and studied the photo through narrowed eyes, his lips slightly pursed. 'Check the date if you like,' I said. 'And you can see the harbour at Saint-Martin in the background.'

'I see it,' said Nicolas, "E looks very 'appy to be standing next to you, Natalee.' His eyes grazed the hint of cleavage visible in the dip of my dress, which revealed quite a bit more than it would have on Marie. 'And 'oo wouldn't?'

'Plenty of people,' I said crisply, reaching for my phone.

He handed it back, almost grudgingly, as if he'd like to flip through the rest of my pictures – not that he'd find them very thrilling. They were mostly of scenery and sunsets, and several of Charlie and me goofing about, or Dad looking bashful – he didn't like having his picture taken either. 'I am sorry I doubted you,' he said, with what sounded like genuine regret. 'But you understand, I cannot risk the reputation of my magazine by letting an unknown—'

'But why?' I cut in. 'Why not give an unknown writer a chance?' As I leaned forward to make my point, Babette gave a warning bark. As much as I loved dogs, I wished she'd bugger off. It was hard to concentrate under her ferocious glare. 'How do you know you're not missing some amazing talent by only giving assignments to your regular team?'

'You 'ave amazing talent?'

'Well, no, of course not…'

'Why not? Don't be modest, Natalee.'

'Well, I mean, I'm OK, but I wouldn't say *amazing*.' *Why was I putting myself down?*

'Ah, you British. You are so modest.' His smile projected amusement, but no surprise – as if he'd expected nothing else. 'As it 'appens, I sometimes 'ave guest writers, usually American or Canadian, very high-calibre, but what I was going to say before you so passionately interrupted me, Natalee, was that I think, on this occasion, I am more than 'appy to let you… what is it you English say?… *do the honours.*'

'Oh.' I absorbed his words and felt a rush of excitement. 'Well, that's great,' I said, furnishing him with a smile so bright it made him blink. 'Thank you, Monsieur Juilliard.'

'Please, call me Nicolas.' He glanced at my chest and away. 'We must celebrate,' he said, as the waiter returned with a bottle of wine that elicited a nod of approval, and while it was poured – which seemed to take an excruciatingly long time – Nicolas's eyes didn't leave mine. When the waiter had gone, we clinked glasses, and as I took a tentative sip – cool and grapey (I wasn't a connoisseur) – suspicion began to creep around the edge of my excitement.

'I hope you don't expect anything in return,' I said, putting my glass down, noting the way his eyes had fixed on my breasts again. 'I'm not going to sleep with you to show my gratitude.' This time, his laughter was contagious, and several people joined in without any idea what they were laughing at. 'I'm not joking.'

'Oh, Mademoiselle Bright, you are quite adorable,' he said, dabbing his eyes with his napkin when he'd recovered. 'Of course you don't 'ave to sleep with me.' He shoved back a lock of hair that had fallen across his brow. 'Not unless you want to, of course.'

'Who wants to sleep with who?' A woman pulled up a chair and sat between us and as she did so, the temperature seemed to drop by several degrees. She didn't bother introducing herself – she didn't have to.

It was Fleur Dupont.

'Fleur! What are you doing in La Rochelle?' Nicolas didn't sound too surprised as he scooped up Babette and kissed the dog's nose before handing her to the waiter with a look of remorse. 'Look after 'er, please, Fleur is allergic,' he said, and I noticed that Fleur was looking at the dog as though she was the Devil himself. All the same, I was glad when Babette was whisked away, thrashing and snarling in the waiter's arms.

'I told you I was visiting my father today.' Fleur turned to look at me through long-lashed eyes, her gaze impenetrable behind her rectangular glasses. There was no hint of the warmth she'd presumably deployed to get Brad Pitt to talk. 'You mentioned your meeting with Mademoiselle Bright, so I thought I'd come and see the competition,' she added, and my eager words of greeting died on my tongue. So that's what I was. *Competition.* I supposed she was used to getting her own way at the magazine – getting all the high-profile assignments. 'Nicolas tells me you know Jay Merino.' Her accent was almost neutral, unlike Nicolas's, but I detected a very slight croak at the end of the sentence. She must really want the job, but of course she would: an exclusive with Jay would bring her closer to winning Nicolas's job.

'I... yes, I do,' I said, feeling somehow diminished. It wasn't because she was beautiful, though she was, with her curtain of black hair pulled back to reveal high cheekbones and a swan-like neck. She was wearing a simple fine-knit sweater tucked into slim trousers that accentuated her slender figure, making me feel by comparison like an overweight teenager dressed for prom night. Close up, she appeared closer to forty than her photos suggested, with faint lines around her eyes and mouth, but they spoke of experience and probably enhanced her approachability – though not to me. 'He, er, Jay is...' I cleared my throat. 'I spoke to him this morning,' I stammered, picking up my glass. I sipped some wine, trying to hold on to the feeling of triumph I'd experienced moments earlier. 'I thought, because we know each other, and he happens to be here filming, it was the perfect opportunity to—'

'I have been trying for some time to arrange a meeting with him,' she interrupted. 'We were very close.' It took a moment to realise she meant close to a meeting, not close to Jay. 'That job was as good as mine, until you called Nic.' Her nostrils flared. '*I know him, he'll talk to me, pleeease,*' she whined, '*give me a chance to write for your amaaaaazing magazine, even though I have no experience.*'

Wow. It was as if she'd been listening in on our phone conversation. Though her impression of me needed work. Unless I sounded like a whinging brat on helium.

'Fleur does not like losing,' said Nicolas, who'd been watching our exchange with a loose-lipped smile and a look of sly delight. I wondered whether this was some sort of fantasy for him – two women fighting for a job, with him holding all the authority.

Yet he didn't. Boldness crept back in. *I* was the one holding the cards. Jay had agreed to talk to *me* and if Nicolas wouldn't publish the interview, I'd offer it elsewhere. Jay wasn't concerned about the publication – he'd simply agreed to honour his promise to me – but I was guessing that Nicolas wanted to publish it very much indeed.

'Ultimately, it's up to Jay Merino who he talks to,' I said, concentrating on keeping my voice steady. 'He's chosen me.'

'It sounds like you didn't give him much choice.' Fleur's gaze turned stony and I understood. Jay Merino had become an enigma. An interview – even a quote – from him would be breaking news and she wanted the accolades as much as she wanted to run the magazine. But surely, I had as much right to pitch for my dream job as she did hers.

'P'raps you should both write up an interview and I shall judge ze best effort. Maybe I put zem both on ze website and see which brings ze most traffic,' said Nicolas, practically salivating with anticipation, and a faint flicker of distaste crossed Fleur's face.

'I don't think Jay would like that,' I said quickly. 'He's hardly going to let both of us interview him.'

'You know that for sure?' Fleur's voice was hard and I struggled to hold her gaze.

'Yes, I do.'

'You know, she wants to replace me as head of the magazine,' said Nicolas, with a confiding twinkle in my direction. 'I told her, if she can triple ze readership, she can do it. *Maybe*.' He tapped the side of his nose. 'It was our leetle gamble.' I didn't say I'd read about his challenge and cringed a little when he laughed, as if it was all a big joke. 'Now, she will 'ave to try and get your Kate Moss instead,' he said. 'She eez next on my leest. She 'as refused us fourteen times now. A record, I believe.'

Fleur's expression didn't budge, as if she didn't want to give him the satisfaction of responding, but I noticed a twitch underneath her eye.

'Darling, 'ave some wine,' urged Nicolas, beckoning the waiter back. 'Eat with us, we're 'aving the monkfish.'

I hoped Fleur would refuse – any excitement I'd felt at meeting someone I'd so admired had fled – and felt a flash of relief when she shunted her chair back.

'No, thank you.' She rose in a graceful movement, slipping a black leather bag over her shoulder. 'The exclusive should have been mine and you know it,' she said, pinning Nicolas with her frosty gaze. 'It is your loss.'

Nicolas roared in apparent delight. 'Fleur, you are my best girl.' He tried to catch her hand, but she swiped it away. 'We will 'ave someone else lined up for you very soon,' he said in a low, intimate voice.

'I don't want anyone else. I wanted Jay Merino, as well you knew.' A mantle of tiredness fell across her face and I wondered whether she had a crush on Jay, like everyone who'd seen his films, and wanted to spend some time working her magic on him; to get to know him for her own lustful reasons. Then I caught the icy look that Nicolas missed before she turned to leave, and realised it was simpler than that. She was angry that his focus had slipped away from her and onto me.

Chapter Ten

Part of me wanted to rush after Fleur and tell her she was being ridiculous; that I was hardly a threat to her career with her track record, even if I interviewed Jay Merino, but all I could do was stare at her departing back, noting what great posture she had, and how she drew admiring glances as she swished out through the door.

I felt sure she wouldn't have thanked me anyway; she would have hated the fact that I'd caught her in a vulnerable moment, and probably denied it. Even so, the shine had been taken off the evening and, worse, I couldn't honestly say that Nicolas hadn't been playing us off against each other, especially as once Fleur had gone, he said I was *audacieux* (I think he meant 'ballsy'), his eyes full of admiration, and dismissed Fleur's abrupt departure with a casual shrug.

'Do not mind 'er,' he said, as our plates of food arrived. 'It is good to 'ave ze feathers a leetle ruffled.' I wasn't sure about that. I had a feeling that ruffling Fleur's feathers would only end badly – for me. 'She will work 'arder to prove 'erself.'

'I don't think she needs to prove herself,' I said, staring at my meal, not sure my stomach was up to digesting food, no matter how delicious the glistening white fish looked, nestled among tiny quails' eggs and sprinkled with truffles. 'She could easily take over a rival magazine.'

Nicolas chuckled as he forked an asparagus spear into his mouth. 'She 'as been wiz *Magnifique* from the start, when I was 'er mentor.' He dabbed his chin with a napkin where butter had dripped. 'Fleur will never leave,' he said, and I couldn't help thinking that maybe she *should*. Poor Fleur, if he'd been dangling the editor-in-chief carrot for years, providing she landed an interview with this elusive star or that, only to move the goalposts. Perhaps he'd insist on the Pope next. 'Is she in a relationship?' I asked, trying to picture Fleur with a partner, wondering whether what she'd said in an article was true – that she fell a little bit in love with everyone she interviewed, and ordinary people simply couldn't match up.

Nicolas drew his head back, as if the idea was preposterous. 'She is married to 'er job, just as I 'ave been,' he said. 'Like me, she 'as no time for a family.'

There were rumours online that Nicolas had an ex-wife tucked away in Italy, silenced by a generous divorce settlement. Perhaps Fleur should interview *her*. The thought made me want to giggle, and I decided I'd better not drink any more wine.

'Natalee?'

I realised I was staring at my plate, and hadn't heard what he'd said. I hoped he wasn't about to order Babette be brought back to the table – I'd been snapped at enough for one evening. 'What did you say?'

'I offered you a sum for the interview,' he said. 'But I can see it ees not enough.' He named a figure that was triple what I'd had in mind and I tried not to gasp.

'That sounds… reasonable.' I stabbed a quail's egg with my fork and took a tentative nibble. 'I'd rather have a permanent position at the magazine, though,' I said when I'd swallowed, made bolder than usual by the wine, ignoring a queasy flicker of worry as I imagined Fleur's reaction. I wouldn't be welcome there, but I couldn't let that put me off. I'd just have to work hard to win her round, pick her brain for the best interview techniques, that kind of thing. *Flattery makes friends.* Wasn't that the saying? Or was it, *flattery gets you nowhere?*

Nicolas planted a hand over mine, making me jump. 'Let us take it one step at a time,' he said in his lover's voice, and I nudged my knife to the floor so I had an excuse to shuffle my fingers away. 'There is much to do in the meantime.'

As we resumed eating, he outlined his plan to publish Jay's interview in the July issue, and which photographer he would send ('beautiful visuals are a *vital* accompaniment to good-quality writing, Natalee') as well as a translator for the French edition, and I started to relax a little – though it might have been the wine and the absence of Babette – and managed to finish my meal without making a fool of myself.

'I don't eat dessert,' he said, waving away the waiter once we'd finished, and although I was tempted to say that I did, I couldn't face eating one while he watched.

'So, Natalee,' he said, resting his hands on the table as if to show he meant business, 'as you 'ave probably guessed, I love women.' His raised eyebrows required an answer, and I couldn't help it this time. I rolled my eyes.

'Honestly, when men say that I always think what they really mean is, they love the *idea* of women. *Their* idea of women, not actual, *real*-life women, who don't bother shaving their legs in winter, or eat too many cakes, or cry at sad puppies online.'

'What a fascinating insight into your life, Natalee, but I can assure you, I *adore* women, particularly smart, successful women—'

'Like Fleur?' I said, cutting him off.

His brows rose. 'Of course, like Fleur. She eez one of the best.'

'Good enough to do your job?' *Natalie, shut your mouth.*

Nicolas gave me a sizzling look. 'Nobody ees good enough to do what I do, if I may be honest, Natalee.' He pressed a big hand to his heart. I had the sense it was a reflexive gesture – unless he had indigestion. 'It ees a blessing and a curse, because I cannot truly imagine my baby being in somebody else's 'ands.' He cradled his arms and made a rocking motion. 'I 'oped to 'ave a son to leave my empire to, but eet 'as not 'appened yet,' he said with apparent sorrow, and I wondered if he still hoped to father a child, despite being Dad's age. Then again, if it was good enough for Mick Jagger… 'Now,' he shrugged and picked up his wine. 'I do not know what will 'appen.'

Except he did, I thought, watching him empty his glass in two big gulps. He was the sort who'd keep going until he died, and had no intention of handing the reins to Fleur. Though maybe that wasn't an entirely bad thing. I couldn't imagine her wanting to employ me, for a start.

'Well, that's a shame.' I balled my napkin and reached for my bag. I should leave, before the conversation became even more personal. I had the feeling Nicolas was in an expansive mood. 'How much do I owe for the meal?'

'Natalee! You are *enchanting*,' he said, spreading his hands. 'I invited you, so I shall pay, of course. A leetle old-fashioned per'aps, but I insist.'

Suspecting the cost of the meal would bankrupt me, I didn't argue. 'Well, thank you, Monsieur Juilliard, it's been… lovely,' I said, with as much dignity as I could muster. 'I promise I won't let you down. Regarding the interview,' I added, in case there was any doubt.

'I believe you.' His eyes warmed up as they travelled over me once more. 'Are you sure you won't stay for coffee?'

He probably thought I should sober up, but I really wasn't that drunk. 'I'm fine.' I stood, wavering a little. 'I'll be in touch when I have the details. Regarding the interview.' *Had I already said that?*

'I will look forward to it,' he said. 'Now, 'ow are you getting 'ome?'

*

As I cycled to Saint-Martin the following morning, I found myself humming Kylie Minogue's 'Can't Get You Out of My Head'. The sun was shining as I breathed in the salty scent of the air, and I didn't even have a hangover. In fact, I'd slept extremely well after arriving home in a taxi that Nicolas had poured me into, chuckling softly as if I was an amusing toy he'd like to play with again. I was sure he'd said, 'I think I am going to enjoy you being part of my team, Natalee,' but thought afterwards I might have imagined it.

And now, I was going to meet Jay Merino, and this time I wasn't nervous. I'd even managed some breakfast with Dad before leaving the house.

'You're seeing him then?' He'd poured me some coffee in an eager way that had made me feel guilty for escaping to the café every morning, reluctant to fall back into the role of dependent daughter. 'The actor?'

'I am,' I'd said, feeling my face flush red. 'But you're not to tell anyone, Dad. Even Marie.'

He'd shot me a baleful look that had compounded my guilt. 'It should go without saying that I won't, Natalie.' It had almost sounded odd, hearing my name without an extra e, the way Nicolas said it. 'You will be careful, won't you?'

'Why do I need to be careful?' I'd dug into the rather rubbery scrambled eggs he'd made with too much force. 'Jay wasn't like his brother, you know. I doubt they're even still in touch.'

'I don't mean that.' He'd gone into full Dad mode. 'He inhabits a different world from what you're used to and I don't want you getting hurt again.'

'He's nothing like Matt, and it's only an interview, Dad. I'm not dating him.'

I wondered, as I approached the harbour, what it *would* be like to date Jay Merino. He wouldn't want anyone to know about me for a start, so we'd never be able to go out, and while that would have its upside – lots of bedroom action – I couldn't imagine a life in the shadows while Jay pursued his career. He'd been hotly tipped to be the next Bond, which would catapult him to a whole new level I wasn't equipped to deal with – though trying might be fun. I indulged a fantasy where Jay confessed he'd fallen for me that night on the swing but had been scared off by the intensity of his feelings after our kiss, which was why he'd rushed into the night without asking my name. Then I reminded myself he met beautiful, talented women all the time, and while I was OK for a normal person, I was hardly in the same league. Plus, I wouldn't want to be wondering what he was up to all the time. Even the most committed boyfriend might struggle to remember he had a partner while surrounded by stunning actresses. Although Max Weaver was a 'loner' whose heart had been broken the night his wife and son were brutally murdered, he occasionally succumbed to erotic encounters with women who then tried to kill him. ('You'd think he would know by now,' Charlie had said, during the second *Maximum Force* film, when a sexy, mysterious Russian called Anya began her doe-eyed seduction, while hiding a vial of poison in her clutch. 'Shows how stupid men are.')

I parked my bike round the back of the hotel, and checked my clothes for oil stains. I'd decided not to dress up again. I didn't want to look as if I was trying too hard, plus Jay had seen me in a similar outfit and hadn't looked repulsed. After last night it had been a relief to slip on a pair of jeans and a stretchy top, and leave my hair alone. The waves I'd created for my meeting with Nicolas had miraculously survived the evening, as well as a night in bed, and when I checked my reflection in the mirror before I came out, it looked as though I'd applied a filter to my face. Probably because I'd forgotten to remove my make-up the night before and my eyeliner was still intact.

Sucking in a breath, I entered the double doors, and immediately spotted Simon in the chic reception area. Not that he was easy to overlook, with his big, bald head, bristling beard and tank-like proportions. When he saw me, he came over and gave a surly nod.

Would it kill him to crack a smile? 'Morning,' I chirped, a nervous tightness in my stomach now that I'd arrived.

He didn't respond, and I only managed a cursory glance at the delicate blue décor, deep-set sofas and fireplace before he was leading me up a flight of stairs, muttering, 'He's in the Duke of Buckingham.'

On the landing, a heavy-looking door flew open and Susie Houlihan stepped out, wearing a white towel and a hair turban, casting a toothy smile at Simon. 'Hi, honey,' she drawled. 'Would you be a darlin' and fetch me some grapefruit?'

'That's what room service is for,' he growled.

She pouted and stepped back in her room without giving me a second look, and Simon continued to the furthest door and rapped on it four times with his knuckles.

When Jay said, 'Come in,' my heart shot into my throat.

'You'd better be who you say you are.' Simon's eyes were hard as stones as he slid the key card in and turned the door handle.

'I'm sure you've checked me out,' I said tartly, my lingering guilt at getting him into trouble the day before fading in the face of his hostility. 'I wouldn't be here, otherwise.'

'He doesn't need any distractions.'

'I'm not here to distract him,' I said. 'I'm here to do a job.'

His grunt of disbelief made me want to kick him, but I doubted my canvas shoes would make much impact. I made do with pulling a face at the back of his head as he pushed the door open with one hand, looking as if he'd like to curl the other around my windpipe. I slid past without breaking eye contact to prove I wasn't intimidated – even though I was.

As the door closed behind me, Jay moved away from the window, and for one wild second, I wondered whether he'd been looking out for me, instead of the more likely option of admiring the yachts in the harbour.

'I was starting to think I'd dreamt what happened yesterday,' he said, stepping towards me, a smile crinkling his eyes.

'Me too.' His greeting was the opposite of Simon's and instantly put me at ease. 'I hope there was no lasting damage.'

He put his fingers to his collarbone and pressed. 'Not even a twinge,' he said, his smile widening. 'You look nice.'

I glanced at my blue-and-white stripy top, wishing I'd picked something different. 'It's a bit French. I might as well have a string of onions slung around my neck.'

He laughed as though he had been taken by surprise and liked it. 'It suits you,' he said.

'Thanks.' In the pause that followed, I wondered whether I should compliment him in return – tell him I liked his hair a bit longer, that his citrusy shampoo (or shower gel) smelt good, and the sight of his jeans, bare feet and rolled-up shirt sleeves was making my head spin (in a good way.) 'So do you,' I said at last. 'Look nice, I mean.'

'This shirt's about a decade old.' He fingered a button. 'I was asked to be the face of Hugo Boss last year, but I'm not really into fashion. I'd rather leave that stuff to Gerard Butler.'

'I bet you're offered things like that all the time.'

'Not for a while now,' he said. 'I did a watch commercial in Japan a couple of years ago. It paid for a house for my mum.'

His neutral tone didn't invite praise, but I said, 'That's nice,' all the same.

'I'm not sure she wasn't happier on the estate.' He smiled. 'She's still got friends there and visits all the time.'

'She's... recovered now?' I said carefully.

'She's doing really well.' He hesitated. 'This is off the record, right?'

'Of course.' I showed him my phone to show I wasn't recording, even though I'd planned to write in my notepad.

He waved it away. 'Would you like something to drink?'

'I'm fine, thanks.' I looked around the suite, which presumably honoured the duke the room was named after. It was done up like an English gentlemen's club, with dark wood panelling, crimson wallpaper and a leather sofa in the galleried living room. It was furnished with antiques and rugs and the sumptuous bed could have accommodated a family of six.

'It's a bit blokey.' Jay sounded apologetic.

I tore my gaze from the bed. 'It's nice,' I said, feeling my cheeks heat up. Fleur would no doubt have handled this situation with a lot more flair. She'd probably have had Jay in the bath tub by now, up to his neck in bubbles, chatting about his childhood.

'Let's go into the garden,' he suggested. 'It's a lovely day.'

I gave a hard nod, to show I meant business. 'Sounds good.'

He pulled on a pair of leather trainers and we headed for the door, which I noticed was slightly ajar. I wondered whether Simon had been listening to our conversation. There was no sign of him, but he materialised as we reached the foot of the stairs and followed us outside.

'Is he with you all the time?' I murmured, as we strolled into the sunlight.

Jay turned and inclined his head and Simon peeled away without comment. 'He's an old friend, from way back,' he said. 'I don't have many, so I try to keep them close.'

'Give them jobs?'

'Something like that,' he said. 'People can be fickle in this business. You work with them for months, then never see them again.'

'You must have made *some* friends?'

'None I'd hang out with like this.' He sat on one of the rattan chairs that circled the courtyard garden and rested his elbows on his knees, and I guessed he was still talking 'off record'. 'Everyone's keen to get back to their real life at the end of a shoot, including me. It's hard to make true friends, the sort who know the real you.' His gaze was serious. 'Simon was one of the kids I got to know in care. He looked out for me at school when I was bullied for a bit.'

'He was in care?'

'His mum died in childbirth and his dad couldn't look after him.'

'That's sad.' It went a long way towards explaining Simon's attitude. 'It sounds like you haven't let fame go to your head.'

'What do you think?' The force of his gaze made me feel untethered. I sat on the chair beside him and was instantly transported to the night we'd met, on the swings in Gemma's back garden. I wondered what she would say if she could see me now. We'd lost touch after school, our friendship not strong enough to stand the test of time, though I'd heard via the grapevine (Mum) that she'd married a farmer and moved to Somerset.

When Jay broke into a smile, as if he'd had the same flashback, it felt as if the universe had tilted. 'I don't really know what you were like before.'

His gaze grew serious. 'I think you do,' he said.

Chapter Eleven

Unsure how to respond to Jay's comment, I let my gaze move around the garden, surprised no one else was enjoying the sunshine, then remembered there were no regular guests staying at the hotel. 'Where is everyone?'

'The crew are setting up a shoot in one of the gift shops in town,' he said. 'I have to pretend to be browsing, spot a killer's reflection in a mirror and break his neck.'

'Charming,' I said. 'Don't you have lines to learn?'

He grinned. 'It's an action scene, so there aren't too many. I've memorised them already.'

I felt giddy, as if I'd breakfasted on champagne. 'You can run through them with me, if you like.'

'Honestly, it's mostly grunting and I'm good at that. But thanks for the offer.'

'I don't mind listening to you grunt.'

He started to laugh. 'No one's ever said that to me before.'

I laughed too. 'Sorry, that sounded stupid,' I said. 'I suppose I'll have to wait until the film comes out.'

'Do you like the films?'

I hesitated, not wanting to offend him by admitting they weren't my cup of tea. 'I've seen them,' I said. 'But mostly because you're in them and I was curious, because I'd...' I'd been going to say *kissed* but changed it to 'met you once'. Though I hadn't been able to connect him with Max Weaver, however closely I'd watched – even when he'd snogged the actress trying to kill him. 'But you play the part really well.'

'You're not a fan.' I was about to protest, then saw he was still smiling. 'It's fine,' he said, ruffling the back of his hair, which was an inch longer than he'd worn it in *Maximum Force 2: The Middle*. 'The films have served their purpose and it's been fun, but I'll be glad to see the back of them, to be honest.'

'You're not making any more?'

'I think three is enough, don't you, considering it's called *The End*?'

'Maybe.' In truth, one had been enough for me, but fans couldn't seem to get enough of Max Weaver's pursuit of bad guys.

'Although, I think Brian's considering a fourth: *The Resurrection*.' He made a face and I grinned.

'Aren't you doing Bond?'

'Too much to live up to,' he said, eyes scrunched against the sun. 'No, I'm giving up acting once I'm done with this film.'

I sat up straight. 'Giving up?' This was massive. 'But why?'

He rubbed the back of his neck, seeming a little uncomfortable for the first time, and it hit me again what a big deal this was; him talking to me so openly – almost like a close friend he'd stayed in touch with.

'You don't have to tell me, if you don't want to.' *Well done, Natalie. First rule of interviewing: don't encourage your subject to shut up.* Not that I was interviewing him yet. It wouldn't feel right to pull out my notepad now and interrupt the flow.

He shook his head. 'It's OK,' he said. 'At first, I liked it, but—'

'How did you even get into acting?' I was suddenly desperate to know. 'Did you go to drama school?'

His face relaxed. 'I got lucky,' he said, his bashful smile a long way from Max Weaver's repertoire of fearsome expressions. 'I was approached in the street by a guy who said I was perfect for the lead in a film he'd written about zombies and told me to audition.'

'With no experience?'

'Yep.' He gave a self-deprecating shrug. 'I did do drama classes at school and was in a couple of plays,' he added. 'I enjoyed pretending to be someone else back then, but I never intended to take it any further. It was just an escape.' His words lingered, hinting at all the things he'd wanted to escape from.

'You never mentioned it,' I said, feeling shy. 'The night we talked.'

'Becoming an actor wasn't even on my radar.' He made a baffled face. 'I'm not sure how I was planning to make my living, but it definitely wasn't in films.'

'What did you have in mind?'

He gave a half-laugh. 'I thought I might be a professional footballer, but I wasn't good enough.'

'And if you hadn't been approached in the street?'

He steepled his fingers underneath his chin. 'Don't laugh, but I wanted to be a cattle rancher,' he said. 'I saw this old film once, called *Silverado*, and it really appealed to me.'

I couldn't help smiling, though it wasn't difficult to picture him in a tartan shirt and a Stetson, astride a stallion. 'So, why retire?' I said, wishing I could make some notes. I had a feeling he'd stop talking if I did. 'You could always play a cattle rancher, if the part comes along.'

He shook his head. 'Acting was only ever a means to an end,' he said. 'I mean, I did enjoy making the first Max film, but quickly realised that pretending to be something I'm not takes its toll. Especially when that someone's a stone-cold killer.'

'He only kills the baddies,' I pointed out.

Jay shrugged. 'It's not just that. It's hard to put down roots in this job and that's what I really want.' An image of him holding identical mop-haired twins bounced into my head. 'I know, I've been lucky,' he continued, though I hadn't spoken. 'But being lucky's not the same as being happy.' It would make the perfect headline for my interview. 'I've travelled, I've met some great people and had a lot of fun, especially in the early days.' I wondered whether he was referring to his ill-fated affair with the tormented singer, but didn't want to interrupt his flow by asking. 'But I hate the celebrity side, the public wanting a piece of me, the total lack of privacy. Everyone's a paparazzi these days, with their phones,' he continued. 'I don't even have a mobile, and never use social media.'

'I'd noticed,' I said, giving away that I'd looked him up.

He blew out a breath. 'I don't want to live my life in hiding, but I don't want to be seen,' he said. 'Not even on screen.'

'So, you're retiring because you're *too* famous?' My brain bulged with questions. 'Other actors manage to stay out of the limelight and still have long careers.'

'When you say "out of the limelight", they still do the chat show circuit and other publicity stuff whenever a new film comes out, and I can't even bear to do that.' He grimaced. 'That makes me sound totally up myself, but I promise, I'm not.' He twisted to face me full-on, as if to better convince me of his intentions – as though he really cared what I thought. 'I want to live a regular life, spend time with my mum, get into property developing, the sort of housing that people can actually afford, open a drama school, do something for underprivileged kids like my brother…' he paused, a cloud passing over his face, and there was such an easy rapport between us now, it felt natural to ask, 'How is your brother these days?'

His head dipped, so I couldn't read his expression. 'He… he died, six years ago.'

'*What?*'

'He never really escaped from that crowd he used to hang around with, the lot who crashed your friend's party.' He lifted eyes etched with regret, and the sorrow I felt was instant and overwhelming. 'I wanted to help him. I tried, I really did. I got him jobs and into rehab a couple of times, but nothing stuck.' He seemed lost in memory for a moment. 'The last time he relapsed, I was filming in the Czech Republic, and by the time I found out he'd overdosed, it was too late.'

'That's awful.' I hadn't been aware of reaching out to hold his hand, but I squeezed it hard, as if I could force out the pain. 'I'm so sorry, Jay.'

'I don't want all this to have been for nothing.' He thrust an impatient arm out. 'His life, mine.' He glanced at the hotel and garden, the verdant green of the grass a vivid contrast to the bright white walls of the courtyard. 'It has to mean something,' he said. 'I want to do good things with the money I've made; set up a foundation in Sonny's name, make sure there's help out there for kids like him to get clean.'

Sonny. I'd forgotten what his brother was called. 'He was in prison,' I said, recalling the story I'd seen in the press soon after Jay became well-known.

He nodded. 'He committed a robbery to pay for his habit. He was better when he came out, but soon got sucked back in.' Jay's jaw was clenched and I imagined the frustration and helplessness he must have felt – that despite his best efforts, his fame, the money he must have been making, he'd been powerless to save his little brother.

'There was nothing more you could have done.' I was sure he'd heard it before, but I longed to make him feel better. 'Some people can't be helped.'

'I know, but it's no consolation,' he said, as I'd known he would.

'How did your mum cope?'

'Weirdly, she stopped drinking the day he died.'

'That's good, isn't it?'

'It is, but…' He gave a short laugh. 'All the ways I tried to help and it took my brother's death for her to clean up her act.' It must have been bittersweet, but there was no animosity in his voice. 'We get on well now, but it hasn't been easy.'

'I can imagine.'

I could, and felt an explosion of gratitude for my happy childhood, with parents who'd put me at the centre of their world and made sure I felt safe and loved. My only real gripe growing up – apart from the usual niggles around homework and staying out late with Gemma – had been not having a pet, because Dad's eyes swelled shut if he so much as looked at a cat, and dogs made him sneeze and wheeze. It was one of the reasons he didn't frequent the café as often as I did, because Gérard brought Hamish, and sometimes Madame Bisset brought fluffy Delphine.

'What about your dad?' I said, hoping I wasn't pushing my luck.

'He pops up now and then, wanting money.' Jay's voice was resigned. 'I don't hate him, but he hasn't earned the right to be called a father.'

I reluctantly untangled my hand from his and watched him flex his fingers. He seemed miles away, and I was torn between letting him carry on talking and bringing him back from the past. I guessed he didn't open up often – definitely not to virtual strangers – and was deeply moved that he'd chosen to talk to me.

'You know, that should be the angle,' I said, aware our knees were brushing, and how small my legs looked compared to his. 'For the interview.'

His gaze refocused. 'Angle?'

'You should talk about the Foundation, about wanting to help young people – the good things you can do once you've retired.'

He seemed to shake himself back to the present. 'No one knows I'm retiring,' he said. 'If it gets out, that's all anyone will want to talk about and I need to get this film wrapped without any distractions.' His mouth curved. 'Any *more* distractions.'

'I know, I'm… I shouldn't have… I'm really sorry, I…' Full sentences and proper breathing were suddenly beyond me.

'I'm enjoying *this* distraction.' His eyes were gently amused, his earlier torment banished, and I felt my temperature rise once more in response.

'So, er, you'd been thinking about giving an interview before I, um…' I mimed a dive through the air.

He laughed. 'Like I said, I was thinking about meeting that woman from *Magnifique* magazine,' he said. 'They have a good platform and Fleur Dupont has written some really good stuff.'

'She's the best,' I agreed, echoing what Nicolas had said the night before – minus the accent. I shifted position, feeling a bit deflated. Maybe the interview wasn't so much about Jay keeping his promise, but more about getting word out about his Foundation to attract funding and support. I wondered whether he'd have been so open if that hadn't been a factor. Not that it mattered. He'd agreed to let me interview him, and if my words could help him in any way, it would be worth it. In fact, I *wanted* to help him. I would make it the best piece of writing ever published, anywhere, if it was the last thing I did.

'So, how come you're living in France?' said Jay, just as I was wondering how to articulate my thoughts. 'You said you're here with your dad?'

It took me a moment to regroup, then I gave him an abbreviated version of why I'd left the UK, skimming over the details of my break-up, but he frowned when I said that Matt was about to marry his ex. 'That must be tough,' he said. 'I don't blame you for making a fresh start, but don't you miss your old life?'

'To be honest, although I do sometimes miss the job and the people I worked with, I love it out here.' I looked up at the cloudless, pale blue sky. 'Even when the weather's not great,' I added. 'I thought the novelty might wear off quickly, but I've made friends here. Plus, I get on well with my dad, and people come out to visit us all the time.'

'He's a police officer.'

I was touched that he'd remembered. 'That's right,' I said. 'He's retired now.'

'Brothers and sisters?'

'Neither,' I said. 'My parents decided they couldn't improve on perfection.'

He smiled. 'Are they still together?'

'Not any more.' My throat felt suddenly tight. 'They're separated. In fact, my father's started dating again, but it's not going very well.' I told him about Dad's efforts so far and when he'd stopped laughing, Jay said, 'It sounds as though he doesn't really want to meet someone new.'

'He's putting a lot of effort in, if he doesn't.'

'But from what you've said, he keeps finding fault with them all.'

'I just don't think he's met the right one yet.'

'And you?'

'Oh, I'm still off men at the moment,' I said, hoping Jay would think my cheeks were sunburnt rather than flushed with embarrassment. 'I'm trying to get my career on track.'

'Hopefully, I can help with that.' His smile was like a reward I hadn't earned. How could I ever have thought he looked feral? 'And if you ever want to get away and write in private, I've bought a place over here.'

'On the island?'

'A cottage in Sainte-Marie,' he said. 'I've invested in a few properties I rent out to people on low incomes, but I like it here and wouldn't mind coming back.' It suddenly felt as if the air pressure had changed. 'Anyway, it's standing empty if you ever want to use it.'

'That's…' *amazing, when can I move in?* 'Thank you, that's very kind, but I tend to work at the Café Belle Vie, near where I live. They do these amazing *pains au chocolat*, in fact, all the food is amazing. You should try it, it's great.' *Stop babbling*.

'I'll bear it in mind.' He smiled again, and I guessed he was just being generous. Why else would he offer me the use of his cottage, or to come to a café that didn't have a Michelin star, even if it had won a mention in *The Good Food Guide*, as well as some of my columns? Though I had a feeling that, unlike Nicolas Juilliard, Jay didn't frequent Michelin-starred eateries – far too exposing.

'So, who else do you write for?'

I told him about *Expats*, and that I wrote a blog about living on the island and he said he'd check it out (being generous again) and then I regaled him with some of the stories I'd done for *Chatter*, which he found hilarious. With a rush of warmth that had nothing to do with the weather, I realised the sound of his laughter was something I'd love to get used to.

'Are you…' I crossed my ankles and looked at the toes of my canvas shoes. Spotting a small hole, I tucked my feet underneath the chair. 'Are you seeing anyone?' My attempt at being off-the-cuff was spoiled by a squeak in my voice and I hastily cleared my throat. 'Do you have a girlfriend hidden away?'

'I'm not a kidnapper,' he said, eyes brimming with amusement. 'No, Natalie, I'm not seeing anyone at the moment. In fact, I haven't had a proper girlfriend in a while and, in case you're wondering, I've never been engaged, or anywhere close to getting married.'

'Right.'

'I was in love once with a singer, which you probably read about, but it didn't end well and I've steered clear of relationships since.'

'OK.'

'That doesn't mean I don't enjoy being with women,' he continued. 'But they tend to be mutually short-lived affairs.'

'I see.'

'And when I say affairs, I don't mean with married women. My dad was a cheater, but I'm not like him.'

'Great.'

We locked eyes and burst out laughing. 'Well, that was intense,' he said. 'But I'm glad we know where we stand.'

A bulky shadow fell across us and Simon appeared. 'Jay, it's time to go.'

'Already?' He sounded put out. 'That went quickly.'

'I won't keep you,' I said, mindful that I'd held up filming once already.

'Thanks for the chat, I've really enjoyed it.'

'Me too,' I said, feeling shy as we stood up and faced each other. I wished Simon would disappear, but he remained, solid as a wall, hands clasped behind his back.

'I hope that was OK.' Jay tweaked his shirt collar and brushed his hands down his jeans. His fingers were long, the nails clean and short. 'You will let me see it once it's written, won't you?'

My stomach seized. 'That was the interview?' I waited for him to tell me he was joking. 'I'd assumed this was an informal chat, off the record.'

'Isn't that the best sort of interview?' His smile did nothing to quash my rising panic.

'But I haven't made any notes.'

'I'm sure you'll remember the important bits and put them in the right order.'

I would. Our conversation would be etched forever on my memory, but I'd hoped to elicit some witty anecdotes, as well as probe into his background and expand on his plans for future projects. I hadn't expected to have to pick out snippets from a chat about our lives, which had included some pretty personal stuff.

'You said yourself the angle would be the Foundation,' he said. 'That's what I really want it to be about. You can add some context around our chat – the hotel, the film, some background on Max Weaver, if you like.'

'But that's not very personal, and everyone knows everything about your character.' I caught Simon's eye-roll and imagined him as a tiny baby sitting on a potty. 'I'm not sure Nicolas Juilliard will publish something so... *bland*,' I said. 'He's hoping for something explosive, that no one else has.'

'Isn't the fact it's my first interview enough?'

'It might not be.'

'No one else knows about the Foundation.'

'True,' I said. 'Can I mention that you're retiring?'

'I don't want that getting out until the film's released next year.'

Simon muttered something that sounded like, 'For Christ's sake.'

'But—'

'Natalie...' Jay's face was serious. 'My personal life isn't for public consumption, even for you,' he said gently. 'I'm sorry, that's just how it is.'

'I get that, and obviously, I wouldn't dream of writing anything really private, but can't you at least give me a noteworthy quote or opinion, or a revelation of some sort?' I scratched around my brain. 'Something that will get people talking, which will be good publicity down the line, if you want people to remember you when it comes to sticking their hands in their pockets for the Foundation.'

'Ooh, you're good.' His smiling comment fuelled another blush. 'OK, like what?'

'Jay…' began Simon, but Jay's eyes stayed fixed on me.

'Well, I don't know.' I tried to think what the public might want to know, apart from everything. 'What's your view about Trump? How would Max Weaver solve global warming? What's your guilty pleasure, your favourite author, favourite food? What does Jay Merino do to relax?'

He was grinning now and seemed to be enjoying himself. 'OK, well, I'll pass on Trump, and I think Max Weaver is more interested in hunting down killers than in global warming, but my guilty pleasure is eating Nutella from the jar, my favourite author's Bernard Cornwell, and I go sailing to unwind when I can. Will that do?'

On a personal level, his reply had only whetted my appetite for more, but I knew I'd been given answers any journalist would sell their granny for. 'That'll do,' I said. 'Oh!'

'What?' He looked startled.

'There have to be pictures,' I said, urgently. 'Nicolas was going to arrange a photographer to come with me, once I'd given him a time for the interview. And there was supposed to be a translator.'

'Well, translation can be sorted out later, and we know you've got a camera on your phone.'

'I can't use that!'

'Why not?'

For a start, because Simon looked to be on the verge of strangling me. 'Fine,' I said, whipping it out of my bag and looking around for a suitable location.

'I'll sit here.' Jay dropped back on the chair and grinned at Simon, who dropped his head to his chest in apparent despair, and I snapped a load of shots from different angles, dipping and weaving, almost tripping over my bag at one point, hoping at least one of them would be useable. I daren't even imagine what Nicolas would say, but it was better than nothing, which seemed to be the only alternative.

Jay sat still, watching me as I moved around, so that my limbs felt too long and uncoordinated, my hair falling across my face so I had to keep thrusting it back – all to a soundtrack of Simon's barely concealed impatience. He was breathing so heavily, I wouldn't have been surprised to see flames leap from his nostrils.

'That's great, thanks.' I stuffed my phone in my bag without checking the pictures, to show Simon I was done.

Jay got to his feet, seeming as reluctant to leave as I was for him to go. 'Listen, I was planning to take a yacht out after we've finished filming here on Friday.'

'You have a yacht?'

Jay grinned. 'I'm not some billionaire oligarch,' he laughed. 'No, but I have a licence, and was planning to charter a boat and take a look at the ocean before I leave.'

'Just you?'

Simon gave a disgruntled huff.

'Just me.' Jay lifted one eyebrow. 'Unless you fancy joining me.'

'On the yacht?' *Idiot.*

'On the yacht.'

'Hmm…' *Yes, yes, yes, yes, yes,* 'I'll have to check my diary.'

'Don't take too long.' My senses picked up that we might be flirting again. 'I'd like us to talk some more.'

I felt as if there were electrodes attached to my body, firing up my nerve-endings. 'I'd like that,' I said, deciding not to bother playing hard to get. 'What time?'

Simon appeared to have stopped breathing.

'Seven?' Jay looked relieved, as if he'd actually thought I might say no. 'I'll meet you here.'

'In the garden?'

He laughed, though I hadn't been joking. 'In Saint-Martin, at the marina,' he said.

I nodded. 'Of course, the marina.'

'And, Natalie, thanks for coming today.'

He was thanking me?

'Thank you for inviting me.'

For a second, neither of us spoke. The atmosphere seemed to inflate once more, then Simon thrust himself between us and said brusquely, 'You ready now, mate?' and I had no choice but to leave, waving a little goodbye, certain they were both watching as I hurried away, half-expecting Simon to strike me down with a thunderbolt.

It wasn't until I was halfway back to Chamillon that I realised I'd left my bike behind.

Chapter Twelve

I staggered into the café and slumped at the nearest table with a smiling nod to Margot, an artsy, middle-aged writer with steeply piled-up hair, who frequented the same spot two days a week to work on her latest romance. She rarely chatted, apart from to Dolly, who would only say that Margot had been badly let down by men and preferred living in her fantasy world.

'You look shattered,' Charlie hailed me. 'Have you been exercising?'

'You could say that.' It hadn't seemed worth turning back to the hotel, so I'd carried on walking, powered by my conversation with Jay, replaying it over and over, trying to read the things he hadn't said, as well as the things he had. I couldn't help returning to the notion that he liked me. And not just because we'd kissed before he was famous, but because he found me interesting and attractive. It had been obvious in the way his eyes had lingered on my face, occasionally moving to my hair and back to my eyes – as if he was taking mental snapshots to look at later. Nicolas had looked at me in a similar way, but his interest had felt less pure, more primal. It was different with Jay. But was I imagining it?

'Gut feelings are always right,' said Charlie, after I'd offloaded my thoughts over a still-warm apricot croissant. 'If you think he's into you, he is.'

A thrill of excitement made my skin burn as I put down my glass of orange juice. 'Why are you beaming like that?'

'Because, in the year or so that I've known you, I've never seen you like this,' he said. 'I do believe you're falling for Max Weaver.'

'It's Jay,' I said, and dropped my head in my hands. 'And please don't go around saying things like that, you'll get me in trouble.'

'Imagine though, you and Max Weaver.' He leaned across the table and said in a growly voice, 'I love you, and now I'm going to have to kill you.' His appalling Irish accent made me laugh and Giselle, who happened to be passing, gave me a chilly stare that reminded me of Fleur Dupont.

I snapped my fingers. 'I need to email Nicolas,' I said. 'Tell him I've spoken to Jay, and that the interview's done.'

'Can't you tell me first?' said Charlie. 'What did you talk about?' He was as avid for gossip as any girlfriend (probably because he too was in love with Max Weaver) but Jay's words – so many of them, filling my head, looping round and round – felt too big and important to impart in a public place, and revealing such personal details, even to Charlie, felt disloyal. On the other hand, I had to tell someone or I would implode.

'Not here,' I said, looking round. 'Too many ears.'

'I'm taking a quick break, Mum,' he said to Dolly, as we nipped through the kitchen to the courtyard, swiping a freshly made macaron on the way.

'Take all the time you need.' Her eyes twinkled with delight as she slid a batch of buttery brioche rolls into the oven. 'I'll fetch you both some coffee.'

'Maybe I should tell her about you and Max,' said Charlie, once we were seated at the picnic table outside. 'Get her off our backs.'

'There is no me and Jay, and don't you dare,' I said, wagging a warning finger. 'This is all top secret, Charlie. In fact, I'm going to refer to him as X, just in case.'

'Can't I call him Max?'

'No, you can't, it's too obvious,' I said, still hesitant, even though we were outside.

'X it is.' He gave a solemn nod and pressed two fingers to his forehead.

'What was that?'

'Scout's honour, or something.' He leaned forward, adopting a listening face. 'Now, spill.'

'Don't say spill,' I said, though it perfectly described the way I was overflowing with words. Even so, when I opened my mouth, my throat felt frozen.

Charlie's face sobered. 'That bad?' he said.

'Not bad, just… a lot.'

'I'm listening.'

After a couple of false starts, still feeling as if I was betraying Jay's confidences – especially surrounding his brother – I recounted our conversation, tripping up in some places so that Charlie had to urge me gently to carry on, and as I talked, I remembered how it had felt, being with Jay – as if we could have talked for hours without it being awkward. And maybe it was wishful thinking on my part, but I was certain he'd felt it too.

'I'm gutted he's retiring,' said Charlie when I'd finished, his hair a mess from pushing his hands through it. 'And the stuff about his brother's just awful.'

'I know.'

'It sounds like he's been through such a lot.'

'At least he has a good relationship with his mum now.'

'He's obviously a solid bloke, judging by this foundation he wants to set up. He can't be an arsehole if he wants to help young people and invest in affordable housing.'

'He's definitely not an arsehole,' I said. 'We're very different, though.' I traced a figure of eight on the table. 'I doubt we've got a single thing in common.'

'You're both good people.' Charlie looked serious. 'Maybe he spoke to you *because* you're different from the people he usually hangs around with.'

'How come you're such an oracle on relationships, when you're not even in one?'

'I'm naturally wise and all-knowing,' he said with a pious smile.

Although I tutted and swatted his arm, I felt better for sharing, knowing it wouldn't go any further. Charlie's perspective had clarified that Jay had talked to me because, for some reason, he liked and trusted me, and I allowed a nugget of hope to blossom, that this was the start of something important.

It was hard to fathom that two days ago, I'd been talking Dad out of a clothing crisis and worrying about my career.

We chatted a bit longer, and Charlie said he hoped that Max would come to the café and sample its delights, and asked if he could join him on the yacht instead of me.

'It's *Jay*,' I hissed, clamping my mouth shut as Dolly brought out two coffees and put them down, passing an expectant smile between us, as if hoping we'd been discussing marriage plans and babies.

'Take your time, it's quietened down in there.' She squeezed Charlie's shoulder and winked at me, and I experienced a stab of guilt that my feelings for him would never be what she hoped. 'Talk as long as you like,' she added.

'You heard her.' Charlie grinned as she went back inside, the sun glinting off his untidy hair. 'Anything else you'd like to share?'

A memory of the night before shot into my head. 'Oh my God, I haven't even told you about meeting Nicolas Juilliard and Fleur Dupont.'

Dad wasn't in when I got back, no doubt out on another date. I ran upstairs, fired up my laptop, and quickly emailed Nicolas, knowing it would be easier to put in writing what I'd struggle to say on the phone. I explained that the interview had happened already and promised I could work with what I had, and that he wouldn't be disappointed once he read it.

I was certain he'd be angry, but he replied straight away to say how much he was looking forward to seeing it.

It is unorthodox, but that could work very well. It is good to surprise our readers, and whatever you have, it is nothing that anyone else has, so it will be good, Natalie. You must come to my office soon, and meet everyone.

I read his message as though he was speaking, almost surprised to see only one 'e' at the end of my name. Then I read it again and clapped my hands. I was going to be in *Magnifique!* Well, my words were. *And my photograph!* I'd need a good headshot, like Fleur's, perhaps in black and white. Maybe I should get my hair professionally straightened, so I looked less like a poodle. Not that I'd written anything yet. I still had no idea where to start, but the words would come, as they always did. I just needed to let them percolate for a while.

I scrolled through the photos I'd shown Charlie, and had to admit they had an amateurish sort of charm. I was no Annie Leibovitz, and I wasn't sure the pictures were magazine quality, but they were natural and well lit, thanks to the sun bouncing off the walls. In most of them, Jay was smiling and relaxed – the exact opposite of Max Weaver's short-tempered scowl. Mostly, his face was angled away, but in one he was looking directly at the camera and when I zoomed in, my heart missed a couple of beats. He seemed to be staring right at me, and I wondered what he'd been thinking. Hopefully not, *I wish to God she'd hurry up and leave me alone.*

Maybe I'd find out on Friday evening.

Simon was in a couple of the shots, looking comically out of place in the sunny surroundings, with his all-black outfit and murderous eyes. I wondered what on earth *he* did for relaxation. I couldn't imagine him putting his feet up with a novel, or playing tennis. I giggled, imagining he was a robot, and that Jay plugged him in at the end of the day to recharge.

I sat for a moment and cracked my knuckles (a habit that made Charlie cringe), opening paragraphs for my interview rolling through my head.

Women love him and men want to be him, but in the flesh, Jay Merino couldn't be further from his alter ego, Max Weaver… a bit hackneyed.

Jay Merino is SO much hotter in real life… definitely not. Even though he was.

Despite mega box-office success, the man famous for playing Max Weaver is as much an enigma now as he was when he auditioned for… I couldn't remember the name of the zombie film he'd starred in off the top of my head, and anyway, it wasn't a good enough hook. More *Chatter* than *Magnifique*, the sort of paragraph Jackie would have loved. In fact, she would have killed for an interview with Jay Merino – it could possibly have saved the magazine from going under, and given it a bit more gravitas. Imagining her reaction made me think of Jools, and I got out my phone and tapped in a message.

You'll never guess who I spoke to today! Jay Merino!! He's filming in Saint-Martin-de-Ré! He's SO nice, not at all like he is on screen! Hotter, too!! Hope all's well over there! X Too many exclamation marks, but it was that sort of message. Even so, as soon as I'd sent it, I wondered whether I'd done the right thing, and reassured myself it wouldn't go any further. When she'd left her beauty editor job at *Chatter*, Jools had retrained as a massage therapist, and now worked at a top-end spa in Hertfordshire. She no longer had any connections to the magazine world (apart from me), having being scarred by her year at *Gossip*, where she had to schmooze Z-list celebrities at all hours, just to get an exclusive about their upcoming fitness DVD. Even when we'd worked together, she'd been the soul of discretion, much preferring the make-up freebies that came her way to inventing headlines for stories that were often made up. We'd kept in touch by text, and she'd been over to visit the year before, and was coming again in the summer. I knew she'd be thrilled that I'd talked to Jay Merino and wouldn't tell anyone, just as I'd never revealed that she once massaged a famous boyband member with terrible back acne.

I reminded myself Jools had a busy job and wouldn't reply immediately, and busied myself with housework for the rest of the afternoon in an effort to calm my racing thoughts. I'd just finished, and was debating whether to give Mum a call, when the front door opened and Dad ushered in a birdlike woman with a crest of ash-blonde hair that made me think of a cockatiel.

'Natalie, this is Yvette.' He looked a bit bashful. 'I've offered to teach her English,' he said. 'Yvette, this is my daughter.'

This was a departure. Dad hadn't brought back a date before, or offered to teach one English, as far as I knew. '*Bonjour,* Yvette.' I stuck out a hand, determined to give her the benefit of the doubt. It wasn't her fault she wasn't Mum – or even Marie next door – and she had a pleasant enough smile, though her teeth looked pointy and sharp. She was dressed in a black blazer with a white turtleneck, black trousers and high-heeled boots, and her handshake yanked me forwards.

'*Bonjour,* Natalie.' She had a loud, sing-song voice. 'It is so kind to meet you.'

'*Good,*' said Dad, too loudly.

Misunderstanding, she nodded demurely. '*Merci.*'

'No, I meant, "it's *good* to meet you".' My insides scrunched up. Dad had over-emphasised 'good' as if she was five years old. '*Good.*' He nodded slowly. 'Not *kind.*' He shook his head. *This was going to be excruciating.* 'It is *good* to meet you.'

Yvette gave rein to a shrill giggle. 'Marty, you break me up,' she said in heavily accented English.

'*Crack,*' Dad almost shouted. '*Cra-a-a-a-ck,*' he repeated, stretching the word to breaking point. 'Not *break.*' He shook his head. '*Crack.*'

Yvette's throaty laughter quickly turned to wheezing. 'Crack,' she echoed, bashing her chest with her palm. 'You *crack* me, Marty.'

'UP. *You,*' he prodded the air near her nose. 'CRACK, *meeeeeeee,*' his finger turned inwards, 'UP!' Now he was pointing at the ceiling, while Yvette nodded ferociously.

'CRACK, *meeeeeeeee,* UP!'

'I'm going for a walk,' I said, pretending not to see the panicked look Dad threw me. But I didn't miss the way his gaze fell on a photo partially hidden in the window recess, of Mum holding out the enormous cake she'd made for his fiftieth birthday, the words 'To

My darling Marty' iced on top, circled by so many candles we'd joked about having the fire brigade on standby. As I closed the front door on another blast of laugh-coughing, I couldn't help hoping this date with Yvette would be his last.

In my hurry to get away and think some more about Jay, and how to write up our conversation, I almost crashed into Larry and Barbara.

'We've been in Saint-Martin today,' said Barbara, without preamble, her sculpted, straw-hued hair not moving in the gentle breeze. She was clutching Larry's arm as though she might topple over without his support. Wearing high heels on the island's cobbled streets was never a great idea.

'Sounds lovely,' I said, trying to edge past.

'You'll never *guess* who we bumped into?'

I froze. Had Marie told them that Jay was staying at L'Hôtel des Toiras? Was that why they'd gone there? *Did it matter?* The toothpaste was probably out of the tube anyway, as Dad would say. Word would have spread about filming by now, and while locals might not be bothered, it was bound to be a big deal to anyone visiting.

'I think I probably can.' In spite of myself, I couldn't suppress a grin.

'You might know him.' Larry hitched up the straining waistband of his jeans. He was big all over, teeth and hair included, though his eyes were hard to see as his cheeks bunched up in a smile. 'He's pretty well-known, from what I gather.'

'That's an understatement!' I suddenly wanted to sing from the rooftops that, not only did I know Jay Merino, I'd spent an hour with him that morning, and would be seeing him again very soon – that we were going on a date.

Wait. It *wasn't* a date, by any stretch of the imagination. It was two people who'd forged an unexpected connection, spending some time together, to hopefully get to know each other better. *That's a date*, I imagined Charlie saying and my mood swung sky-high. In my head Charlie was right: *I was going on a date with Jay Merino!*

'… absolutely divine,' Barbara was saying, closing her eyes in apparent ecstasy, revealing a layer of pea-green shadow in the crease of her eyelids.

'I can't argue with that,' I said, a little smugly.

'You've eaten there?'

'Sorry?' My gaze swung to Larry.

'You've eaten at his restaurant?'

What was he talking about? 'Restaurant?'

Larry's monstrous eyebrows shot up. 'The one run by Jacques Blanc,' he said, referring to a well-known chef, who'd appeared on several French cookery shows and was as renowned for launching careers as he was for being roguishly handsome to women (and men) of a certain age.

'Ah, right, of course.' I had a giddy urge to giggle, which was odd. I was acting like a lovestruck teen, assuming they'd meant Jay, looking for an excuse to talk about him. Was I in love? I couldn't be, not this soon. But I hadn't felt this strongly about Matt, even in the beginning. Maybe I was infatuated with Jay or – more likely – just overwhelmingly grateful that he'd thrown me a career lifeline by agreeing to let me interview him.

'He was talking about his new cookbook,' Barbara went on, pretending to swoon. 'Talk about dish of the day!'

Larry gave an indulgent eye-roll. 'Good job I'm not the jealous type,' he boomed, and I joined in their laughter as I carried on down the street, not sure where I was going. I thought about popping back to the café, but I'd distracted Charlie enough for one day, and rolling up again would only fuel Dolly's daughter-in-law fantasies.

As I dithered at the end of the street, debating whether to go to the beach where I could walk and think in peace, a nippy white Citroën drew up and the passenger window slid down. Simon leaned over, his face ruddy with heat – or anger, it was hard to tell – and barked, 'Get in.'

My heart gave a big thud. I peered inside, but the back seat was empty. Was Simon trying to kidnap me? 'My parents warned me never to get in a car with a strange man.' It was meant to be light-hearted, but came out sounding rude. 'I mean, in a stranger's car.'

'You've met me before. Twice,' he pointed out. 'I saw you just this morning.'

Yes, but I don't know *you*, I thought, but kept it to myself. 'Is… is that my bike?' Peering closer, I could see the handlebars poking up from the boot.

'You left it outside the hotel.'

'Well, it's very kind of you to bring it back.' I was getting a crick in my neck from peeking in through the window. 'How did you know where to find me?'

'You told Jay yesterday where you lived, so it wasn't exactly hard.' He was starting to sound bored. 'Are you going to get in?'

'I can just get my bike out and wheel it back,' I said. 'The house is just up there.'

'I know, I saw you come out, but time's marching on.' He looked closely at the clock on the dashboard, as if to push home the point. 'You can get it out later.'

Later? I supposed I ought to be reassured he was planning to bring me back. 'Does Jay know you're here?'

He snorted. 'Of course he does.' He leaned over and thrust open the door. 'Do you think I'd be here, otherwise?' he said grimly. 'He's asked me to take you to his cottage in Sainte-Marie.'

Chapter Thirteen

Not completely convinced it wasn't a ruse by Simon to get me in the car, so he could somehow dispose of me, I said, 'Why didn't Jay come and get me himself?'

'Filming overran and he wanted to have a shower and meet you there.' He didn't hide his annoyance at being questioned and when I didn't move, due to a dizzying sense of excitement, he added, 'He wants to make dinner for you, OK?'

What? Galvanised, I clambered into the car, my heartbeat loud in my ears. Simon might be lying, but I was willing to risk being murdered on the off-chance Jay Merino was actually going to cook for me at his cottage.

Just in case, I rummaged for my phone in my bag with shaky fingers and shot off a text to Charlie. *Off to Sainte-Marie to see X's cottage!!!* Better not write Jay's name, but Charlie would know who I meant. *I think he's cooking me dinner there!* I wanted to add a gazillion emojis to sum up how I was feeling, but felt the burn of Simon's gaze as he pulled up at the junction leading out of the village. *He's sent his miserable git of a bodyguard, Simon, to pick me up xx* At least if I went missing, Charlie would know where to start looking, and who to point the finger at when my grisly remains were found.

'You'd better not be giving out details,' Simon warned, with faintly sinister undertones. 'You ever heard of security?'

'Have you ever heard of good manners?' I fired back. 'I don't even know if you're telling the truth about where we're going.'

'Why did you get in then?' His knowing smirk suggested he knew exactly why I'd dived into the car. 'Do you normally drop *everything*,' he made *everything* sound suggestive, 'to meet someone you barely know, or only famous people?'

I supposed he had a point. 'I'm just saying, I'm not vanishing for the evening without letting my dad know where I am.' To prove a point, I typed a message to Dad. *Eating out with a friend, should be back by 10.30, have a great evening! X* Maybe with me out of the way, he'd relax a bit with Yvette, and show her his pen collection, or... maybe not his pen collection. Perhaps he could talk to her about his days in the police force... maybe not, considering it was 'nothing like CSI' and she might be either horrified or bored. Maybe his love of fishing. Or not. Most of the women he'd told had apparently glazed over after the first five minutes.

Glancing at Simon, I noted his pained expression, and guessed he was trying to hold back a sneer at me texting my dad my whereabouts, like a fifteen-year-old.

'Should we make small talk, or shall I just look at the scenery?' I said.

'Look at the scenery.' His beard twitched and I thought I saw something that wasn't fury in his eyes, but then he was staring stonily at the road ahead.

'You could tell me a bit about yourself, and what it's like working for Jay,' I said. It was a twenty-minute drive to Sainte-Marie, but would feel a lot longer if we weren't going to speak. 'Do you carry a gun?'

'You want me to talk, so you can publish it somewhere,' His voice hardened. 'I know what you journalists are like.'

'I'm not a journalist, I'm a writer,' I said, which prompted him to open his mouth and close it again, presumably at a loss. I felt a childish pinch of victory, until he said, 'Either way, you have an agenda when you talk to people and I don't like it.'

'Don't flatter yourself,' I said. 'I've no interest in writing about bodyguards.' His hands tightened on the steering wheel and, for a second, I thought I'd gone too far.

'It's nothing like you see in films.' There was slightly less steel in his voice. 'There's a lot of standing around, and it's not as if you can just zone out.'

Encouraged, I said, 'My dad says the same thing about being in the police force. That it's different in real life, I mean. Like, overnight stake-outs with piles of empty coffee cups and food wrappers in the car, it just doesn't happen in reality.'

He nodded, but didn't ask any questions.

I thought about his dead mum and felt a softening. 'Did you ever want to do anything else?'

'Scenery,' he said gruffly.

Hiding a smile, I turned my attention to the view outside. Saint-Marie was the most rural village on the island, home to oyster farmers and wine growers, and the view seamlessly transitioned from sea, sand dunes and low-level rock shelves to vineyards and bramble-filled moors, where I'd taken long walks with Dad when I first came to the island, pouring out my heartbreak about Matt reuniting with Steph – though, in truth, once I'd left the UK, it had started to take on a lot less significance. The quick sale of our house and subsequent injection of cash had helped. At least I hadn't had to worry about money, even if I'd been left with trust issues and an abiding dislike of Xboxes.

As the Gothic church tower came into view, spotlit by early evening sunlight, my heart began to freewheel and my mind leapt forward to what might lay ahead. Simon – who'd proved to be a surprisingly careful driver – pulled the car down a winding road and turned into a driveway sheltered by trees. The cottage, like a lot of homes on the island, was a simple, one-storey dwelling with exposed stone walls, topped by a roof of round tiles, the shutters painted a delicate clover-green. But the real surprise was the pretty, enclosed garden, filled with laurels, mimosas and fig trees, all of which I could identify as I'd written a column about gardening for *Expats*, inspired by Dad's attempts to recreate something similar to the garden Matt had created at home (not very successfully).

'It's lovely,' I said to Simon, but he only grunted and snapped off his seatbelt, as if he regretted being nearly civil to me earlier. 'Shall I wait here?' Now we'd arrived, I was oddly reluctant to get out of the car. What if Jay wasn't here and this was where Simon was planning to hold me hostage? I knew nothing about him, other than that he was fiercely loyal to Jay. This could be Simon's place – although, knowing how expensive property was here, I doubted he'd be able to afford it. Unless Jay had bought it for him. It wouldn't be surprising, considering how he felt about helping people, especially those closest to him.

'Are you going to stay there all night?'

Simon's voice jolted me. He'd come round to open the car door and was giving me a stranger look than usual. 'Maybe you could let Jay know I'm here and he can tell me if it's OK to come in,' I said, smoothing the wrinkles out of my top, wishing I'd had time to get changed. I was wearing the same outfit I'd had on that morning, but then again, if this was a hostage situation, my clothes were the least of my worries.

'I'm not planning to keep you here against your will,' said Simon, as if he'd read my mind. 'Don't worry, I won't be hanging around.'

'I'm not worried,' I lied, flushing to the roots of my hair. *Oh God, my hair.* I wanted to take out my compact mirror (an urge I'd never had until yesterday) and check that I looked respectable, but not with Simon watching my every move. Instead, I climbed out onto the white shingle drive, my legs as unsteady as if I'd been on a roller coaster, and tried to inspect my appearance in the window as we approached the front door. I looked tiny behind Mount Simon, but although my hair looked vaguely the right shape, I couldn't make out any details – which was probably just as well.

Simon knocked, the same four sharp raps he'd made on the hotel-room door (was it only that morning?) and turned a brass key in the latch. 'We're here,' he called, stepping over the threshold, and I wanted to snigger. He was like a husband, back from the office, but without a briefcase or any social graces. 'You there?'

There was silence from within and I'd just dug my hand in my bag to retrieve my phone, trying to remember the number for the police, when I heard Jay call from a long way off, 'Come in!'

Relief swept over me when Simon stepped back. He gestured for me to go past with a sarcastic twirl of his hand.

'Sure you don't want to search me?' I said, my sudden giddiness tinged with guilt that I'd doubted his motives. 'I could be packing a weapon.'

'Don't tempt me.' He eyed my bag as if it might contain a revolver. 'Jay trusts you.'

'But you don't?'

'I don't trust anyone where he's concerned.'

'Maybe you need to get over that.'

'Maybe I will.'

'Good.'

'Good.'

A subtle alteration around his eyes suggested he might be close to cracking a smile, but it didn't make it to his mouth. Though it was hard to tell inside the giant beard. 'I'll be back for you later,' he said and headed towards the car.

Grinning, I closed the door and turned to look at my surroundings. I was in an airy, white-and-wood kitchen, which opened onto a large sitting room with oak floorboards, a tasteful grey sofa and contemporary paintings on the walls. At the far end of the room, a pair of patio doors stood open, leading to a sun-filled terrace. As I made to move towards them, Jay came striding in.

'Simon gone?'

'Yes,' I said, willing my heart to calm down before it burst out of my chest.

'I'm glad you came.' He stopped in front of me, smelling deliciously of woodsmoke and a subtle, spicy scent that made my senses reel. 'I didn't want to presume you had nothing better to do, but… I don't know.' He ran a hand over his hair, his sheepish smile yanking at my already overworked heart. 'After you'd gone this morning, I couldn't stop thinking about you, and when I came back to the hotel and realised you'd left your bike, I thought I'd take a chance and invite you to see the cottage, but I don't have a phone, or your number, so…' he paused and I realised he was nervous. *Jay Merino was nervous.* I had to stop thinking of him as Jay Merino instead of just Jay.

'It's fine,' I said, relaxing a fraction. 'I was only going for a walk, to have a think about our, er, interview this morning. My dad brought a date home and I couldn't face hanging out with them.'

Jay pulled a comical face. 'What was she like?'

I gave him a rundown, playing up the language mismatch, and he doubled over, laughing. 'I wouldn't have minded hanging around there, it sounds like comedy gold.'

A small silence fell as we discreetly assessed each other. He was casually dressed in black jeans with a plain, grey T-shirt and looked more approachable somehow; like someone I could have met at a bar, rather than an out-of-reach, mega-famous actor.

'I'm sorry I didn't have time to get changed,' I said, self-conscious under his gaze. 'I promise I do have more than one pair of jeans.'

'You've nothing to apologise for. I like the way you look.' He gave a little laugh. 'Sorry, that sounded too much.'

I laughed too, because it was so unlikely. Maybe he preferred the natural look and the women he met were too groomed, but whatever the reason, I believed him. 'It's just as well,' I said. 'I don't own any designer outfits, and my hairdresser's given up trying to sort out this mess.' I flicked at my hair, thinking, *why draw attention to it, you idiot?*

'Your hair's lovely.' Reaching out, he tucked a strand behind my ear, and it was such a gentle and intimate gesture, I felt as if I couldn't breathe for a moment.

'I'd like to say the same about yours, but honestly, it's still a bit too short.' I couldn't believe I'd said it, but he laughed as though it was the funniest thing he'd heard in ages.

'My mum says the same,' he said, resting his hand on the wooden kitchen counter. 'She looks at photos of me when I was younger, when it was long and wavy, and says she laments the day I had it cut.'

'She actually said "laments"?'

His eyes crinkled. 'She did.'

'You can grow it back once you retire.'

'I've already started. I might grow it down to my waist.' He rubbed the back of his head. 'Only another three weeks of filming and then I'm done.'

My heart jerked. 'You're here for three weeks?'

'I'm afraid not.' His mouth turned down. 'Budapest next, then Hong Kong, then I'll visit home for a few days and come back here.'

Our eyes locked. Did he mean… he was coming back because *I* was here? No, of course he didn't. He was talking about the cottage. *Obviously.* He had a home here now. 'It's lovely,' I said, tearing my gaze from his to look around, trying to ignore the wings flapping in my stomach. 'Was it like this when you bought it?'

'Pretty much.' He followed my gaze. 'The paintings are my mum's,' he said with a hint of pride. 'She took up art therapy as part of her recovery after Sonny died, and unlocked a hidden talent.'

'Wow, they're good.' I wasn't usually a fan of abstract art, but could see they were from the heart, and the colours – great sweeps of blue and grey – were somehow calming.

'The place needs personalising a bit more, but that's something I can sort out down the line.' He smiled. 'For now, I'm just glad to have somewhere to call my own, where I can be myself. No one here cares who I am.'

I care. 'Well, thank you for inviting me,' I said, suddenly wondering *why* he'd invited me. 'Did you want to continue the interview? Jay Merino at home.' I struck a pose, leaning against the worktop. 'It's a bit more *Hello!* magazine than *Magnifique.*'

He grimaced. 'Definitely no more interviews. I invited you here because I wanted to see you and to cook you dinner,' he said simply.

'Oh.' I managed not to clap my hands to my cheeks like a star-struck fan. 'That's… thank you.'

'When I say cook, I mean barbecue,' he added with grin. 'I've not had much opportunity yet to hone my cooking skills.'

'Well, it sounds great.' My stomach gave an obliging growl. 'I thought I could smell something smoky.'

'I was getting it going when I heard Simon,' he said. 'That's why I didn't come in right away.'

'Do you want a hand?'

'You can come out and keep me company and have a glass of wine,' he said. 'With any luck, there'll be a nice sunset soon.'

An inner voice was crying *OH. MY. GOD!* but outwardly, I smiled modestly and said, 'A sunset should always be shared.'

'So true.' He thought for a second. 'Sunsets are proof that even bad days can end beautifully.'

'Today's been a bad day?'

He laughed. 'That's what you took from my stolen quote?'

My cheeks turned to fire. 'Sorry,' I said. 'It's a beautiful quote.'

'Today's been a good day and it's definitely going to end beautifully.' His eyes held mine until I thought I might combust. 'You're not vegetarian, are you?'

Chapter Fourteen

I completely lost track of the next few hours. After I had assured Jay I didn't just eat vegetables, he led me outside to a balconied terrace with a clear view across flat green fields to the sea. The sun had tinged the sky apricot and the air was soft and full of competing scents – specifically, mimosa and barbecued meat.

Jay confessed that Simon had shopped for the ingredients, but only because he hadn't had time himself. 'I hate letting people do things for me, but it won't be for much longer,' he said. 'I fully intend to do my own shopping in future.'

'You might have got more used to being looked after than you realise.'

'Believe me, Natalie, I haven't,' he said, looking at ease as he flipped a thick burger, his brow lightly furrowed with concentration. 'I know actors often say they've never forgotten their roots and where they came from, but I can promise you, hand on heart, I haven't.'

'That doesn't mean you want to still be that person.'

He considered this for a moment. 'I often hated my circumstances, but never myself,' he said. 'I always found ways to be happy, even when things were really bad.'

'Like watching a sunset?' I teased, sitting at the table he'd dressed with silver cutlery and a fat candle in a jar, feeling as if I could stay here forever as I relaxed more and more in his company, helped along by the glass of fruity red wine he'd poured, and which I'd drunk too quickly.

'Yeah, something like that.' He gave me a lazy smile that made my heart trip. It kept happening. We'd chat for a while about ordinary things while we ate and drank, exchanging stories about growing up (he had some happy memories despite the tough times), laughing as we discovered things we had in common (loved Brussels sprouts, hated being cold, hadn't watched *Game of Thrones*), then he'd give me a look that made my breathing falter. It was so different to anything I'd experienced in the past. I had a comfortable friendship with Charlie, and with Matt… well, we'd had more differences than similarities. He often used to say, *why are you like this?* and it wasn't until after we'd broken up that I'd realised, if he'd had to ask, he couldn't be right for me.

It was hard to fathom that Jay might feel the same way I did, but when he refilled my plate and handed it back and our fingers brushed, I could tell from his startled look that he'd experienced the same fizz of electricity I'd felt, from my fingertips to my toes.

'Funny how we have fingertips, but not toetips,' I jabbered, trying to gloss over my reaction to his touch. 'Yet we can tiptoe but not tipfinger.'

'What are you talking about, you mad woman?' Jay's look of baffled amusement almost made me snort out a mouthful of wine.

'I've no idea.' I broke down in helpless giggles.

Jay laughed softly, his eyes not leaving my (probably ruddy) face, then he reached over, removed my glass from my hand and pulled me to my feet. 'I'm having the best time,' he said, his forehead touching mine. 'I'm so glad you threw yourself at me.'

'Me too,' I murmured, eyes level with his mouth, and before I could process what was happening, his lips were on mine, gently exploring at first, then building in intensity, his arms wrapping tightly around me.

There was no hesitation this time, no pulling away and leaving – just more kissing that felt like it might go on forever, and I slid my arms round his neck, feeling a volley of fireworks go off in my chest. The kiss grew tender as Jay cupped my face in his palms, sweeping his thumb over my cheek, and when our mouths pulled apart, I had to lean against him or I'd have fallen over.

'Did you hear the fireworks?' he murmured into my hair. 'Do you think they were going off for us?'

A giggle broke free. 'I thought I'd imagined that,' I confessed, turning my face up, stomach clenching when I saw my desire reflected in his eyes. 'What's going on here, Jay?'

'I don't know, but I like it.' The hoarse catch in his voice made me feel light-headed and, for a moment, I thought my knees would buckle with the enormity of what was happening.

'I like it too,' I whispered.

'I felt bad for leaving you the way I did that night, but I wasn't ready...'

'Ssh.' I placed my fingers against his lips. 'It's fine,' I said. 'You didn't break my heart or anything.'

His laugh was laced with regret. 'I'm glad to hear it, I think.'

'Maybe it was meant to be this way.'

'Maybe you're right.'

We drew apart and studied each other, and I had a sense that the world had changed, that there was a different feel to the air – and sensed he felt it too.

'We've missed the sunset,' he said, and I tilted my head to see that the sky was charcoal, and the world had narrowed to the two of us on the terrace, lit by the flickering candle on the table and a smouldering glow from the barbecue.

'There'll be other sunsets.' It sounded like a cheesy line from a film – not *Maximum Force* – but Jay smiled, as if he thought so too, and I wondered how I could feel so in tune with someone I barely knew. Except – it felt as though I *did* know him. As if we understood each other. Which was clearly silly after such a short time, and probably due to the wine I'd drunk heightening my emotions, and to being a very long way from my normal routine.

'What's for dessert then?' I said, to avoid doing something silly like dragging him off to the bedroom (not that I knew where it was) but before he could reply, four sharp raps on the door reverberated through the house.

'Simon's got a really loud knock,' I said.

'It's his massive hands,' Jay replied, and this struck us as so hilarious that we laughed for what seemed like ages, until Simon knocked more loudly and we heard him bellow, 'I'm coming through,' as if we needed rescuing from bears.

'Out here, Si,' Jay called, and by the time Simon materialised in the doorway, after flicking on the overhead light inside, Jay and I were sitting opposite each other, holding a wine glass each, smiling inanely, as though we'd been discussing the view.

Simon looked at me suspiciously, then at Jay's half-empty glass, as if I might have laced it with venom like a villain in one of his films. 'You told me to come back at ten,' he said to Jay.

'Thanks, mate.' It was obvious from the friendly grin he gave Simon that theirs was an equal friendship, and not the master/butler arrangement it appeared to be on the surface. 'All good at the hotel?'

'Quiet.' Simon's voice grew more conversational. 'Everyone was knackered after today and Brian flipped at Susie when she said she wanted to get pis… drunk at the bar.' It was easy to picture the director losing his temper, less so to imagine Susie Houlihan taking it lying down, but I was probably mixing her up with her character, Nova. 'Remember there's a 5 a.m. start in the morning.'

Jay groaned. 'I can't wait to have a lie-in,' he said, rubbing his face. Our eyes briefly met and I wondered whether – like me – he was picturing a lot more happening in bed than sleeping.

'Hey, I never got to see your room.' I regretted my loaded tone when Simon visibly tensed. I shouldn't have had that third glass of wine.

'I'm sorry, I meant to give you a tour,' Jay said, unfurling from his chair. 'We got a bit distracted.'

'We did indeedy.' I caught the appalled look that Simon threw Jay. 'Oh, lighten up, you big muffin.' I giggled. 'He's so grumpy.' I thumbed my nose and blew a raspberry, but Simon still looked dead behind the eyes. 'Doesn't he ever smile?'

'Believe it or not, he does.' Jay slapped him gently on the back before holding his hands out to me. 'I think it's past your bedtime,' he said, gently. 'And it's definitely past mine.'

'Had enough of me already?'

'Definitely not.' His eyes glinted. 'But Simon's right, I've an early start and I'm rubbish without enough sleep.'

'I admire your dedication to your work, sir.' My pompous tone made him smile.

'Why thank you, ma'am.'

'I can clear up here, if you want to take her home.' Simon sounded less annoyed than I might have expected. 'Unless…' he nodded at the bottle of wine.

'I've only had one,' said Jay, and I felt a twinge of shame that I appeared to be drunk. I was a complete lightweight with alcohol. 'Come on, you.'

By the time I'd fluttered my fingers goodbye at Simon and thanked him for bringing me over, and Jay – at my insistence – had shown me the rest of the cottage (which I barely took in, other than noticing the bed looked comfy, the shower inviting, and there were photos of his mum and brother around that I wished I'd looked at earlier), I felt sober enough to enjoy every second of the drive back to Chamillon, cocooned in the car with Jay, rock ballads playing on the radio as the night outside flashed by. Every now and then, he turned to look at me and smile (perhaps checking I hadn't fallen out of the car). I smiled back goofily and wished our destination was further away.

I directed him to the rue des Forages and he parked outside the house. The lights were off and I wondered whether Yvette was staying the night and had to quash an unpleasant imagine of her tucked up naked beside Dad.

'I'll get your bike out,' said Jay, and had deftly removed it from the boot and propped it by the front door by the time I'd heaved myself out of the car. Soft music and voices floated from Marie's house and I guessed she must still be up, entertaining her Americans. Part of me wanted to shout, 'Look who's here, with me,' but I was starting to see Jay less as Jay Merino, the actor, and more as a man I happened to like a lot, so instead I said in a jokey tone, 'I'd invite you in for a coffee, but…' and let the sentence hang.

Jay took my hot hand in his cool one and said, 'I'd love to meet your dad, once I'm done with filming.' My heart soared. He sounded as if he meant it. 'Come and watch me filming tomorrow, around two o'clock,' he said, impulsively. 'I'm doing a scene at the lighthouse at Saint-Clément-des-Baleines. I have to pretend to throw Nova off the top, but of course, she escapes.'

'Oh, I've been up the lighthouse a few times, on holiday,' I said. 'Are you sure your director won't mind?'

'I'll tell Brian you're there as my special guest.' Jay's fingers tightened round mine, and they felt like a pledge. 'Simon will look out for you.'

I could imagine how that would go down. 'Great,' I said, wondering whether my smile could get any wider.

'We could grab something to eat afterwards.'

My smile got wider. 'I'll see you there.'

'Great.'

Still smiling, I watched him get back in the car and waved as he drove off, though he probably couldn't see me as there were no street lights to break up the darkness. When he'd gone, I let myself into the house and floated upstairs, and still had a smile on my face when I dropped into bed, five minutes later, and fell instantly asleep.

Chapter Fifteen

The dream I'd been having hurtled into the distance as I groped from under the duvet for my phone, which was blasting out the theme from *Maximum Force*. Simon had been chasing me along a quayside, and I'd had to jump in the sea to escape. Jay, wearing a pirate-style eye-patch, had leaned over the side of a super-sized yacht to grab me, but I'd never know now whether I made it to safety.

Why was I dreaming about being saved by a man? It seemed so twentieth century. Even if the man was Jay in a sexy eye-patch.

I finally yanked my phone from my bag, just as the call cut off, and a smile crept over my face as memories of the night before rolled in. I hadn't expected to sleep at all, sure I'd spend the night going over and over everything that had happened, but events had clearly caught up with me. That, and the wine. And the kissing. *Ah, the kissing.*

I needed to talk to Charlie. He'd be dying to know what had happened, especially after the message I'd sent him. I saw that he'd texted back, *Dinner with Max Weaver??? What is happening to your life??? Be good (not!) X*

I chuckled, thinking how Charlie would laugh when I told him I'd been worried I was being kidnapped, and that I'd hoped he would come and find my dead body. Dad had replied too. *Take care, Natalie. Remember what I taught you. Dad xx* He was referring to the self-defence techniques, should I find myself being attacked: kick with both feet at once, thrusting my hips off the floor for extra power, then get up and run away as quickly as possible – which, sadly, would only work if I was lying down. Failing that, it was a kick to the groin and/or fingers jabbed in eyeballs… then run away as quickly as possible. He'd insisted for a while that I carry a special alarm that made a terrifying sound, but I once set it off in the cinema by accident, resulting in a panicked stampede to the exits.

Still smiling (I couldn't seem to stop), I pushed my duvet off my face, blinking as hazy daylight streamed through the window. I rarely drew my curtains because I liked waking up to a slice of blue sky, though today it was the colour of sterling silver, as though it might start to rain. Squinting again at my phone screen, I saw it was Charlie who had been calling. He'd tried earlier too – several times – but I'd been so deeply asleep I hadn't heard my phone. With a lurch, I realised it was almost ten o'clock. He was probably wondering what had happened to me, or – more likely – wanted to know if I'd spent the night with Jay.

The thought sent heat searing through me, and I indulged a few seconds of reliving his kiss and the feel of his body against mine, imagining him naked. I'd already seen his chiselled arms and rippling abs when he'd stripped to the waist as Max Weaver, about to bed one of his 'dangerously seductive' women, but I somehow couldn't associate the sight with real-life Jay – though the firmness of his chest beneath my palms the night before had hinted at what lay beneath. Conscious of my inferior level of fitness, I pitched out of bed and dropped to the rug, where I attempted to do a press-up, but although I managed to lower myself down, pressing up was beyond me. At least my thighs were vaguely toned from cycling or walking everywhere and my skin – though generally as white as a sheet of A4 – was smooth and blemish-free.

A surge of energy propelled me to my feet, and I messaged Charlie to say I was on my way, before clicking on an email from Sandy at *Expats*.

She loved my *How Not to Impress an Actor on Location* submission and was sure it would get a great response.

'Yes!' I fist-pumped the air, then put my phone on charge before diving into the shower, where I sang 'Let Your Love Flow' at full volume while washing my hair with the super-expensive, frizz-control shampoo I saved for special occasions.

'You're in an excellent mood,' said Dad when I pitched up in the kitchen, dressed in fresh jeans and a barely ironed shirt, my hair still damp as I hadn't got the patience to dry it. 'I take it you had a nice meal with your *friend*?'

'Lovely,' I said, unable to prevent a blush sweeping over my face.

'I hope he was nice to you.' His eyebrows rose.

My blush deepened. 'No self-defence required.'

'Glad to hear it.' Luckily, Dad returned his attention to his notepad, tapping his teeth with one of his special pens. 'How was your date with Yvette?' I looked around, hoping she wasn't about to appear, wrapped in his towelling dressing gown.

'Oh, it didn't work out.' He absently scratched his head. At least his hair had almost returned to its natural colour, with just a faint trace of brown around the temples. 'The language barrier was a bit of a problem.'

'I thought her English was pretty good,' I said. 'She didn't sound like she needed many lessons.'

He gave me a mournful look. 'The lessons were just an excuse,' he said. 'She made a pass at me, nearly as soon as you'd gone.'

'She did?' I wasn't entirely surprised, considering the hungry looks she'd been throwing his way. 'Isn't that a good thing?' Even as I said it, my mind rejected the idea. 'She obviously liked you, Dad.'

'She put her tongue in my mouth.'

'That's…' *revolting*. 'That's normal, Dad, if someone finds you attractive.' I really didn't want to be having this conversation with my father. 'Maybe it was a bit too soon?'

He shuddered, as if the memory was too terrible to contemplate. 'It felt all wrong,' he said. 'I've never kissed anyone before but your mother, and she never put her tongue in my mouth on our first date.'

'Oh God, Dad.' Despite the miles between them, he clearly hadn't moved on from Mum as much as he'd been pretending. Not if their first date – a trip to the cinema to see *The Terminator* – was fresh in his mind.

'Don't worry, I called her a taxi and popped next door when she'd gone,' he said, brightening. 'Larry used to be a cop in LA. We compared notes and had an argument about gun control.'

'I bet that was fun for Marie and Barbara.'

'Oh, they joined in,' he said with a chuckle. 'We all had plenty to say. I didn't get home until midnight.'

So that was why the house had been in darkness when I got home. Not that my mind had been on anything but Jay, but it hadn't occurred to me that Dad might not be there. I'd fallen asleep so quickly, I hadn't heard him come in. 'Well, I'm glad you had a nice time,' I said, and when he looked like he was about to ask more about my evening, I glanced pointedly at the old-fashioned clock on the wall, which used to belong to his mum and which he'd insisted on bringing to France. 'I've got to go to the café, I'm meeting Charlie.'

'You and your men,' he said fondly, as though I had a string of them competing for my affections. 'Get him round here for dinner sometime, I want to try out a new recipe.'

'It's not another take on a French classic, is it?' I recalled his attempt to recreate *bouillabaisse*, using sardines and turnips. I hadn't realised my gag reflex was so strong.

'Marie's going to show me how to make a soufflé.' He threw down his pen and pretended to crack an egg. 'I'm popping round there later.'

'That sounds great,' I said. The more time he spent with Marie the better, as far as I was concerned. 'I'll see you later.'

After gathering my things, I set off for the café, swinging my laptop bag – I wanted to make a start on my interview with Jay, once I'd filled Charlie in on last night. I was glad to see a brightening in the sky as the sun began to creep through. It was a sunshine kind of morning. A sing-song kind of day. *Sing-song kind of day?* I laughed at myself. I wanted to twirl round lamp posts and buy ice creams for passers-by. Luckily, there were no lamp posts – or ice-cream parlours – nearby.

The colours of the fishing boats in the marina looked more appealing than usual, and the café especially welcoming in the feeble sunlight, the tables outside separated by olive trees in terracotta pots. They were a recent addition by Dolly that Charlie had been opposed to, on the grounds that they might be a health and safety hazard, but they added a touch of class. In my elevated mood, I resolved to compliment Dolly. The continuing success of the café was due to more than her baking, and she deserved to be told so.

As I stepped through the door, the smell of warm, buttery pastry assailed my nostrils, and I closed my eyes and inhaled, wondering whether I really could bring Jay here one day, and introduce him to the best *pains au chocolat* in France.

'Natalie!'

My eyes snapped open. Charlie was beckoning urgently from behind the counter. 'Where have you been?' he said, once I'd weaved through the tables, aware I was beaming in a way he'd probably never seen before. 'I've been trying to call you for ages.'

'I know, I slept right through,' I said. 'Until your last call, but you'd rung off by the time I found my phone.'

A customer nudged past, and I realised I'd pushed to the front of a small queue. The café was busy, Giselle and the rest of the staff occupied, while Dolly was replenishing the pastries, her cheeks glowing with exertion. She didn't even look up.

'Go and sit down. I'll be over when I'm done here,' Charlie hissed. He sounded stressed, and his hair was more mussed than usual. Giselle slid me a contemptuous look as she shuttled back and forth behind the counter, a tray balanced on her upturned hand.

'OK,' I said cheerfully to Charlie, not wanting to add to his workload. 'I'll have my usual, but there's no rush.'

'Gee, thanks,' he said, with what sounded like sarcasm. But Charlie was never sarcastic, at least not with me. I was in an over-sensitised state, I reminded myself, and must be imagining things.

Humming beneath my breath, I found a vacant table tucked in a corner between the counter and the wall, and took out my phone while I waited, wishing Jay had a phone so we could have exchanged numbers and messaged each other. How was he feeling this morning? The same way I did – as if I was made of marshmallow but also invincible – or would it be business as usual? He would have to switch off from real life in order to become Max Weaver. I should have asked him about his acting method, but that could be a conversation for another day – a private one. My lips seemed permanently fixed in a smile, and I hoped I didn't look deranged to onlookers. Not that anyone cared – apart from Giselle, who was flashing me hostile glances as she took an order from a couple at the next table. Probably wondering if I was planning to make a move on Charlie.

Ignoring her, I turned back to my phone to check my messages. No reply yet from Jools, but, surprisingly, there was a text from my former editor, Jackie. We'd rarely texted since she started working for *Gossip*. I'd had the sense she was embarrassed to have moved to the competition, which she'd once derided as 'publishing for the lowest common denominator'. Intrigued, I opened the message, and felt an instant wash of coldness.

Hey, Natalie, good to hear from you. This is amazing!! I can't believe you got to speak to the man himself! I remember you trying to contact his people back in the day, and not getting anywhere. I think I might have doubted you really knew him, ha ha, but this is fantastic news! I'm assuming you want us to run an interview? Thanks for thinking of me, Nat, you must have heard that circulation's down. Name your price, darling x

I felt as if someone had doused me in icy water. How did Jackie know I'd talked to Jay? Surely Jools wouldn't have forwarded my message. I read it again, and felt as if my blood had pooled at my feet when I realised what had happened. I'd been imagining Jackie's reaction when I decided to text Jools, and had sent it to her instead. No wonder Jools hadn't responded. *Oh God.*

I quickly typed *Hi Jackie, could I ask you a favour? Please don't do anything with this.* Even if – somehow – Jay was OK with a puff piece appearing in a British magazine, I'd promised Nicolas Juilliard an exclusive interview and – more importantly – it was an issue of trust, of keeping my word to them both.

I was shaking as I waited for Jackie's response, which came immediately. *Why did you get in touch, if you don't want to write about him?*

It was a mistake. I replied, deciding to be honest. *The message was intended for someone else.*

Another magazine? I'll pay double whatever they're offering.

Not another magazine, a friend. I didn't know whether that was better or worse.

You can't expect me to sit on this, Natalie, it's HUGE. Just a few details will do, and a photo, if you have one.

I don't. I lied. *PLEASE, Jackie, it's personal. Don't print anything.* I tried to think rationally. *He's doing an exclusive interview with a magazine over here. After it comes out, you can do what you like.* It wouldn't matter, then. My photos, the feature, they'd be in the public domain, and would be reproduced anyway. *You won't even have to pay me! Gossip's* budget was obviously stretched, but I knew an interview with Jay Merino – even a quick Q&A about his favourite things – would be too tempting for her to pass up.

There was a pause, during which I was aware of Charlie sliding a cup of milky coffee in front of me. 'Reply, reply,' I muttered, imagining Jackie rapping her scarlet nails on her desk, lips pursed as she considered my plea.

The reply, when it came, nearly choked me. *Now I know he's filming there, I can put something together myself and get one of my contacts to try and get a pic of him, thanks Natalie. Take care x*

'Noooooooooo,' I wailed, dropping my phone and pushing my hands through my hair – or as far as they would go in my mass of air-dried curls.

'I take it you've seen the damage,' said Charlie.

I raised my head, which felt exceptionally heavy. He was sitting opposite, his usual smiley expression replaced by something grimmer.

A grim-faced Charlie. I hadn't seen that look since... I'd never seen that look. 'Yes,' I mumbled. 'Wait.' I yanked my hands free and sat up. 'What damage? What are you talking about?'

He pulled out his phone, jabbed the screen and held it in front of me.

'I thought you didn't like Twitter,' I said, trying not to look, knowing I wasn't going to like whatever it was. 'You said it's full of trolls.'

'Look.' He pushed the phone so close, the writing started to blur, but not before the words had leapt out and imprinted themselves on my brain.

No more Max Weaver! Jay Merino to retire after Maximum Force 3: The End. The actor – currently filming scenes for his latest movie on the Île de Ré in France – says he's done with films and wants to set up a foundation in dead brother's name!

I stared at Charlie in horror.

'It's gone viral,' he said.

Chapter Sixteen

'I don't believe this.' I grabbed Charlie's phone and read the headline again. The *Daily Mail* had posted the story, and so had *The Telegraph* and French newspaper, *Le Monde*. It had been liked eight thousand times and retweeted more than that. 'Someone's talked to the press.'

'Clearly.'

I couldn't bear to read the whole story, just segments… *not happy with fame… reconciled with his mother… NO to Bond… property investment…* Almost everything Jay and I had talked about was there – all the personal details he'd confided to me. I wanted to be sick as I looked at the comments.

Max Weaver, NOOOOOO, I love you, don't retire!!!
Wasn't his brother a druggie?
I wouldn't mind earning his money.
Didn't he dump Carly Sweet for his co-star on Max Force 2?
I want to marry Max Weaver!!

I handed the phone back to Charlie with trembling hands. 'I don't understand.' My voice was barely audible. 'Nobody knew this stuff but me and you.'

'I didn't leak it,' he said.

'Of *course* you didn't.' It hadn't even crossed my mind. 'Neither did I.'

'Obviously, but someone did.'

His face blurred through a haze of tears. 'But how would they have heard my conversation with Jay?' I covered my face with my palms. 'Charlie, he'll think it was me.'

'Drink your coffee,' his voice softened. 'You need caffeine.'

'Who would do this?' I lowered my shaking hands. 'I thought sending a message about Jay to my former editor was bad enough.'

'You did what?'

'That's what I was upset about just now, but this…' I gestured to his phone. 'This is so much worse.'

'Why did you send her a text?' Charlie sounded confused.

'It was a mistake,' I explained, the words like dust in my mouth.

'Christ, Nat, you've really messed up.'

'You think?' I glared at him, then subsided. He was right. I'd messed up badly, yet the misdirected message wasn't even the worst of my problems. 'Nicolas will be so, so angry,' I said, my stomach twisting with fresh anguish. 'He's bound to have got wind of this. Editors are always on social media, he must have seen it.' But it wasn't Nicolas's reaction I was really worried about. It was Jay's. 'I have to go.'

As I made to stand up, Charlie caught my wrist. 'Natalie, what happened last night?'

'It was amazing.' A sob leaked into my voice. 'I really like him, Charlie.'

'Could someone at his end have done this?'

My mind flew to Simon, but I quickly dismissed the thought. 'Jay told me that no one knew he was planning to retire and he keeps himself to himself, most of the time. I just don't see how anyone could have found out.'

'He's not…' Charlie drew his hand away. 'I know you won't want to hear this, Natalie, but… pillow talk?'

'He's not sleeping with Susie and even if he was, I can't imagine he'd tell her the stuff he told me.' Charlie's slightly pitying look sent fresh tears to my eyes. 'I know you think I'm being blind, because of Matt, but I'm not. I'd know if I was being played.'

He puffed out his cheeks. 'It was the talk of the place first thing,' he said, casting his gaze around the café, though if everyone had been gossiping before they'd now lost interest. 'Giselle saw it trending online and started showing everyone.'

Blinking, I turned to see her clearing one of the tables outside with a little more vigour than usual. 'Charlie, you haven't told her anything, have you?'

'Of *course* I haven't.' He sounded hurt. 'How can you even ask?'

'I'm sorry.' I shook my head, trying to clear my suspicions. 'But you know she hates me—'

'Even if I was seeing her, which I'm not, and madly in love, which I'm not, I'd never repeat anything you'd told me in confidence.'

'I know you wouldn't, Charlie, I'm sorry,' I repeated. 'I just… this is so *awful*.'

'I know, but no one's died, and if there's anything between you and Max Weaver, he'll believe it wasn't you who leaked your conversation.' He nudged my plate forward but the thought of eating made me want to retch. 'You should probably talk to him, and to Nicolas Juilliard.'

As he finished speaking, my phone vibrated. Fighting a wave of nausea, I turned it over. Jools had texted.

I've just read that Jay Merino is filming in your neck of the woods! Any chance of you 'bumping' into him? I remember you telling me he'd promised to let you interview him one day! Hope you're well, babe, speak soon XX

'Oh God,' I moaned. There was another message, from Mum.

You didn't tell me Max Weaver was on the island! Anything to do with the exciting assignment you mentioned? Call me soon, sweetheart (how's your dad?). Love, Mum xx

'At least your name wasn't mentioned anywhere,' said Charlie, concern etching his features. 'I read the whole thing and it just mentions "a reliable source". There's speculation it was an extra from the film.'

'The only reliable source as far as Jay's concerned will be me.'

'Someone must have overheard your conversation.'

Again, I thought of Simon, appearing and disappearing; never far from Jay. He'd made his distrust of me plain, which would be a good cover for his own betrayal. But what would he have to gain by contacting the press? Unless Jay's imminent retirement meant he was worried he'd be out of a job – that Jay would no longer require the services of his old friend.

A million thoughts collided as I switched off my phone and swung my laptop bag over my shoulder. 'I'll call Nicolas, then I'm going to Saint-Clément to try to talk to Jay.'

'Shall I come with you?' Charlie stood too, shoulders hunched around his ears. 'You could use some support.'

More tears threatened to spill over. 'Thanks, but I'll be fine,' I lied, catching Dolly firing frantic eye signals at Charlie. 'Besides, it looks like you're needed here.'

I half-ran back to the house, powered by panic and despair, and burst through the door to find Dad sat on the arm of the sofa, watching the news on TV. A ticker tape rolled beneath a shot of Max Weaver, and I didn't need to read the words on it to know all the channels had picked up the story about Jay's imminent retirement.

'Did you know about this?' Dad turned down the volume as the photo switched to one of Max Weaver hurtling out of a helicopter, arms outstretched, his face distorted by high velocity while someone fired a round of bullets at him.

'Yes,' I whispered, with a plummet of misery as I remembered Jay telling me he did his own stunts. Even before the shot switched to a bank of reporters clustered outside his hotel, I knew that whatever had started between us would now be over. 'He told me it all yesterday, in confidence.'

Dad turned, alerted by my dry and creaky voice. 'How come it's ended up on *Sky News*?'

I burst into tears. 'I've no idea.'

In an instant, I was in Dad's arms, and he was stroking my hair and shushing me, just as he used to when I'd had a nightmare, and he had to reassure me there wasn't a porcelain doll underneath my bed, about to come to life (I'd been banned from watching *Are You Afraid of the Dark?* after that episode). 'What's happened?' he said, when my sobs had subsided to an undignified snivel and I was squashed beside him on the sofa, a tissue pressed to my eyes.

When I told him, his brow puckered. I recognised what Mum and I used to call his 'Detective Marty' face. 'What's the likeliest explanation?' he said, crossing his ankles and wagging his foot – a sure sign he was thinking things over very carefully.

'That someone overheard Jay and me talking in the garden at the hotel.'

'There you are, then.' He squeezed my hand. 'Tell him that and you've nothing to worry about.'

'Nothing to worry about?' I leapt off the sofa and almost fell over the coffee table. 'Things Jay told me in *strictest* confidence, because he *trusted* me, are plastered all over the news and social media, and as a result, there are reporters *here* on the *island*, outside his *hotel* and God only knows how they found out where he was staying, which he'll be *furious* about, he *hates* publicity and…' I was jabbing the air with my finger and emphasising like mad. 'Not only that, his *exclusive* interview is no longer relevant because *everyone* knows about his future plans now, *including* his director, who, by the way, was hoping to make another film with Jay and will be *livid*.'

'I thought this film was called *The End*?'

'He wants to resurrect Max Weaver, but that's not the point, Dad.' Bits of shredded tissue floated to the floor as I waved my arm about. 'Jay told me some things for the interview but some of it he told me as a… as a *friend*.' I almost choked on the word, imagining what Jay must be thinking now. He was probably regretting speaking to me at all.

'He must really like you to have told you all that.' Dad seemed unmoved by my outburst, as if he had every confidence that a simple conversation could resolve everything. And he must surely know from his policing days that life was never that simple. 'You have to talk to him, Natalie.'

'I'm planning to,' I said. 'If I can get near him, which I doubt.'

'You have to at least try.'

I nodded. 'First, I need to explain all this to the editor at *Magnifique*.' I blew my nose on a fresh piece of tissue from the toilet roll Dad had produced. 'I'll be in my room.'

'I'll fetch you a cup of tea.'

As soon as I'd closed my bedroom door and switched on my phone, I saw that I'd missed several calls from Nicolas's office, and my heart dropped through the floor.

'Monsieur Juilliard, please,' I said, as soon as the assistant picked up. It was the same one I'd spoken to before, but this time she didn't bother with small talk, just said, 'I'm putting you through,' in a tone that could have cut through concrete.

Seconds later, Nicolas's voice filled my ear. '*Natalee*, I would not 'ave believed this of you.' His tone was heavy with remonstration and regret, and although I'd found it slightly creepy at the time, I wished he'd go back to finding me alluring. 'I gave you the opportunity you sounded so desperate for, and you throw it in my face like this?' I imagined him flicking a hand up in despair. 'I do not understand.'

'It wasn't me, Monsieur Juilliard.' I was careful to keep any trace of tears or panic from my voice. 'I'm *devastated* that this has happened.'

'But, where else would this 'ave come from?' he said, not unreasonably. ''E 'as not talked to anyone else. I take it only you 'ad this information.'

'*Exactement*.' It was hardly the time to impress him with French words – especially ones a five-year-old would have mastered – plus, I *had* talked to someone else, but only Charlie knew it all and he would never have gone to the press with it. 'Why would I ruin my chance to work at *Magnifique* when it was my dream?'

'Only you can answer that, Natalee.' Nicolas paused, releasing a weighty sigh. 'Maybe you wanted the notoriety, the five minutes of fame, or to be on, what is eet you English are obsessed with? To go in ze jungle and eat insects, or be on ze *Love Island*, *non*?'

'Definitely *non*!' A blast of anger burned through my anguish. 'I'm a writer, I don't want bloody notoriety. I want to be taken seriously.' Something struck me. 'Anyway, none of it was attributed to me, so how would I even achieve notoriety, as you put it?'

'I 'ave no clue, Natalee. I agree something does not make sense, but ze fact remains, all ze news about Jay Merino is now public knowledge, so I 'ave no need for you to write anything.'

I dropped on my bed, the mattress sagging beneath me. I wanted to throw back my head and howl, but instead pinched the bridge of my nose and said, 'Monsieur Juilliard, I can put this right, I promise you. I'll talk to Jay, persuade him all this will be great publicity for his foundation, if he'll agree to the interview going ahead.' *Fat chance*, screamed an inner voice. *He won't give you the time of day, after this.* 'There are things that weren't revealed, for instance, he likes to go sailing to relax and—'

'Fleur has already reached out to him,' he smoothly interrupted. 'She 'as an idea 'ow to turn things around, to make this work in 'is favour.'

Fleur had reached out to Jay? Of course she had. She was probably loving this. I could just imagine her persuading him that I wasn't to be trusted, that she knew – from Nicolas – I'd been to the hotel to talk to him and that, even if it had been indirectly, the leak must have come from me. 'But *I* can do that,' I said. 'Please, Nicolas, just let me try.'

'I'm so sorry, Natalee.' To his credit, he sounded as if he meant it. 'Whatever 'as 'appened, I cannot work with people 'oo are indiscreet.'

My body sagged like a collapsed tent. I *had* been indiscreet. Confiding in Charlie, texting Jackie accidentally, like an overexcited teenager; writing a column for *Expats* about Jay – albeit without his name attached – partly because I'd been short of alternative ideas. What sort of writer didn't have ideas? I didn't deserve to write for *Magnifique*. Or even *Expats*.

'Would you like to 'ave dinner again sometime?' Nicolas's voice turned treacly. 'We can still 'ave a nice time, Natalee. I like to be around young people with spirit, they remind me why I got into zis business in ze first place, and why I find eet so 'ard to give up.'

'For God's sake, Nicolas,' I snapped. 'You don't 'ave to, I mean *have* to give it up altogether, but you could hand over the day-to-day running to Fleur, if that's what she wants. You know she'd do a bloody good job, but maybe that's what you're scared of – that a woman could do a better job than the mighty Nicolas Juilliard.'

I cut him off before he could reply and felt a leap of horror. Talk about burning all my bridges at once. At least while he'd found me 'charming' there was a possibility he'd have given me another chance to write for the magazine down the line, which was more than Fleur would do.

I quickly logged on to the *Expats* website to see that Sandy had posted my column up and read it through half-shut eyes. Actually, it wasn't half bad, and Jay's name wasn't mentioned. Maybe she hadn't seen the breaking news and guessed who I'd been talking about, and had simply uploaded it in good faith. Unlike most editors, she wasn't interested in publishing at any cost – though I doubted my words would reach a very wide audience anyway. Until I scrolled down and saw the comments. There were triple the usual amount already and all of them complimentary (words like *hilarious* and *wish that had happened to me!* jumped out) even though it was clear they didn't know I was talking about Jay. It had been shared numerous times and I allowed myself a small thrill of achievement. I thought I'd done well with a blog post I'd written in January about experiencing winter in a country I'd only previously visited during summer. *Who knew it could rain for days on end on the Île de Ré, and that the sky would be the same shark-grey as it is in the UK?* It had prompted twenty-five responses from readers detailing their experiences, but this was on another level.

Then I reread the news articles and had to squeeze my eyes shut to stop the tears from leaking out. How could I ever convince Jay I wasn't the source? It was almost word for word what he'd told me. When I imagined confronting him, all I could see was the picture I'd looked at online, his eyes like those of a tiger crouched to attack as he spotted the long lens of a camera trained on him. But I knew I had to try.

Chapter Seventeen

Dad offered to drive me to Saint-Clément where Jay was filming, probably wary of my state of mind and the fact that I'd barely driven since moving to the island.

'I'll be fine,' I insisted, trying to moderate my tone so as not to alarm him further. 'I promise I'll be careful.'

He didn't argue as he plucked the key out of the kitchen drawer, where it tended to languish most days, but in the rear-view mirror his face was a mask of anxiety as he watched me drive away. When I stalled at the end of the street, he started jogging towards me, and I lurched into gear and pulled away with a cocktail of emotions churning in my stomach.

If I could just talk to Jay, I was sure I could sort this out. He'd said he trusted me and, after last night, he surely wouldn't believe I could betray him. He must know I'd have nothing to gain and everything to lose by contacting the press and revealing everything he'd told me. As I drove, I wondered how he'd found out – whether it had been when reporters turned up outside the hotel, or whether he'd seen the story online. I imagined his phone endlessly ringing, then remembered he didn't have one. A small blessing, but all the same, panic clawed at my throat as I imagined his reaction. I *had* to see him whatever it took, and try to work this out.

I arrived at Saint-Clément on autopilot, grateful I'd at least remembered to stay on the right side of the road. The thought of being incapacitated by a car accident, with Jay believing I'd royally stitched him up, was excruciating.

The lighthouse was at the furthest point of the island like the bow of a ship, and as I parked by one of the nearby cafés, I could already see two tiny tussling figures at the top – presumably Max Weaver and Nova, battling for supremacy. Gathered around the base of the lighthouse were crew, cameras and cables, and beyond that, an assembled crowd, no doubt drawn by the action unfolding. It was almost a shame that Jay would be too busy fighting his 'opponent' to take in the sweeping view of the best beach on the island. As I jumped from the car, I imagined for a heady second us having a picnic on the long curve of pale sand once filming was done for the day. I could drive to the market five minutes away for provisions and we'd eat on the cashmere blanket Dad kept in the boot of the car as we watched the sun go down.

Then reality roared back. The last thing on Jay's mind would be having a picnic with me – or doing anything else, apart from bitterly regret the day I'd (literally) thrown myself at him. My distress hardened into determination as I rushed towards the lighthouse, skirting the museum in front to avoid being seen, but as I drew closer, Brian spotted me and said something to Simon, who whipped round and stalked towards me. Even from a distance, his face looked thunderous, and any hopes I'd nursed that the news somehow hadn't got through, instantly died. Simon looked like a man on a mission – one that could end in my murder.

We stopped abruptly, a few feet from each other, as though a trapdoor had opened, and Simon's face wrenched in disgust. 'You've got a nerve coming here, after what you've done.'

'I haven't done anything.' Forcing myself to breathe, I shielded my eyes with my hand as the sun slid out from behind a passing cloud. 'And Jay invited me here.'

'Yeah, before you spoke to the press and effed everything up.'

'You really believe I would do that?'

His face was set in a scowl. 'I told him you couldn't be trusted.'

'Oh, you did, did you?'

'You're just like all the rest.'

Wings of anger began to beat in my chest. 'What about you?'

'Pardon?' He drew his head back, as if to get a better look at me.

'You could have leaked all that stuff,' I said. 'You were in the garden when I was talking to Jay.'

'As a matter of fact, I wasn't.' He jutted his hairy chin out. 'I was with someone, as it happens,' he said. 'She'll vouch for me.'

Susie. I remembered how she'd come out of her room, wrapped in a towel, and the way she'd looked at Simon. Despite his gruff rebuttal, they were obviously embroiled in a torrid fling. 'Does Jay know?'

'Yes, he knows.' His brows dipped further. 'Not that it's any of your business.'

'It's my business when I'm being accused of something I didn't do.' Several sets of eyes were on me now, and I knew it was only a matter of seconds before I was carted away, or even arrested, as this was the second time I'd invaded the film shoot. 'I really didn't do it, Simon.' My voice was a plea. 'What possible motive could I have had?'

As if the ring of truth had filtered through, Simon's face fractionally unclenched. 'Who else could it have been?' As he stepped closer, my legs braced and my hands clenched into fists – as if I had any chance of fighting him off. 'No one else knows all that stuff about Jay,' he said roughly. 'Even I didn't know he was planning to retire.'

'Really?'

His tone grew defensive. 'Only because he didn't want to put me in an awkward position and make me worry for my future.' That sounded like Jay. 'But he's promised there'll be a role for me, whatever happens.' A slight husk in his voice brought home how important his relationship with Jay was, and I realised that they must have had a conversation – perhaps even a confrontation – when the news had broken, and that it was somehow my fault.

'Oh, Simon, I don't know who could have done it.' It came out close to a wail. 'Did Jay say anything else?'

His face hardened. 'Only that he's withdrawn permission for your interview to be published, not that there's any need for it now everyone knows his business.'

'It's been killed anyway,' I said miserably, deflecting an image of Jay flinging furniture around his hotel room, cursing the day he met me. 'Apparently, the writer he was thinking of talking to in the first place has been lined up to put a good spin on things for him.' It wasn't much consolation, but Fleur would present Jay in the best possible light, and it wouldn't surprise me if her interview pulled in quadruple the amount of readers. Maybe then, Nicolas really would give her his job.

'Yeah, well, none of this will do you any harm in the long run.' Simon's voice thickened with anger. 'Now the you-know-what's hit the fan, you can always go on telly and talk about your so-called relationship with Jay. You've even got the photos to prove it.' Like Nicolas, he'd decided I wasn't to be trusted, despite his doubts. 'You'll be on breakfast telly by the end of the week, talking about your amazing encounter with Jay Merino.'

I gasped at the sheer injustice. 'I would *never* do that,' I said truthfully. 'And I shouldn't be trying to convince you anyway. I need to talk to Jay.'

'I'm afraid that won't be possible.' Simon was planted in front of me, implacable as a tree. The sort that could withstand a tornado. 'Jay doesn't want to see you. He has absolutely nothing to say.'

'I'd rather he told me that himself.' I glanced behind Simon at the historic 'old tower' as it used to be called, rearing up to the sky. Filming had apparently resumed, but I could no longer see anybody at the top. Was Jay watching from one of the narrow windows on the tier below, sick with disappointment at my 'betrayal', willing me to go away? Perhaps he wished he had some of Max Weaver's skills and could karate-chop me into oblivion. 'I just need a few minutes with him, then I'll go.' I clasped my hands, not caring that I was begging. I couldn't leave without seeing Jay – I might never get another opportunity.

Simon was shaking his head. 'Just leave,' he said, folding his arms. Even his tattooed serpent looked hacked off. 'You had your chance and you've blown it.'

My thoughts were running about like mice. *If I could just get up there…*

'Look, I think the director wants you.' I pointed to where Brian was standing with a cameraman, peering through his spectacles at something on a small screen.

Not fooled by my pathetic ruse, Simon didn't turn to look, but I dodged past him anyway and pelted towards the lighthouse, glad I'd pulled on my trainers before leaving the house. Hearing his roar of outrage spurred me on. Despite his bulk, he didn't look built for running and I had desperation on my side.

'Where do you think you're going?' someone – possibly Brian the director – bawled, and I heard someone else say, 'Oh God, is it her again?'

I kept on running, despite feeling as though my airways had shrunk and I couldn't get enough breath in my lungs, until I burst into the lighthouse, where the magnificent spiral stone staircase curled upwards, looking like an ammonite from below.

I'd climbed the two hundred and fifty-seven steps several times in the past and today, I had the advantage of not needing to buy a ticket, and no tourists blocking my way. Gripping the wooden handrail, I hauled myself up the steps two at a time, as if I was being chased by a pack of starving wolves. Or a furious bodyguard. The thought of Simon's rage propelled me upwards.

'Jay!' I called, but it came out as a wheeze. I really needed to up my exercise routine – or at least start one. The muscles in my thighs seized up as I reached the top stair. I crashed onto the floor of the lighthouse keeper's room and lay on my stomach on the wooden boards, trying to catch my breath.

'Natalie?'

Gasping, I pulled myself onto my hands and knees and raised my scarlet face to see Max Weaver, studying me with a mix of emotions I couldn't tell apart. 'Jay,' I rasped, my voice a ragged whisper.

'Hey, it's your little saviour,' said a familiar American voice. I twisted my head to see Nova (Susie Houlihan), looking more seductive in her beige trench coat than she had at the hotel in her towel, making eyes at Simon. This time, she was wielding a knife instead of a gun, which Jay (or Max) must have been in the process of wrestling from her before – presumably – 'throwing' her over the viewing balcony outside. 'Is she the one who sold you out, baby?'

Baby? 'What possible reason would I have for doing that?' I said, scrambling to my feet, but before I could take a step forward, I found myself dangling several inches above the floor, trapped in the vice-like grip of Simon's arms. 'Put me *down*.' I kicked back at his shins as he spun me towards the stairs, but my heels only met the air. 'Sorry about this,' he said, sounding as out-of-breath as I felt.

'You will be.'

'I was talking to Jay,' he growled in my ear. 'I'm going to call the police once we're back downstairs.'

'We don't need to get them involved,' Jay said flatly. I willed him to make eye contact, but his head was tipped away from me and I couldn't read his expression.

'Jay, I'm so sorry about the reporters, about the stuff online. I promise you, I didn't talk to the press,' I burst out, adding for clarification, 'or anyone connected to the press,' thinking of Jackie, but knowing she couldn't be responsible. All she knew was that I'd bumped into him.

'I want so much to believe that, Natalie.' He spoke in a quiet way that made my insides shrivel. 'But no one else knew that this was going to be my last film.'

'Such a shame, honey,' Nova (Susie) murmured. 'I still haven't managed to get you into bed.' I assumed (hoped) she was talking about Max, not Jay.

'Somebody knew,' I said.

'It wasn't anyone around me.' Jay's hands hung loosely by his sides and I couldn't help thinking how much I preferred him dressed in jeans and a T-shirt, rather than his Max Weaver crotch-gripping leather trousers – however well they fitted.

'I can't believe you told *her*,' Susie murmured, the implication being *her, of all people; a stranger* and knew the ramifications for Jay would be that his co-stars, his director – everyone connected with the film – would probably treat him differently now they knew he'd had enough of the franchise.

A fresh wave of anguish threatened to overwhelm me. 'Somebody must have heard us talking,' I said, realising how ridiculous I must look, clamped to Simon's chest, feet hovering in mid-air. 'Maybe someone who works at the hotel.'

'There was no one else there.' Simon's abrasive voice rumbled through me. 'I checked the itinerary.'

'So, you *do* believe me.' I tried to twist round and look at him, but my face met his solid shoulder and the silky fabric of his sporty black T-shirt. 'Why else would you check?'

'I'm working, Natalie,' Jay said. He finally looked at me, and when I saw how empty his eyes were, I felt my heart break. 'This isn't a good time.'

'I don't think there'll ever be a good time, honey.' Although Susie's words were directed at me, her gaze had travelled to Simon, as if she'd like to be the one clasped to his sturdy chest.

'I can wait until you've finished.' I wildly flailed my legs and tried to wriggle out of Simon's clutches. I'd spent more time in his arms than I had in any man's since Matt's, and my top was riding up, revealing more of my stomach than I was comfortable with.

'Put her down, Si.'

Hope flared inside me at Jay's words. *He didn't hate me. We could work this out.*

Simon deposited me on the floor with obvious reluctance and I wobbled on my feet. 'Jay, I—'

'Please, Natalie.' He didn't look at me again. 'I think you'd better just go.'

Susie's red-painted lips curled in a smirk.

'What are you grinning at?' I snapped. 'And why do you need to wear lipstick to kill a man, for God's sake?'

'I seduce him first, honey.' She fluttered her false eyelashes at Jay. 'Max likes a woman in red lipstick and not much else.' She tugged at the belt of her coat. 'I'm not wearing anything under here.' This time, her words were directed at Simon as she pulled her lips into a sultry pout.

Ignoring her, I took a step towards Jay. 'How do you know it wasn't her, or even Simon? Either of them could have overheard us talking at the hotel.'

'Don't, Natalie.' His voice had tightened and I knew this time I'd gone too far.

'Wasn't me.' Susie's eyes jolted wide. 'I had better things to do.' She winked at Simon, who didn't reply as he cupped my elbow.

'After you,' he said, turning me towards the stairs once more, and I had no choice but to walk back down, which seemed to take an eternity with Simon right behind, breathing out in long, heavy sighs.

I kept my head bowed as we emerged, feeling like an inmate on death row, not daring to meet anyone's gaze, and didn't argue when Simon escorted me all the way back to the car and watched me open the door. The fight had drained out of me. I barely had the energy to put the key in the ignition.

Simon grabbed the door before I could close it, and dropped to his haunches. 'Look, Brian's furious, and Jay's gonna be pestered left, right and centre for interviews now, but it's not the end of the world,' he said, to my surprise. 'He'll handle it, but you've got to stay away from him, OK?'

Tears swam to my eyes and spilled over. He opened his mouth – only just visible inside his beard – but whatever he'd been about to say died on his lips, replaced by a thin smile. 'Just pretend you never met him, yeah, and be glad he doesn't want to... I don't know, sue you, or whatever.'

As he rose, I slammed the car door and drove away blindly, his words ringing in my ears.

It's not the end of the world.

Then why did it feel like it was?

Chapter Eighteen

Halfway home, my tears dried, and a plan began to form. I couldn't leave things as they were, without having one last stab at apologising to Jay. Instead of heading to the café or home, I drove to Saint-Martin and parked round the back of the hotel, glad to see all but one patient reporter had vanished. The last thing I needed was to be 'outed' as the person who'd leaked the news online, or for rumours to start flying that I was Jay's girlfriend – or even a stalker. That kind of publicity would be the kiss of death to any potential relationship with him. If, indeed, there was any potential left.

My idea wasn't spectacular. As much as I would have loved to gain access to his room and lie in wait for him, I knew it would be the action of a desperate – possibly unhinged – person, and I'd already made a pretty poor show of myself. Instead, I would leave my number at reception, with a request for Jay to call me (he could borrow Simon's phone, if he had one). I refused to believe there was nothing more to be said.

Not wanting to dwell on our lighthouse encounter any more, I ripped a sheet of paper from the notebook I kept in my bag and wrote my mobile number with one of Dad's pens. I resisted the urge to scrawl a plea across the bottom – *please, please, please call me, you gorgeous man. I didn't do it, and I think I'm in love with you* followed by multiple hearts – and kept it simple. *Call me, please. Natalie x*

It was quiet inside the hotel – probably because the guests were all filming in Saint-Clément – and the lobby was deserted. I crossed to the desk, and was about to ring the bell to summon a receptionist when I heard voices approaching from outside. A second later, the owner came in, accompanied by Fleur Dupont.

The sight of Fleur knocked the breath from my body, which was already weakened by the emotional fallout of the last few hours, and from climbing two hundred and fifty-seven steps at speed.

'Hello, Natalie,' she said, with a cool little smile. 'This is a surprise.' To prove it, her eyebrows arched, creating fine lines on her porcelain-pale forehead. I felt like a homeless person who'd wandered in looking for shelter, struck once more by how quietly confident Fleur seemed with her place in the world, and her right to occupy it. She looked amazing too. Even if I had the money to employ a stylist, I'd never be able to replicate her effortless panache.

'Hi,' I said, though it sounded more like a sound a startled animal might make.

'Can I help you?' the hotel owner asked in perfect English. She was a tall, elegant blonde with a warm, direct smile. 'I'm afraid there is no one here at the moment and we are not talking to the press.'

'I… I know, I…' My words drifted into silence. Why couldn't there have been an obliging receptionist I could have slipped my number to? She would have taken pity on me and promised in a knowing whisper to make sure that 'Mr Jay' got my note. (I'd possibly watched too many period dramas with Mum. Sunday nights had been 'our telly night' while Dad was on police duty.) 'I wanted to leave a message for…' I raised my chin, a subconscious gesture of defiance. 'For Jay Merino.'

The hotel owner's expression was genuinely pitying. I had the feeling she knew exactly who I was and why I was there and guessed she must have known about my meeting with Jay the previous day. 'I'm sorry, but I cannot do that, Miss Bright,' she said. So, she *did* know who I was. As shame crawled over me; I wished I had the power to become invisible.

'It's a written message,' I persisted. 'If you wouldn't mind passing it to him.'

'I'm sorry, but no.' She murmured something to Fleur then walked away without looking back, as if supremely confident I wouldn't do anything silly, like charge upstairs and shove the note under Jay's door. I considered it. Even though my legs didn't feel capable of tackling any more stairs, I could always crawl up on all fours.

'You are either very bold, or very stupid to come here.' There was private amusement in Fleur's voice as she glided closer, her scent enveloping me in an annoyingly pleasant haze. 'You talked to Nicolas,' she said – a statement, not a question – and I imagined her as a classy spy in *Maximum Force*, bugging her boss's office so she was privy to his calls. 'You know the assignment will be mine now.'

'You could have any *assignment* you wanted,' I said, but her smiling answer wasn't exactly a surprise. 'Did you have anything to do with the leak?'

She tipped her head back and laughed out her disdain, revealing her slender throat. 'Assignments like this, that have to be fought for, they are the most rewarding,' she said, ignoring my – admittedly pitiful – question. She slipped her hands into the slanted pockets of her herringbone trousers and tilted her head like a therapist. 'I live for the exclusives.'

'And yet, this wasn't yours,' I couldn't resist saying. 'You got it by default.'

Annoyance flittered across her perfect features. 'It would have been mine if you had not tried to trade on a previous connection with Jay

Merino.' Her face looked older suddenly, the lines around her mouth more deeply scored in a flare of sunlight pouring through the glass-paned doors. 'You could say he was merely being a gentleman.'

'Well, you've got your own way now. I hope you're happy.' It was a juvenile shot, but her comment about trading on a previous connection had stung.

'Oh, I am *very* happy,' she said airily, but I remembered the look that had cloaked her face in the restaurant, and knew that it wasn't strictly true. She wouldn't be truly happy until she'd taken Nicolas's crown – the ultimate reward for dedicating her life to his magazine.

'I still think I would have done a good job,' I said. 'Don't you ever think about supporting writers who want to be like you?'

I caught a flash of surprise, as if it was an idea she'd never considered, before her face relaxed into a smile that didn't touch her eyes. 'I haven't got where I am by pandering to people who do not wish to work as hard as I have,' she said serenely. 'If you must know, Nicolas is relieved that the interview is now in my hands, where it was supposed to be all along. He knows I am the one who brings him the readers.'

Wishful thinking, I felt like saying. It all came back to him. For all her 'career woman scraping her way to the top by sheer hard work' spiel, there was a part of her just trying to impress a man. 'Well, you must be thrilled that this has happened,' I said. 'Have you spoken to Jay already?'

Her smile was edged with triumph. 'I am meeting him later,' she said, repositioning the gold-chained strap of her bag. 'We are having dinner here, in the hotel, where no paparazzi can take his picture. Just the great Phillipe Baptiste.' Even I knew he was a top photographer, famous for his intimate celebrity portraits. 'He has dropped everything to be here this evening.'

'Well, good luck,' I said dully. She'd got what she wanted. I hadn't. There was no point continuing the conversation. 'I hope it goes well.'

'Luck does not come into it,' she said, eyes glittering behind her glasses, and I remembered Jay saying *being lucky's not the same as being happy*. 'It will go well, because I am good at what I do.' I could see she *was* happy, and genuinely excited – this interview would be up there with meeting Brad Pitt – and was shot through with envy. 'I am going to wait for him here, so...' she dipped her chin. 'Goodbye, Natalie.'

I watched her stride off in the direction of the restaurant, looking as if she owned the place, and a feeling of desolation washed over me. There was nothing else I could do, short of hanging around and delivering my number to Jay in person, but the chances of succeeding after our earlier encounter were slim to none.

I heaved in a breath and turned to leave, almost bumping into a short, stout woman, standing right behind me. 'Oh, I'm sorry,' I said, leaping back. 'I didn't see you.'

'I am sorry,' she replied in careful English. Her face was soft and round like a bap, surrounded by a cloud of greying curls. I realised I'd seen her before, going into Marie's house. 'You're Jeanne,' I said.

She nodded, a smile stretching her plump lips. 'I 'eard you talking,' she said. She was carrying a bale of white towels and nodded over the top. 'You like me to give to 'im?'

I followed her gaze. She was talking about the balled-up piece of paper in my fist, and I remembered she was the one who'd told Marie that Jay was staying at the hotel, despite the non-disclosure agreement, and this thought lit another. Jeanne had appeared out of nowhere, and must have overheard my conversation with Fleur from the shadows. Could she have eavesdropped on Jay and me in the garden? Her spoken

English sounded good; her understanding might be even better. She came into contact with all nationalities, working at the hotel.

'Jeanne, were you here yesterday?' I tried not to think how offended Marie would be if she knew I was questioning her friend. '*Mardi*?'

Her brow wrinkled. '*Non*,' she said, with a decisive shake of her head. 'Eez day off. I go wiz my 'usband to La Rochelle to visit our daughter, Marielle.' It was clear she was telling the truth and I felt a combination of relief and disappointment as I wondered whether she'd told her daughter about Jay, and realised it didn't matter. People gossiped when something out of the ordinary happened – it was human nature. And Jeanne wasn't the one who'd ruined things for me with Jay. Looking at her more closely, I couldn't even imagine her switching on a computer, though I was probably over-generalising.

'You give?' One careworn hand shot out from beneath the towels, and I found myself passing her my phone number. She palmed it into her apron pocket and with a nod and wink, vanished as quietly as she'd appeared on soft-soled shoes, and it wasn't until I was driving back to Chamillon that I realised Fleur hadn't asked me the obvious question: why I'd sabotaged my chances of interviewing Jay. Either, she didn't care, or she knew that I couldn't – wouldn't – have done it.

I stopped at the café on the way back, unable to face Dad until I'd diluted what had happened by talking to Charlie, though I'd replied to Dad's anxious texts, telling him not to worry and that I was fine.

Charlie was outside, chatting to his friend Henri, who owned a restaurant in Saint-Martin. When Henri saw me, he slapped Charlie on the back and strode away with a friendly wave.

'How did it go?' Charlie peered more closely at my tear-ravaged face before taking my elbow and steering me across the road to the marina. After hoisting himself up onto the railings – which usually scared me in case he toppled backwards into the water – he said, 'That bad?'

Resting my arms on the rail beside him, I stared across the water, knowing if I so much as looked at him, I'd start crying again. 'Worse,' I said, and recounted what had happened, fixing my attention on a pair of blue and white fishing boats, bobbing side by side.

When I'd finished there was silence, and I turned to see Charlie's shoulders shaking with laughter. 'I'm sorry,' he said, after making an effort to control himself, 'it's just the thought of you tearing up those steps with that bodyguard chasing you.' He pressed his lips together, as if to stop more laughter erupting. 'Imagine if they'd been filming and you turn up in *Maximum Force*.'

'I'm glad you find it funny,' I said, but felt myself smile. It *was* pretty funny. I'd have found it hilarious, if I hadn't been the one being chased. 'I didn't know I had it in me to run that fast.'

'So, Jay was angry?'

'No,' I said with a sad shake of my head. 'I think I'd have preferred it if he was.'

'He was disappointed.'

'Exactly.' My heart was heavy with the crushing realisation that I'd probably seen him for the last time – at least in real life. Tears threatened again. 'As if I'd let him down.'

'And you don't think Fleur Dupont had anything to do with it?'

'I don't see how she could,' I said. 'Unless she was skulking about at the hotel when Jay and I were chatting. But no one apart from you and Dad knew I was going to meet him at that point. I didn't even tell Nicolas.'

'Maybe she's been following you.'

'Unlikely,' I said. 'She's based in Paris.'

'Except, she keeps turning up where you are.'

I shrugged. 'I'm sure she has better things to do than trail around after me.'

'Maybe you'll never know who it was.' Charlie's voice was sober now. 'It might be better to let it go and move on.'

'I don't know if I can.'

'At least your name still hasn't come up anywhere.'

'But Jay thinks it had something to do with me and that's all I care about.'

'Do you reckon that was the point?' Charlie was massaging his chin, looking thoughtful. 'Whoever it was, they wanted to make him doubt you?'

'But no one knows he likes me like *that*.' *Apart from Simon.*

'No, but maybe they wanted to kill your interview.'

'Only Fleur would have that motive, and I don't see how she could have found out.'

'Maybe someone's got it in for Jay,' suggested Charlie. 'They wanted to make trouble for *him*, maybe with the director, to get their own back about something.'

'Which brings me back to his bodyguard.' But although we hadn't seen eye to eye, I didn't believe Simon capable of something like that, and told Charlie so.

'You don't really know him though, do you?'

'True.' I drew in a breath and let it out. 'Maybe you're right and I'll never know, and it doesn't matter anyway, because the damage has been done.'

'Why don't you come up and have something to eat?' Charlie planted his feet back on the ground and dusted his hands together. 'We're closing shortly. I'll cook us some dinner.'

'Thanks, but I should get back.' My nerve-endings felt raw and I was overcome with a longing for my bed. 'Dad will be wondering where I am.'

'Well, if it gets too much there, you can always stay over here.' Charlie tried to engage me in a grin. 'Mum would love that.'

'I know she would.' I gave him a weary smile, feeling as if I'd aged ten years since I arrived at the café that morning, suspended in a bubble of bliss. 'That's probably why I shouldn't.'

'At least have an early night,' he said, and I was comforted by his steadying hand on my shoulder. 'Will you be OK?'

I nodded, and with a final concerned look, he headed back to the café where Giselle, standing in the doorway, greeted him with a cheerful smile – though I noted he merely nodded at her as he walked past.

It was a relief to find the house empty when I returned. There was a note from Dad on the kitchen table, letting me know there was some leftover soufflé if I was hungry. He must have gone on another date, unless he was back at Marie's. I glanced at the fridge, but couldn't summon the energy to open it. I hadn't eaten for hours and was vaguely curious to know if Dad's soufflé-making session had been a success, but couldn't face food.

Instead, I made a mug of tea and took it to my room, where I settled back on my bed and sipped the milky liquid, fighting a memory of Jay not quite meeting my eyes at the top of the lighthouse – as if, after all, I'd confirmed his worst suspicions about human nature.

I checked my phone – no messages – and went online, heart racing. *#JayMerino* was trending on Twitter, but there wasn't anything new and no one seemed to be interested in who had leaked the news. Comments ranged from speculation about Jay himself to deep love and admiration for Max Weaver, and plenty of crude comments along the lines of what they'd like to do to him that I quickly scrolled past without looking at.

I skim-read a piece posted several hours ago by *The Sun*, but it was only a rehash of what had already been posted, the only fresh news a single line at the end: *The actor has declined to comment.* I imagined Jay fending off reporters; pictured them thrusting microphones at him, spitting questions, demanding answers, bringing up his brother's death, and I wondered whether one of them was Jackie's contact, snapping pictures of Jay's furious face for *Gossip.* I gave a strangled sob as I switched off my phone. *This was all my fault.* I may not have talked to the *Daily Mail*, or whoever, but if I hadn't gone looking for Jay, we wouldn't have had the conversation and there'd have been nothing to leak. If only Marie hadn't told Dad that Jay was staying on the island. If only Jeanne hadn't told Marie…

The slice of sky outside my window grew inky and I wondered what Jay was doing. *I'm sorry*, I thought, willing the words across the airwaves to wherever he was. Probably in a clinch with Fleur Dupont, after being beguiled by her over dinner, determined to cast me from his mind – if he hadn't done so already.

The thought was like a knife in my heart and I put my mug down, slid under my duvet, and cried myself to sleep.

Chapter Nineteen

I woke to daylight and lay in a haze, blissfully blank – until my mind flashed back to the day before. I groaned and rolled over, trying to blot out the memories, and heard voices chatting downstairs, one male and one female. *Dad's date must have stayed overnight.*

'Yuk.' I yanked a pillow over my face, then remembered his reaction to Yvette's attempted kiss and put it back. It was more likely that Marie had popped in, or maybe Barbara, suggesting an outing somewhere with her and Larry. Dad would probably offer to show them the eco-museum of salt marshes in Loix, which was one of those places he found endlessly fascinating. The island was full of salt workers, still using age-old techniques, and I'd written about them for *Expats* ('Things to See and Do on the Île de Ré!') but had a limited interest in salt – other than as an accessory to chips.

'Natalie!' he called up the stairs, as if he'd intuited I was awake. My door was ajar, and when I realised he must have checked on me when he came in, the twist in my stomach tightened. I was living with my dad, still causing him anxiety, as if I was sixteen again. Except, at sixteen, the worst I'd gone through was a phase of rising at sundown at the weekend, like a vampire, leading him to worry I was depressed. (It was laziness.)

'I'll be down in five!' I called back, knowing he'd come up if I didn't. My legs felt like concrete when I swung them out of bed; a reminder

– as if I needed one – of yesterday's wild pursuit, and the sight of my puffy, swollen-lidded face and crumpled clothes in the mirror sent me scurrying to the bathroom, tearing my top off as I went. After a brief shower – no humming this morning – and an attempt at repairing my face with concealer and mascara, I pulled on clean jeans and a long-sleeved top, and scraped my hair into a tight, high bun. I didn't have the energy to deal with it properly.

I slowed as I made my way downstairs, leg muscles throbbing with fatigue, pasting a smile on my face so as not to scare Dad's guest, but when I saw who he'd been talking to, I was the one who cried out in surprise.

'Mum!'

'Oh good heavens, Natalie, I barely recognised you with all your hair off your face.' She moved quickly towards me and pulled me into a tight embrace.

'How can you not recognise your own daughter?' I hugged her back, happy to see her. 'What are you doing here?'

'What do you think?' She drew away and placed soft hands on my cheeks, staring into my eyes like a hypnotist. 'Your dad called yesterday and said he was worried about you.'

'Dad,' I chided. He was stirring something in a pan on the hob, looking faintly embarrassed but pleased – for me, or because Mum was here, it was difficult to tell. Probably both. 'I told you I was fine.'

'You didn't look it.' He gave Mum a look so layered, it was impossible to tell which emotion was uppermost. 'I knew your mother would understand,' he said. 'We speak the same language.' I had the feeling he was referring to more than *actual* language. 'She got the first available flight and I went to meet her at the airport.'

So that's where he'd been when I got back. 'You didn't have the car,' I pointed out.

'Marie lent me hers.'

Mum was hugging my arm and stiffened at the mention of Marie. 'I must pop round and thank her later.' She reached up to pet my bun as if it was a hamster. 'This is adorable.'

'Mum,' I said with a smile, feeling about seven years old. I seemed to be ranging through all the ages but my actual one, since waking up.

'So, what's been going on?' she said, pulling me across to the table. 'Dad was telling me it's all to do with the actor.'

'Ah, so that's why you're here.' I perched on the edge of the table while Mum settled herself on a chair, looking perfectly at home – as if we were back in our kitchen in England. 'You're hoping to get a look at Jay Merino.'

'Don't be silly,' she said, taking hold of my hand. 'Although, if you can arrange it…' Her eyebrows did a little jig. 'I'm joking,' she said, while Dad chuckled indulgently.

They seemed perky for a pair who must not have had much sleep. Both were fully dressed, Dad in the clothes he'd worn the day before, Mum in smart blue jeans and a maroon sweatshirt with a horse's head on the front. Dad's boots and Mum's trainers were side by side on the mat by the door, next to her little silver suitcase on wheels. 'Have you been to bed?' I said, realising at once how it sounded. 'I mean…'

'I know what you mean,' Mum said calmly, stroking a strand of hair behind her ear. 'We've been talking all night.' She and Dad exchanged a look that reminded me of a time when I'd come home from school to find them side by side on the sofa, Mum's head on Dad's shoulder, watching a black and white film, the curtains partly drawn. 'Daddy took the day off,' Mum had said, drawing me down between them. 'It's our wedding anniversary today.' They'd looked at each other in a way that had made me feel soft inside, and I realised now that look – the one that had summed up what they meant to each other – was back, as if it had never been away. 'We want to help,' she said.

'Don't you have things to do back home?'

She flicked a dismissive hand. 'Nothing that can't wait,' she said. 'There are things that matter more.'

Dad briefly stopped stirring, as if hoping her words encompassed him, and I realised that even if I was incapable of sorting out my own life, I could help them sort out theirs.

'Honestly, Mum, I'm glad you're here, but I'm fine.' Before she could reply, I added, 'Has Dad shown you around?'

'Not really,' she said. 'We didn't want to wake you up.' Her eyes skimmed the kitchen appreciatively. 'I must say, it's even nicer than it looks on video.'

'On video?' Dad dropped the wooden spoon.

'I mean, in the pictures Natalie showed me.' Mum was as close to blushing as I'd ever seen her and I wondered whether, if I'd told Dad she'd insisted I show her every room – plus the garden and even the shed – on my phone, he might not have been so keen to start dating again. He might even have picked up the phone and had a proper conversation with her. But although I'd suspected Mum's curiosity might be rooted in jealousy, I'd assumed it was because he appeared to be managing without her, not because she longed to be here with him.

'Listen, you can have my bed if you like, Mum,' I said, impulsively. 'I'm staying at the café tonight. I'm working on an assignment with

Charlie.' It would be a good way to give them some time alone – providing Charlie didn't mind.

'Oh, I'd love to see him while I'm here.' Mum rose and whipped the wooden spoon off Dad, just as she used to whenever he'd tried to make porridge at home, saving it before it burnt.

'What assignment?' Dad's eyebrows crinkled with suspicion. 'I thought you were trying to sort out this interview mess.'

'Oh, it's sorted.' I made sure to inject my voice with conviction. 'I spoke to Jay yesterday, and he knows it wasn't me who leaked the news. He's not angry or anything.'

I wish.

'So, you'll be seeing him again?'

'Well, probably not. He's very busy.'

'Do you know who did it?' Mum removed the pan from the hob while Dad took out three bowls. I was starting to feel like Goldilocks. Or was it one of the bears? 'When I saw that stuff about Jay Merino on the news, I had no idea you were involved.'

Tiredness rose in me like a wave. I couldn't face going over it all again. 'No, but it's OK,' I said, jumping up and taking three spoons from the drawer. 'I'm doing this thing with Charlie now, about… about the, er, the restaurant industry, and how it's… and cafés, and how they're in competition. With restaurants. The crossover between cafés and restaurants and some behind-the-scenes stuff about what really goes on in the kitchen.' I babbled. 'I'm going to talk to Charlie's friend, he owns a restaurant.' It wasn't a bad idea, now I thought about it. Henri was bound to have plenty of stories.

'What about the interview for that posh magazine?' Dad had slipped into Detective Marty mode, stroking his chin and furrowing his brow. 'I thought it was a done deal.'

'Oh, someone else is doing that now.' I busied myself at the sink, rinsing out the dishcloth and swiping it over the taps. 'She's an experienced journalist, so it's probably for the best.'

'But, Natalie…'

'Leave it, Marty.' Mum spoke gently, giving me one of her searching looks. 'She knows we're here if she needs us.'

'Thanks, Mum.' Swallowing a surge of tears, I forced myself back to the table. 'Can I have some porridge?' I said. 'And please make sure it's not too hot or too cold.'

After breakfast, which went down surprisingly well, thanks to Mum's intervention and a scattering of blueberries, I messaged Charlie.

Is the offer to stay with you still open?

Course it is, you donut he replied. *Come whenever you're ready x*

I flung some things in my rucksack and checked my phone. No missed call from Jay, but I hadn't truly expected one. For all I knew, Jeanne hadn't had a chance to pass him my number and even if she had, he might have thrown it away. Even so, I felt a hard dip of disappointment in my stomach. That was it, then. Unless I went old-school and wrote him a letter and took it to the hotel, but even so, what could I possibly say? The fact remained that the things he'd told me had gone public in the most underhand way, and unless it was someone from his side (Simon) and I could prove it, nothing had changed.

My brain raked around for answers. Had someone overheard me talking to Charlie at the café about my meeting with Jay? But unless a customer had managed to slip through the café into the courtyard and somehow camouflaged themselves, it was unlikely.

Even if Dolly had overheard and understood our conversation when she'd brought out our coffees, there was no way she'd have called a newspaper and passed it on. The thought was ludicrous.

Tired of searching for answers, I looked for Mum and Dad instead and found them in the garden, admiring the colourful geraniums Dad had planted because they were easy to grow. After hugging them both, and promising Mum we could go shopping the following day, I cycled to the café beneath an overcast sky, hopeful that at least if my parents reunited, something good would have come of my fall from grace.

In the café, the air rang with chatter and the clatter of cutlery. Dolly was in the kitchen, preparing for what she called the lunchtime siege, and said Charlie had gone to the bank to get some change for the till. 'He told me you're staying the night,' she said, oblivious to Giselle's cold-eyed look as she coasted through with an armful of plates, catching Dolly's words.

'It's platonic,' I said, making sure Giselle could hear. If she felt about Charlie the way I'd started to feel about Jay, I didn't want her to think there was anything between us.

'That's what I'm worried about,' chuckled Dolly, thinking I was talking to her.

'Seriously,' I said to Giselle, who was standing with her back to me, radiating dislike. 'If you want to ask Charlie out, be my guest, but if he says no, it's nothing to do with me.' I realised she wouldn't understand and tried to find the right words in French, but she'd already turned and was heading back into the café, blowing out a disdainful laugh on the way.

'I've no idea what that was about.' Dolly stared after her with a look of bafflement. 'Of course Charlie won't go out with her, she's not his type.' She cast me a meaningful look. 'Not his type at all.'

'Neither am I, Dolly.' I was suddenly tired of fudging the issue, and giving her false hope. 'You must know by now, there'll never be anything between Charlie and me but friendship,' I said. 'I love him, but like a brother, that's all. I'm sorry.' Her face sank into a mix of hurt and acceptance, but I felt a freeing sense of relief at getting the words out at last – though the time and place could have been better. Luckily, the staff were too absorbed to take notice, or so I hoped.

Dolly searched my face, as if looking for signs that I was telling the truth, and I had the feeling she was seeing me properly for perhaps the first time. At last, she nodded. 'I always wanted a brother,' she said, and I knew the topic was closed. 'My sister was OK, but she used to steal my boyfriends.'

Charlie returned to find me up to my elbows in flour as Dolly tried to show me how to make puff pastry (her secret was grating in partly frozen butter) as she was making some *millefeuilles* for one of her tasting sessions, held after hours for regulars – like a pub lock-in but without the alcohol.

'She didn't make a single suggestive comment about you staying the night,' he said later, leading me up to the apartment, my rucksack hoicked over his shoulder. 'What did you say to her?'

'That you're like a brother to me and will never be anything more.'

He paused on the landing and gave me a soulful look. 'That's the nicest thing you've ever said.'

'Not true,' I said. 'I told you once that you had very nice hands for a man.'

'That's true, you did.' He held one out and studied it. 'Then you spoilt it by saying it was because I didn't work hard enough.'

'So I did.' I smiled, glad I'd come to the café after all. I hadn't thought about Jay for at least half an hour. 'By the way, my mum's turned up and I think she and Dad might be getting back together.'

'So, that's why you're really here.'

'I thought I'd leave them to it.'

We chatted for a while on the cheerful orange sofa that dominated the living room, not mentioning Jay or the magazine, until Charlie said he'd better get back to the café. 'Are you coming down?'

'I might stay here and work on a new column for *Expats*,' I said, looking around the small but cosy space, which was filled with mismatched furniture and clutter on every surface, the air sweet with the smell of baking. 'And I might update my blog.'

'Business as usual then?'

'I suppose so.' I gave a weak smile, trying not to think of the interview I'd hoped to be writing.

'Don't go online and don't keep checking your phone.'

I sank back on the sofa. 'I don't want to look online, or check my phone.'

'So, just writing then.'

'Just writing.'

'Good,' he said and flicked me a thumbs-up. 'Do you want some coffee?'

'I'll come down if I do.'

When his footsteps had faded, I quickly checked my phone. Jay hadn't called (obviously) but there was a message from Jools.

Is everything OK, babe? Jackie's been in touch, asking about Jay Merino and that time you told us you knew him before he was famous. I think she was digging for information, you know what a viper she can be. With all the stuff in the news about him, I reckon she's hoping for some sort of exclusive. I didn't tell her anything, FYI!

Thanks, J I typed back. *You're right, she's digging. My fault, I sent her a message about seeing him here I'd meant to send to you, then refused to write a piece for Gossip x*

Good for you she replied. *We need to talk SOON. Call if you need to chat, anytime. Can't wait to see you in July xxx*

I felt an unexpected pang for the days when we'd worked together, grabbing lunch from the deli next door or at the pub down the road – anything to get out of the office for an hour – and was tempted to call her, to talk to someone who didn't live on the island, but I doubted there was anything she could say that Charlie hadn't already.

I sat for a moment, staring at a framed photo on a pile of magazines that doubled as a table, of a Yorkshire terrier wearing a little blue waistcoat. The dog had been Charlie's when he was a little boy – a fact I'd deeply envied. *Could I write something about pets for my column?* It was an idea I'd had before and I'd made some notes, and I didn't have anything else. I took out my laptop and moved to the two-seater dining table by the window, but all I could think of were the opening paragraphs I'd planned to write for my interview with Jay. The interview that Fleur would now be writing. Should I write it up anyway, for practice?

I opened a new document and arched my fingers over the keyboard, but something powerful stopped me. It felt wrong, like stealing Jay's words. Words he'd given to me, like a gift – a gift I'd abused. Sighing, I stared at the blinking cursor at the top of the page, then logged onto my blog instead, but no words would come. I read the comments beneath my last post, marvelling that so many people had read and enjoyed it, and felt the corners of my mouth turn up in spite of everything. I'd always believed in the power of words, even if I'd never quite worked out what I wanted to do with them, but reading 'this made me smile, even though I was having a bad day' was enough to spur me on. I opened a document and began to type:

The French are generally unsentimental about pets, and animals in general, and keep them as much for practical purposes (e.g. to guard premises or catch vermin) or as fashion accessories as for companionship. I stopped and stretched my fingers. It sounded too factual, and wasn't even true. Nicolas treated Babette like a baby, while Gérard seemed almost surgically attached to Hamish, and there wasn't a more photographed feline in France than Madame Bisset's Delphine.

My gaze drifted to the window and I twitched the gauzy curtain aside and looked out. The weather had worsened and in the gloomy light, raindrops glittered like glass. The courtyard gate was ajar, a curl of smoke drifting through. Seconds later, Giselle appeared, looking furtive. She'd obviously been smoking and knew Dolly wouldn't approve. She extracted a packet of chewing gum from her apron pocket and pushed a piece in her mouth, before disappearing from view. She'd be furious that I knew her little secret – not that I planned to tell anyone.

I thought of her icy stares; the way she attempted to monopolise Charlie whenever I was around, as though I had no right to breathe the same air as him, never mind be his friend. And Fleur, with her cold little smile and her easy dismissal of me. She seemed to assume that only *she* had the right to aim high and do whatever she wanted. That *her* desires were more important, the only ones that mattered.

Suddenly, I knew what I wanted to write. I turned my attention back to the document, and almost of their own volition, my fingers began to dance across the keys.

Chapter Twenty

'So, what did you write?' Charlie's voice penetrated a dream I'd been having of a giant yacht, powering towards me through choppy waters. It was coming to save me, but I'd grown a mermaid tail and was able to flip easily to the shore and squeeze water from my luxuriant waist-length hair.

'Mmmmfff, sorry, *wha…?*' I peered at him blearily through sleep-puffed eyes. After my burst of writing, I'd lain on the sofa, intending to have a little rest before heading down to the café, and must have nodded off. Where most people developed insomniac tendencies during times of crisis, it seemed I could sleep for France. 'Siesta,' I muttered, pushing myself upright, wishing I felt refreshed. My legs still ached and now my head was throbbing. I checked my hair, but my bun wasn't where it was supposed to be.

'It's slipped down.' Charlie gave it a helpful nudge.

'Ow, it hurts.' I wrenched the band from around my wodge of hair and shook it free, which increased the pounding in my temples. 'I've got a headache.'

'I'm not surprised, carrying that lot around.' Charlie bounced a hand off my curls. 'How much does it weigh?'

'Gerroff!' I stood up, wavering as pain circled my skull. 'I shouldn't have gone to sleep.'

'You didn't do any writing then?'

'Actually, I did.' I jammed my forearm over my eyes as he flicked on the overhead light. Rain was lashing the windows, and it looked even more gloomy outside. 'Is it evening?'

'Pretty much,' he said, crossing over to my laptop on the table. 'Can I read it?'

'Knock yourself out,' I said. 'Do you have any headache tablets?'

'Kitchen drawer.' He was already sitting down, eyes fixed on the screen as I staggered through the adjoining door to the cramped old-fashioned kitchen, which was barely used for more than storage, as the cooking and baking mostly happened downstairs.

I found a packet of aspirin in the cutlery drawer, and swallowed two with several gulps of water from the tap, then filled a glass. I felt dehydrated from all the crying I'd done, plus I hadn't drunk anything but the cup of tea Dad had made after our porridge that morning.

'This is brilliant,' Charlie said when I returned to the living room, feeling marginally better. 'Where did it come from?'

The heart. 'It just sort of flew into my head,' I said, a burst of warmth heating my cheeks. 'I kept thinking about Fleur Dupont, and how mean she was to me when really she had no reason to be, and Giselle, who hates the sight of me because she's in love with you. Or fancies you, or whatever. But why hate *me*? Why not hate *you*, for not loving or fancying her back? Although that wouldn't be fair either.' I was warming up now. 'It's just so unfair that women blame each other, or hate each other for the wrong reasons, not that there are any right reasons, unless you've murdered a member of their family, or run over their dog on purpose or something. I mean, why can't we just support and help each other? I'm sick of it,' I finished glumly.

'It really comes through.' Charlie's expression was admiring. 'I always said you were a good writer, that you can make people think.'

'It's just my opinion.' Enthusiasm draining, I returned to the sofa. 'Who cares what I think?' But even as I sat down and picked at my cuticles, I remembered the comment I'd read: 'You made me smile, even though I was having a bad day.'

'Lots of readers.' Charlie's tone was urgent. 'Honestly, Nat, you should send this to Nicolas Juilliard, or… or better still, post it on your blog. It'll get more views that way.'

'You know that's not how I want my career to evolve.' I sounded like a nineteenth-century scholar. 'I was hoping Nicolas might still give me an assignment one day, if I haven't pissed him off completely.'

Charlie's eyes rolled. 'I get that you want to bag an A-list interview that will be talked about on *Front Row*, or *Good Morning America* or whatever, and be the next…' He flung out an impatient hand. 'Fleur Dupont, who, by the way, isn't even a very nice person, if that's who you're talking about here, and from what you've told me, but I don't—'

'What's wrong with wanting to bag an A-list interview?' I butted in.

'Nothing, I guess, but…' He bit down on his lower lip, stopping himself from saying anything else, and I got up and bent over his shoulder to read my article again. I had to admit it was good – maybe the best thing I'd ever written. The words had flowed like water, as if they'd downloaded spontaneously into my head, and although I'd missed the 'f' out of 'shift' (*attitude shit?*), it barely needed editing.

'"Supporting each other's goals and objectives should be standard. It's not only rewarding, it's the best way to receive the support you need when you need it. Can't we just shine, be happy, be in love, be successful, without some woman feeling threatened and acting like a bitch?"' Charlie gave me a delighted grin before carrying on. '"Don't you realise it says more about you than me when you blame me for 'taking' your job, or slut-shame me for 'stealing' your man?"' He stuck his palm up and I gave him a half-hearted high-five. '"No one is solely successful on their own, someone will have helped you get there, and if a man wants to have a relationship with you, he will. Stop blaming his best female friend, or his mum, or any other female for stopping it happening, because if it's meant to be, it'll happen."' Charlie winked at me. 'I think I know who you're talking about.'

'I'm not stopping you seeing Giselle, am I?'

'Of course not,' he said, pulling his chin back. 'And after our chat the other day, I've made sure she knows I'm not interested in her, that way.'

'Yet she still somehow thinks it's my fault.'

He turned back and read, '"There's so much tearing down of women in society, when it should be our duty to uphold each other." Hallelujah!' He slapped the table. 'Here's to the sisterhood!'

I couldn't help being pleased by his reaction. 'Maybe I should have ended with that line.'

'You've got to do something with this.'

'Delete it?'

'You're kidding.' He looked at me as if I'd grown wings and flown around the room. 'Come on, Nat, it needs to be read.'

'It was just something I had to get off my chest.' I slouched back to the sofa and flumped down. 'Didn't you say something about cooking dinner?'

'That was yesterday.' He turned to face me, pressing his hands on his knees. 'I'm being serious, Nat. I love you coming to the café every day, but we both know you're escaping real life, hiding behind that column of yours, which, by the way, would be a lot more entertaining if you wrote them all like the one about mistaking Jay for a potential murder victim.'

Hurt by this criticism, I said, 'The column's just a stop-gap until I get a job at *Magnifique*. At least, it was.'

'A stop-gap that's lasted a year?' He rose, pushing his fingers through his hair. 'You're worth more than that, Nat.'

'What do you mean?'

'You once told me that when you worked for *Chatter*, the reason you cared about what you wrote is because the readers cared, and that's why you did your best to write a good feature, however silly the topic.'

'I did,' I said. 'Even the one about zombies invading a campsite and terrifying a woman into giving birth in her tent.'

'I bet they were on their way to a fancy-dress party.'

'Yes, but the best bit was that the woman who gave birth – the one who called the magazine with the story – had been there on a break with her girlfriends after being dumped, and she fell in love with and married the zombie who helped deliver her triplets.'

'Wow.' Charlie took a moment to digest this. 'But that's my point,' he said, swiftly rallying. 'You should be writing for ordinary people who care, not some hot-shot magazine publisher, who dumps you the second there's a whiff of scandal, or because he knows you won't sleep with him, and is playing you and Fleur against each other for fun.'

I stiffened. 'Nicolas Juilliard didn't want to sleep with me.' I recalled his hand on my elbow and the weight of his gaze on my body, and wasn't so sure. 'And he's not playing us against each other.' I wasn't sure that was true, either.

'I'm playing devil's advocate.' Charlie sounded so exasperated, I couldn't help wondering whether he'd wanted to say something like this for a while. 'Why don't you just keep writing about stuff that matters to you, or that you find amusing, and get it out there? Start linking editors to your blog and see what happens, and stop acting like being a freelancer, and not having your own desk in a fancy office, is the worst thing in the world because, from where I'm sitting, it really isn't.'

Anger rose, taking me by surprise. 'You accuse me of hiding out here, but you escaped to this café too when things went wrong in England.' I knew I was hitting below the belt but couldn't stop myself. 'And *you're* still here, nearly four years later,' I ranted. 'Living with your mum, serving cappuccinos and chatting to people for a living.' It was a grossly unfair statement. Charlie's job involved a lot more than chatting, but it was also one of the reasons people came back to the café, day after day. 'You have a degree in precision engineering, for God's sake.'

Anger pressed his mouth into a grimace. 'A degree I hated, but stuck with because my ex wanted a boyfriend who could make a lot of money,' he said. 'And maybe living with my mum isn't ideal, but I love working here. I just didn't know I would until I came.'

'You're scared of having a relationship.'

A muscle twitched in his jaw. 'You know why.' He stuffed his hands in his jeans pockets and hunched his shoulders. 'My ex—'

'Broke your heart, I know,' I cut in, matching his exasperation. 'But that doesn't mean all women are like her, or that you can't be happy with someone else.'

'You can talk,' he muttered. 'You haven't exactly been putting yourself out there.'

I couldn't find an answer to that, apart from a very weak, 'True.'

'Not until you met Max Weaver, anyway.'

'You mean Jay Merino.'

'Maybe.'

'You do.'

'Fine.' The rain had stopped and the sky had brightened, and a sliver of sunshine pushed into the room. 'OK, so maybe we've both been hiding.' Releasing a sigh, Charlie let his shoulders drop before moving to the wall to switch the light off. 'If I promise to think about meeting someone, will you do something about this thing you've just written?'

'*Think* about settling down?'

To my relief, he grinned. 'When I next meet someone I like, I won't immediately imagine her running off with my cousin.'

'Deal?'

He gave a decisive nod. 'Deal.'

I stood and we shook hands, and he pulled me in for a hug.

'Friends?'

'Friends,' I said.

'Sorry for getting mad at you.'

'Me too.' He started rocking me from side to side until I couldn't stop giggling, and as we were pulling apart, Dolly appeared in the doorway. To her credit, she merely smiled and said, 'Do you fancy coming down for the taster session, before Madame Bisset feeds everything to her cat?'

'Does a one-legged duck swim in circles?' Charlie rubbed his hands together, back to his usual self. 'Nat?' He cocked an eyebrow, and I sensed he was double-checking we were OK.

'Sounds good.' I mustered a smile. 'I'll just go and freshen up.'

'We'll see you downstairs,' said Dolly, briskly refastening her apron as she retreated.

When she and Charlie had gone, I glanced through the window and a thought floated into my head, but vanished before I could grasp it. I stared at the bruised purple sky, the remnants of my headache pulsing behind my eyelids, and almost collapsed with fright when a burst of dramatic music erupted behind me. I'd forgotten that Charlie had changed my ringtone to the theme tune from *Maximum Force*.

Shaking my head, I carried on to the bathroom. It would only be Mum or Dad, checking up on me, but my stomach had started to rumble, reminding me I hadn't eaten since breakfast. I'd call back after dinner.

I was in the middle of a wee by the time the call rang out, and it started again straight away. I sighed. They obviously weren't giving up and would worry if I didn't respond.

Then it hit me. *Jay!* What the hell was I doing on the toilet, ignoring my phone?

I staggered back to the living room, knickers and jeans bunched around my thighs, but by the time I got there and snatched up my phone, the music had stopped.

I didn't recognise the caller ID, which meant it *must* have been Jay.

Heart jumping like a tennis ball, I pressed call.

'Ah, Natalee, thank you for calling me back.'

Nicolas. I planted my bare bottom on the sofa. 'What do you want?' I said, not bothering to hide my annoyance.

His laughter was hearty. 'Natalee, you are *so* funny,' he said. 'I wanted to ask you, about somezink you said when we last spoke.'

'Go on.' It was funny, but I no longer seemed to care what he thought, despite a part of me still hoping he'd give me a writing assignment.

'You said I was worried zat a woman might do a better job zan me at running ze magazine.'

'Correct.' My sentences were getting shorter.

'I do not like zis insinuation.'

I remained silent.

'Natalee?'

I caved in. 'It's obviously struck a chord if you've been thinking about it,' I said. 'I just get the feeling that if Fleur were a man, you wouldn't hesitate to hand her the reins.'

'It ees 'ard work, overseeing an empire, Natalee.' *Empire?* 'Eet requires a different skill set entirely.' I'd been right about Nicolas. Where women were concerned, he was stuck in medieval times. 'It requires a certain amount of… *balls*.' He clearly relished the word, rolling it around like a sweet.

'You can only have *two* balls, and they're really not necessary to run a magazine,' I said, rolling my eyes so hard they were in danger of falling out. 'But if we're talking metaphorical balls, Fleur has them and they're massive.'

He chuckled. 'Call me old-fashioned, Natalee, but I prefer ladies wizout ze balls.'

'You're old-fashioned,' I obliged. 'Look, it's not the 1950s, Monsieur Juilliard. If you shift your thinking a bit, you'll realise you've found a worthy successor to your "empire".' I couldn't help giving the word some sarcastic emphasis, and Nicolas guffawed so loudly, I had to hold the phone some distance from my ear.

'I would very much like to marry you, Natalee,' he said when he'd finished. 'Things would be so *hot* in ze bedroom.'

'Only if I set fire to your pyjamas.'

He roared. 'Oh, my days,' he said. 'You must come to Paris soon. I zink I can find a place for you 'ere on ze team.'

I imagined Fleur's reaction to that, and how Nicolas would love to see the two of us, circling each other like a pair of wild cats, vying for his attention, and realised it wasn't an attractive proposition. 'I have to go,' I said, and rang off.

After wriggling my jeans back up, I washed my hands and splashed my face with water in the bathroom, which made me think of Dad saying, '*Have you noticed in movies, how people are always splashing water on their faces, usually before or after they've murdered someone?*'

'Nat, there's hardly anything left,' Charlie hollered. 'And Hamish is looking hungry.'

'I'm coming!'

With renewed energy, I shot back to my laptop, titled my document 'Other Women are NOT my Competition' and posted it on my blog. Then, before I could change my mind, I linked it to my Twitter page and went downstairs to sample what was left of Dolly's *millefeuilles*.

Chapter Twenty-One

'I can't believe you turned down a job offer from the mighty Nicolarse,' said Charlie. We were slouched on the sofa in front of the BBC News on TV after the tasting session (I hadn't been able to resist sharing with Hamish) and I'd spoken to Mum on the phone – she and Dad were going out to eat, she'd reported, with a lightness to her tone I hadn't heard in a while.

I hadn't mentioned Nicolas's call while we were in the café, happy to listen to Dolly's plans for a trip to England before the summer season started, Charlie's idea of applying for a liquor licence to serve wine at the café, and the plot of Margot's latest romance, which seemed to involve a lot of al fresco sex.

'I'm not sure Nicolas even meant it,' I said, rubbing my temples as my headache threatened to return. 'But I don't think I want to work for someone who holds as much power as he does, and has such old-fangled views about women in the workplace.'

'Well, I'm proud of you.'

'Why thank you, Charles.'

'What do you think?' Dolly came through from her bedroom and shook her hips in a way that made Charlie groan. Frank was taking her to a salsa festival in La Rochelle and she'd dressed for the occasion in a gold velour jumpsuit that should have looked terrible, but somehow worked.

'It's a bit tight,' said Charlie, his eyes seeking a safe place to land. I knew he liked Frank and was pleased for his mum, but still wasn't quite comfortable seeing her in 'girlfriend' mode – a feeling I could wholly relate to, since Dad had flung himself into the dating ring.

'You look lovely,' I said.

Charlie studied the label on his beer bottle. 'Shouldn't you wear a coat?'

Dolly and I shared a smile.

'A coat would spoil the effect,' she said, patting her fringe down. 'Like scaffolding around the Taj Mahal.' She winked at me and picked up her sequinned bag, just as the doorbell chimed. 'Don't wait up, I won't be back before midnight.'

'Her social life's better than ours,' said Charlie, once she'd left on a cloud of perfume, singing 'I'm in the Mood for Dancing'. 'How she manages to be up at 5 a.m. is beyond me.'

'To be fair, she doesn't go out that often,' I said. 'And she seems really happy with Frank, so...' I caught an odd expression on his face as he looked at the TV screen. 'What is it?'

'Look.' He reached for the remote control and turned up the volume. 'It's Max Weaver.'

I sat up fast enough to give myself whiplash. 'Where?' Eyes bolted to the screen, all I could see was a shot of a hotel... *the* hotel. In Saint-Martin-de-Ré. And suddenly there was Jay, in front of a bank of microphones like a police commissioner, or president, about to make a serious pronouncement. 'Oh my God.'

'Shush,' ordered Charlie, increasing the volume to maximum.

'... want to address the rumours,' Jay was saying, his deep, cocoa-brown eyes directed straight down the lens. My heart was racing. He looked so attractive in dark jeans and a khaki T-shirt that showed off his muscly (but not overworked) arms – arms that had wrapped around me just two nights earlier. He was projecting an air of tension, not used to being himself on camera, and I longed to reach through the screen and reassure him – until I reminded myself he was there because of me.

'It's true that I'm giving up acting,' he said, and the resulting roar of disappointment made him smile a little and his posture softened. 'Max Weaver's been good to me and I've loved playing him, loved putting all those bad guys away, but I want a different life now,' he continued, his voice solid and sure. 'It's also true that I want to establish a foundation that funds programmes to help people like my brother…' As he broke off and swallowed, tears sprang up in my eyes. 'Young people who need help to turn their lives around,' he went on. 'A place where they can get help, maybe learn new skills and be mentored, and have an opportunity to make something of themselves, so they don't end up like he did.' I caught the glint of brightness in his eyes. The reporters and onlookers were silent now, hanging on his every word, as I imagined everyone watching at home would be. Max Weaver hadn't cried onscreen since the funerals of his wife and son – but Jay Merino was real, his emotions on display, and I suddenly wanted to yell at everyone to leave him the hell alone; tell him he had every right to protect his privacy, to not bare his soul for the world to see, and that nobody had a right to know what he was feeling, just because he'd generated a level of fame even he hadn't envisaged.

'I won't be giving any more interviews,' he concluded, holding up a hand as a barrage of questions followed his pronouncement. 'But I'd like to thank everyone for supporting my career, for loving Max as much as I've loved playing him. I wouldn't be here without you.' There was a roar of approval. 'And, just for the record, I never bribed my stuntman to pretend to be me – that was you guys following the wrong man. And I've never once,' he arched his eyebrows, 'requested a hot tub to be installed near my trailer.' Laughter rippled through the crowd. 'I mean, can you really see Max Weaver in a hot tub?'

More laughter. 'Only if it was with a naked woman,' someone called.

'Except she'd try to drown me,' Jay deadpanned and the crowd expressed their delight. Even I was smiling.

'He's actually good at this.' Charlie's voice made me jump. I'd almost forgotten where I was. 'I can see what you like about him.'

'Hush.' I was on the edge of the sofa, unable to tear my eyes from the screen as the camera panned out. Simon was standing close by in his customary pose, eyes scoping the area as if for a gunman, and the hotel owner was there, smiling benignly, as if she had famous actors staying all the time – which, to be fair, she probably did.

A familiar face made my heart drop. *Fleur.* She was standing to one side in a mannish suit that somehow enhanced her femininity, wearing an enigmatic smile that could have meant anything, including that her interview with Jay had been a great success and she was proud of him. Was she the one who had persuaded him to confront the press; convinced him it would be good publicity for his proposed foundation? It would also generate more interest in her interview when it was published. I wondered whether she was waiting for him to mention it, but Jay was backing away now, hands raised in a goodbye gesture.

'Do you know who leaked the news of your retirement?' The lone voice seemed to ring out above the others and Jay's expression tightened. Charlie reached over and squeezed my hand. 'There are rumours you've got a stalker here.' The same voice – it was one of the reporters I'd seen hanging around the hotel. Perhaps he'd been at the lighthouse and seen me charging inside or – more likely – being escorted out. 'Was it her?'

My breath had stuck in my throat.

'There's no stalker,' said Jay, leaning towards the nearest microphone, eyes seeming to look directly into my soul. 'She's someone I've known a long time and grown close to.'

'Whaaaat?' Charlie's gaze met mine, equally wide.

A frenzy of questions were being flung at Jay as we turned back to the TV.

'Who is she?'

'Does she live on the island?'

'Are you getting married?'

'Is she French?'

He ignored them all. 'I don't know who leaked the news, but it definitely wasn't her.'

And just like that, he was gone, swept inside the hotel, leaving behind a clamour of voices.

'Who was it then?'

'Was it your bodyguard?'

'Is your new girlfriend an actress?'

'Good luck with your foundation!'

'Love you forever, Max!'

'That was Jay Merino, confirming that he is indeed retiring from acting after his latest movie is wrapped,' said a shiny-haired presenter back in the studio. 'Which means we can rule him out as the next Bond.' She made an inappropriately sad face. 'And, now, the rest of today's news...'

Charlie switched off the TV. 'I did just see that, didn't I?' He wobbled his head and did some comedy blinking. 'I didn't hallucinate that you just made the top story on the national news?'

'I did not.' Shock gave way to a glowing warmth that spread through my veins. 'I mean, he didn't mention my name, thank God.' But I couldn't believe he'd mentioned me at all. Jay Merino, so famously reticent about his private life, had gone public, and more or less told the world that he didn't believe the woman he might have been seen with had betrayed him. *But why not tell me to my face?*

'Did you see the look down the camera?' Charlie was clearly tickled, shaking his head and grinning. 'He's obviously into you.'

I shook my head, my previous glow fading. 'I reckon Fleur Dupont persuaded him it was better to address the rumours than ignore them, that's all,' I said.

'What, and to talk about *growing close* to the potential source of the leak?'

The glow reignited. It was true that Jay hadn't needed to say it. I wondered what Fleur had made of his comment. She must have discussed possible culprits, perhaps even mentioned me by name, knowing I'd interviewed him, but he must have rejected the idea. Or had he? My thinking was getting muddled. Perhaps he'd just said it to put an end to the speculation. 'I'm glad he spoke up, but he did it publicly instead of directly, which means he still doesn't want to see me,' I said, aware of Charlie scrutinising my face. 'He's done his interview with Fleur now, and whatever closeness there was between him and me doesn't exist any more.' The flame inside flickered and died. 'I'm over it,' I lied. 'The public's had their piece of Jay Merino, or Max Weaver, or whatever. Hopefully, he'll be left alone now there's nothing to report.'

'Apart from the fact that he's *grown close* to someone.'

'Leave it, Charlie.'

He frowned, and looked as if he was about to pursue it, but changed his mind. 'Do you want to watch *Maximum Force: The Beginning*?'

I tossed a cushion at him. 'I'd like a beer and to watch something fluffy and feel-good, with no men in it whatsoever.'

'In that case, I'll go out and leave you to it.'

He didn't. We watched *Horrible Bosses 2*, because we both loved Jason Bateman, and I even managed to laugh in all the right places. We drank beer, ate a bowl of crisps, and I pretended not to notice Charlie's occasional concerned look.

As the credits rolled, he stretched and said casually, 'Have my bed, I'll take the sofa.'

'Are you sure?' My headache had crept back, and he'd made a big deal a while ago of some amazing pillows he'd bought online, which had cured his stiff neck.

'Positive,' he said. 'I've slept on the sofa before when friends have stayed. It's pretty comfy. And I've changed my bedding in your honour.'

I was touched. 'Thanks, Charles.'

'You're welcome, m'lady.'

I barely had the energy to pull my pyjamas on and brush my teeth, and was on the edge of sleep, lulled by the hum of something sporty on the television in the living room – Charlie watching rugby on *Sky Sports* no doubt – when the *Maximum Force* theme music blasted from my phone, charging on the floor by the bed. Sticking a hand out, I picked it up, expecting it to be Mum or Dad, but I didn't recognise the number.

I sat up, clutching the duvet to my chest.

'Jay?' I whispered.

'It's Simon.'

'What?' I blinked at the pitch-black bedroom, which was like being underground, thanks to Charlie's blackout curtains. 'What do you want?' I said. 'It's nearly midnight.'

'I think Jay suspects it was me.' His voice was hard with a catch at the end.

'What do you mean?'

'He asked me earlier if I knew who'd talked to the press.'

'That doesn't mean he thought it was you,' I said. I remembered his instant defence when I'd suggested the leak could have come from Simon. 'He trusts you.'

'I could tell he did suspect me,' he persisted, his voice an angry bite. 'You put the idea in his head. He'd rather believe it was me than you.'

'But Simon, it wasn't me either.' I groped my mind for something that would persuade him. 'I promise, on my parents' graves.' I hated using them like that, but couldn't think of anything more convincing. 'It wasn't either of us.'

'I know it wasn't,' he said, surprising me again. 'But until we know who it was, I reckon he's always gonna suspect it was to do with one of us.'

My heart tightened like a fist. Simon was right. Not about Jay thinking Simon had betrayed him, but that it must have been me – maybe not directly, but that I'd talked to someone who'd blabbed to the press, for reasons unknown. *Mud sticks*, wasn't that how it went? *No smoke without fire*. To the public, Jay's retirement, the foundation… it was already old news, a bunch of words that had been released to the world and confirmed by Jay himself. They had no idea (and wouldn't care) about the ramifications – the effect on those he was closest to; the doubts and suspicions that could poison or even destroy a friendship, or a potential relationship.

'Jay knows you better than anyone,' I said. 'In his heart…'

'You're in his bloody heart,' Simon cut in, brusquely. 'If he doesn't want to believe it was you, then it has to be me, 'cos there's no one else I can think of who would have done this that makes any sense.'

'But it's over now he's appeared on the news. It'll all die down in time.'

'It won't die down while we don't know,' he snapped. 'Even if you two get together, it'll be in the back of his mind.'

My heart jumped at the possibility of getting together with Jay, then seemed to freeze like an ice cube. 'We won't be getting together,' I said. 'He's made that clear.'

'I thought *you* were the one who'd made it clear.'

'What do you mean?'

'He got your number,' Simon said, grudgingly. 'The cleaner left it on his pillow. He tried to call you from my phone, but you didn't reply.'

I thought of the calls I'd missed earlier. I'd assumed they were both from Nicolas, and hadn't checked.

'I was on the toilet,' I said and winced. 'I didn't think he'd really want to ring me.'

'Yeah, well, it's probably for the best that you didn't pick up.'

I digested that for a moment. 'Do you know what he was going to say?'

'No idea,' said Simon. 'I'm not even sure *he* knew, he just wanted to talk to you.'

'I'm here now.'

'He's not.' The anger had left Simon's voice. He was matter-of-fact now. 'He's with that journalist, Dupont.'

My heart dropped like a stone. 'She's still there?'

'Apparently, she's not due back in Paris until tomorrow and Jay was in a drinking mood. They're at the bar.'

My throat thickened with dismay. 'Why aren't you there?' I wanted to lash out. 'I thought you never left his side.'

'I know when to leave him alone.'

Great. 'Can't you invent a reason to get him back to his room – alone?'

'He wouldn't take any notice if I did, the mood he's in tonight.'

'Can you at least ask him to call me again?'

'Maybe it's best if he doesn't.'

'Ask him, Simon, please.'

'Why should I?' he said. 'Everything was fine until you threw yourself at him.'

'Isn't that up to him to decide?'

'I think he already has.'

I pictured Jay and Fleur coming back to his room, arms around each other, tumbling onto his bed and tearing at each other's clothes, and bile hit the back of my throat. 'I have to go,' I said, hoarsely.

'Wait—'

'I'm sorry if you think Jay doesn't trust you, Simon, but there's nothing I can do.' I ended the call and threw my phone on the floor to the sound of cheering in the room next door, and Charlie shouting, '*Yeeees*!' then, 'Sorry, Nat, but Farrell scored a try.'

I fell back on the (incredibly comfy) pillows and glared at the ceiling. Or rather, the dense, coal-like blackness where the ceiling should be. Charlie's room was how I imagined purgatory would look, with nothing to see but my own tortured thoughts. I sat up again and shouted, 'Charlie, can we please swap places?'

Chapter Twenty-Two

I arrived home, sleep-deprived and grouchy, not in the mood for a high-powered shopping trip with Mum. The sofa at Charlie's had been every bit as uncomfortable as I'd suspected, and hadn't done my hair any favours either. Mum took one look at me and declared that a 'mooch' around Saint-Martin would be much more fun than 'traipsing to La Rochelle'.

'If you're hoping to see Jay Merino, it's not going to happen.' I threw myself on a chair at the kitchen table, like a bag of laundry. 'He'll be off somewhere, filming.' Today was his last day on the island. Tonight, he'd be flying to Budapest and out of my life.

'I wasn't hoping to see anyone but you.' Mum placed a mug of freshly brewed coffee in front of me. 'Have you eaten?'

'Not much,' I said, feeling like a child again as she flitted around the kitchen, clearly used to the layout (thanks to my phone videos), sliding a pair of plates into the dishwasher and rearranging the bananas in the fruit bowl. 'Just a couple of pastries for breakfast at the café.'

'Shall I make you something?'

'I'm fine, thanks.' I looked around the tidy kitchen. 'Where's Dad?'

'He's, er, getting dressed, I think,' Mum said, and I realised I could hear a muted sound, like someone tuning a trombone. Dad was singing in the shower. 'He'll, er, be down shortly.'

It wasn't like Mum to stammer, or blush like a teenager, and in spite of last night's events, my spirits lightened a little. 'Did you have a nice evening?'

'It was lovely,' she said, coming to rest on the chair opposite, cradling her mug of coffee. 'We went for a meal at L'Ecailler with the American couple next door.'

'Barbara and Larry?' I said, as though there was more than one set of Americans staying with Marie. 'I thought when you said you were eating out, you meant you and Dad.'

Mum had been smiling since I walked in, and showed no signs of stopping. 'He told me about them and they sounded fun, and they were at a loose end so…' She shrugged one shoulder, and I suddenly realised she was wearing the peacock embellished jacket Dad clearly hadn't got around to returning, over her shirt and faded jeans.

'Lovely, isn't it?' she said, seeing me looking and fingering the fabric. 'Your dad said he saw it and thought of me.'

Thinking back to how tight it had looked on him, I had a feeling that was true. 'It suits you,' I said. 'Did you meet Marie?'

'Oh, she's lovely.' Mum spoke in her accepting way and I was glad she wasn't jealous after all, or blaming Marie for trying to 'steal her man'. I remembered the article I'd posted online and felt a leap in my stomach as I wondered if anyone had read it. I hadn't been online yet; had only checked my phone (about forty times) to see whether Jay had called back. He hadn't.

'No news?' Charlie had asked over breakfast, looking well-rested after a good night's sleep on his comfy pillows, but didn't push it when I shook my head and turned down a third *pain au chocolat*.

'Apparently, that actor was on the news last night,' Dolly had said, also looking well-rested, despite not getting home until 2 a.m. She'd salsa-ed into the living room and yelped with fright when she saw me on the sofa, having forgotten I was staying over. 'He's not doing Max Weaver any more.'

If she'd wondered why Charlie and I didn't respond, she hadn't said anything, but Giselle had hurried in at that moment and announced she had to go to the dentist's again at lunchtime, and would need a few hours off. At least, that's what I'd gathered from the burst of French I'd overheard.

'Apparently, Marie's been teaching your dad to cook,' Mum said, cutting across my thoughts.

'And to speak French, although it's not working very well.'

'Avez vous oon cuppa?' she said in Dad's voice and we giggled. 'So, how did your writing project go?'

'Oh, it, er, it went well,' I said. 'Actually, I changed my mind in the end and wrote a piece about how women should be more supportive of each other.'

'Good for you.' Mum patted my hand. 'When is it being published?'

'I posted it online.'

She put her mug down. 'But surely you won't get paid.'

'No, but someone might see it and commission a piece for a magazine, and I will get paid for that.'

She nodded. 'I suppose that's how it's done these days,' she said. *Unless you're Fleur Dupont*, I thought. 'Well, I'd love to read it.'

'I'll send you the link,' I promised.

'And the assignment you mentioned?'

'It fell through.'

She looked at me closely. 'Something else will come along.'

'I hope so.'

Dad bounded in, looking chipper and smelling of my coconut shampoo, and planted a kiss on my forehead. 'Everything OK, sweetheart?' he said, but I noticed his eyes were on Mum, whose face colour now matched the red-painted ceiling beams.

'I'm fine.' I knew it was what he wanted to hear and didn't want to spoil the mood by revealing that, actually, I felt as if my heart was being squeezed and my headache was tightening like a vice. 'You two look happy.'

'I've got a new myth,' Dad announced, pouncing on his notepad, clearly desperate for a distraction. I guessed he was trying to preserve the notion that parents didn't discuss their love lives with their children, which was a bit rich when he'd very recently filled me in on Yvette's ill-fated attempt at seduction.

'Go on,' I said, smiling at Mum as he scribbled something down. She always asked how his book plans were going and I'd kept her posted about his notes.

He held up his pad and read out, 'Victims don't fly through the air when they get shot, and the officer doesn't go over and kick the gun away.'

'Nice one,' I said. 'What about an officer pulling a bartender across the bar, like they do in films?'

'Never happens.' He picked up his pen and wrote it down. 'Or officers chasing a criminal and jumping onto a moving bus or train. They'd end up with a serious injury, or maybe even dead.'

I couldn't help smiling at his serious tone.

'I bet real officers can't pick a lock with a paperclip,' said Mum.

'Good one, Claire.' Dad wrote it down, eyebrows scrunched. 'And a parking space isn't magically available whenever required, either.'

She nodded. 'These are really good, Marty. I was reading your notes last night while you were getting changed,' she said. 'I didn't know about the fingerprint one.'

'Ah, yes.' Dad flicked to the previous page and read out, 'You don't scan a fingerprint into a computer and get a match in seconds, because making an identification requires countless hours of work from a fingerprint examiner, and weeks to complete.'

'Could be catchier,' I said.

'And you're going to help your dad get published?' Mum looked expectant.

'I, er, yes, I'm trying.' I felt a guilty flush rise up my neck. I hadn't been trying very hard. Or at all. It couldn't hurt to send out a few feelers to some non-fiction publishers. 'I'm on it,' I said.

'She is,' Dad confirmed, though he hadn't even mentioned it for a while.

'Two writers in the family,' said Mum, her smile still in place. 'I'm so proud of you both.'

'Listen, why don't I go and get changed and then we can make a move,' I said, getting to my feet. Left to my own devices, I'd only end up replaying Simon's phone call, and Jay's TV appearance, or picturing Jay and Fleur on his yacht somewhere, eating oysters – an image that had lodged in my head as I'd pushed my bike home, too tired to get on it and pedal. 'I honestly don't mind if you want to go to La Rochelle.'

'No, really,' Mum said, her smile becoming a beam. 'I haven't been to Saint-Martin for so long, I'd love to see it again.'

'You don't mind if I come too, do you?' Dad put his notepad down.

'Of *course* not.' Mum had replied before I'd opened my mouth. 'It'll be wonderful to go out as a family.'

Things were taking on a foggy non-reality, as if I'd wandered onto the set of a gentle comedy-drama. 'Just give me ten minutes,' I said. 'And is it OK if we go in the car?' I tentatively stretched my legs. 'I'm not up to cycling today.'

✳

I couldn't deny that part of me hoped I might bump into Jay, or that he would be hanging around outside the hotel on the off-chance I might pitch up, but when we arrived and Dad had found a parking space on the quayside, there was no sign of a film crew and just the one reporter still lurking about. I glanced at a rack of newspapers outside the convenience store, but although Jay's TV appearance was all over social media it hadn't quite made it to the front pages of the tabloids; the printed word was always a day behind. There was a new issue of *Magnifique* and I bought a copy, in spite of myself, while Mum browsed the old-fashioned postcard stand with Dad. Whatever I thought about Fleur Dupont, her interviews were worth the price alone, and reading the French version improved my language skills.

Mum linked arms with me as we wandered around, keen to reacquaint herself with the place she'd last visited when I was a teenager, exclaiming over the things that had changed (not much) and the things that hadn't: the indoor market, the gift shops and the Île de Ré Chocolats & Caramels shop, where we'd once watched the chocolate being made, and sampled so many, we'd all felt sick by lunchtime.

'What I'd really love is to see the lighthouse at Saint-Clément,' she said, as we queued to buy ice creams at La Martinière. 'Do you remember how we used to run up all those steps?'

My sore thighs twinged in recognition. 'Of course I do.' I banished an image of Jay's expression when I'd collapsed in front of him in the lighthouse keeper's room. 'Do you really want to go up there again?'

She flashed me a look. 'Don't you?'

'Maybe not today,' I said.

She looked at me a moment longer. 'OK, love.' She squeezed my arm. 'I'm happy to do whatever you want to do.'

When we'd chosen our ice creams – pecan vanilla for me, apple and honey for Mum, bitter orange and ginger for Dad – we sat on one of the benches overlooking the harbour, and as I licked the creamy concoction and watched the sun glance off the boats and dance across the water, I tried to empty my mind of everything else and enjoy being with my parents. I had no idea how long Mum was staying, or what her being here meant, but it had been so long since we'd all been together, I wanted to make the most of it.

'Look at that seagull,' said Dad, when we'd finished eating and I was starting to feel drowsy, my head on Mum's shoulder, letting the atmosphere wash over me. 'It could almost be British, don't you think?'

We burst out laughing, it was such a silly comment, but I was taken aback by the wistful note in his voice. 'Do you miss England, Dad?'

He gave Mum a sideways glance, as if determining whether or not to be honest, and I was surprised when he nodded and said, 'A bit.'

'But it's so lovely here.' Mum had eased her trainers off and tipped her head back to soak up the warmth. 'Why would you want to go back?' I felt a sudden tension in her body, as if his reply was vital.

'It is lovely,' Dad agreed, sticking his legs out and crossing his ankles, as though he was in an armchair in front of a roaring fire. 'But I sometimes feel as if I'm still on holiday, and start to think it's time I went home.'

I straightened. 'I didn't know that.' I wondered whether I *should* have known. 'I thought you loved it here.'

'I do, but it's not *home*. Though it's *much* more like home since you moved in, love,' he added, as I opened my mouth to protest. But I knew that what he meant was, it wasn't home without Mum. She was looking at him with an expression that made my throat swell.

'You don't feel at home here, Marty?'

Now Dad was looking at her the same way. 'Don't get me wrong, Claire, I've met some amazing people and had some good times, done some interesting things...' his gaze slid to me and away and I guessed he was hoping I wouldn't mention his ill-judged attempt at looking young and cool. Luckily, I'd almost wiped it from my memory and had no intention of raking it up.

'Home isn't a place, it's a feeling,' I said, as they continued skirting around what they really wanted to say, just as they had three years ago, when they'd ended up going their separate ways, thinking they were doing each other a favour. 'So, why don't you crack on and sort yours out and I'll meet you back at the car in half an hour.'

I pressed a kiss on Mum's cheek, then leapt up and strode away before either of them could protest. When I glanced back, they'd shuffled closer together and Dad's arm was round Mum's shoulder. It was a perfect photo moment. I took out my phone and snapped a picture, then surreptitiously checked for missed calls and messages. *Nothing.*

Fighting a dip in mood, I headed to the nearest coffee shop and ordered a cappuccino, which I took to a table in a sunny spot outside. Coincidentally (or not), I found myself facing L'Hôtel des Toiras, where a bunch of visitors had gathered outside, perhaps hoping for a glimpse of Jay Merino. For a second, I wondered whether they knew something I didn't, then forced my attention back to my phone and checked my emails. There was one from Sandy at *Expats* written in her typically formal style.

Your column went down very well online, Natalie. We've never had such an enthusiastic response (I don't suppose your actor was Jay Merino, was it?) but could we have a return to form for the paper next time, please? I know from feedback that my readers love your trademark facts with a bit of fun thrown in, and you do it so well. Very much looking forward to seeing what you've got next. Do swing by if you're ever in town, it would be nice to see you.

Unexpected tears sprang to my eyes. Dear, old-fashioned Sandy, with her rigid hair and Hawaiian shirts. I had no idea she, or 'her' readers, felt so strongly about my columns. I'd assumed they were just fillers. I vowed to start buying the paper again and to 'swing by' and visit her soon. The contrast between Sandy and Nicolas Juilliard was striking, but at least now I knew who I'd rather hang out with – and write for.

I tapped back *My next one is about pets. I'll have it with you by Monday! See you soon, Natalie x* The kiss was probably a step too far, but I wanted to show Sandy I appreciated her faith in me.

I sipped my coffee – never as good as at Café Belle Vie – and was about to have a look through *Magnifique* and check out Fleur's latest interview (with a famous vlogger who'd climbed Mount Everest for a bet) when my attention was snagged by someone standing close to the hotel. A twist of black hair and upright posture, and the sort of wide-legged trousers I'd never get away with, unless I was auditioning to be *Dr Who*'s assistant. *Fleur Dupont.* As if magicked from the pages of the magazine in my hands.

A klaxon went off in my head. Why wasn't she on her way back to Paris? Unless the photographer hadn't been able to drop everything the second he'd been called, and was maybe turning up today?

Fleur was in the shadows and I strained to see her expression, heart racing as I scanned the area for signs of Jay, or Simon. Someone familiar.

And there *was* someone, drawing up beside Fleur on a bicycle, blonde hair streaming down her back, her skinny black jeans encasing her endless legs, giving them a spider-like appearance as she swung them over the saddle and pecked Fleur on both cheeks.

Giselle. Giselle, who supposedly had a dentist's appointment, and was now talking animatedly to Fleur Dupont, gesticulating with one hand, gripping the handlebar of her bike with the other. Their exchange seemed to happen in slow motion, activity around them frozen in time like something from one of Jay's films, as my brain tried to assimilate what I was seeing. Giselle knew Fleur. Fleur appeared to have been waiting for Giselle. Fleur seemed angry, her lips moving in a torrent of words, and now Giselle looked to be crying, brushing the back of her hand across her face.

As I watched, transfixed, a memory popped from some inner recess of my brain and the thought I'd been grasping for the day before suddenly zoomed into view. I got up and hurried closer, in time to hear Giselle practically shout, 'It wasn't my fault, you cannot blame me.' Her voice rose. 'I did not know it would be like this.' Fleur said something in French, her voice much lower, then glanced at her watch before stalking off, just as she had that night at the restaurant with Nicolas, letting her silence speak volumes. I shrank back, but she moved past without seeing me. Giselle stared after her, but didn't follow. Instead, she pulled a tissue from the little black belt-bag around her hips and blew her nose, then jumped back on her bike and began to cycle furiously in the direction of Chamillon – presumably headed for the café, where she would no doubt act out being in pain to go with her cover story of visiting the dentist. She was a far better actress than I'd given her credit for.

When she was out of sight, a rush of adrenaline sent me racing back to the car, where Mum and Dad were kissing in the front as if kissing had just been invented.

'Jesus,' I panted, throwing myself in the back and slamming the door. 'I don't need to see that.' But I couldn't help grinning as they pulled apart, at Mum's hair all mussed, their eyes bright and unfocused. 'I guess you won't be needing my bed tonight.'

Mum turned, her eyebrows lifting. 'I didn't use it last night.'

'Your stuff was in my room.'

'Ah, yes, I hope you don't mind, the light in there is really good for putting on my make-up.' She touched her mouth, which was currently a lipstick-free zone.

'You didn't sleep in there?'

She and Dad exchanged coy smiles. 'We nodded off on the sofa,' he said, which explained Mum's blushing and stuttering when I'd asked if they had a nice evening. 'Not that we did much sleeping.'

'*Dad*!'

'Marty!' Mum said, slapping his hand, but we were grinning again and it didn't seem necessary to say anything else – their expressions said it all.

'Back to the house?' Dad started the engine.

A wave of anger crashed me back to the moment. 'No,' I said. 'Drop me at the café.'

Chapter Twenty-Three

'Where is she?' I barged around the café kitchen, as though Giselle had sensed I was coming and hidden in the fridge.

Dolly, busy wiping the worktops down after the lunchtime rush, gave me a startled look. 'Where's who?'

'Giselle.'

'Oh, she's had a filling, which is giving her a bit of pain.' Dolly was giving me a funny look, as if she'd seen the steam I was sure must be blowing out of my nostrils. 'She's having an early break.'

'She's just had a break,' I snapped. 'I saw her in Saint-Martin.'

'It was hardly a break.' Dolly's look changed to one of puzzlement. 'She lives over that way. It makes sense that she'd go and see a dentist there.'

'She wasn't seeing the dentist,' I said, in danger of grinding my own teeth down to the gums. 'She was meeting someone.'

Dolly's head jerked back. 'A boyfriend?'

'Definitely not a boyfriend.'

'You're not making any sense, Natalie.'

Charlie came through at that moment, carrying a loaded tray, his face alight with the sort of excitement I associated with toddlers on Christmas Eve. 'Have you told her?' he said to Dolly.

At once, her face took on a similar expression to Charlie's. 'I haven't had a chance,' she said archly. 'Natalie's in a bit of a tizz about something.'

'I'll tell you what I'm in a—'

'He was here.' Charlie clattered the tray down and clasped his hands under his chin in a parody of excitement – except, he really *was* excited in a way I hadn't seen since the England rugby team made it to the World Cup.

'Who was here?' I was annoyed that the wind had been taken out of my sails. 'Spit it out, for God's sake.'

'Max Weaver,' he said, flinging his arms wide, as if to catch me when I fell.

My mouth dropped open. 'Jay… Jay was *here*?' I jabbed a finger at the floor, as though he might be buried underneath it. 'He's been *here*, at the *café*?'

'*Yes*, he *has*,' Charlie mimicked, flexing his biceps and adopting his Max Weaver scowl. 'Tell her, Mum.'

Dolly's head was bobbing up and down, and I looked around to see that all the staff were giving off the same air of barely contained glee – exactly as if a movie star had unexpectedly dropped in. 'Stefan got a selfie,' she said, far too breathless for a woman who claimed to have better things to do than be awed by celebrities.

Stefan obligingly held out his phone and I stared, thunderstruck. All the staff were in the picture, and several regulars too. Gérard was holding Hamish aloft like a furry trophy – though Gérard probably had no idea who Jay Merino was – and Madame Bisset's lips were painted in a deep, red bow.

Jay was standing between Charlie and Dolly, an arm around each of their shoulders in a way that suggested he'd been coerced – probably by Dolly. Stefan must have used a selfie stick to fit everyone in, their smiles manic and tinged with disbelief, including Jay's.

'He came in here, and let you take a selfie. With a stick?' It wouldn't quite compute. Selfie sticks were fiddly. What had they talked about while Stefan fixed it to his phone? 'Who carries a selfie stick?'

'One of the customers lent it to Stefan,' Dolly explained, her tone suggesting it wasn't the most important part of the story.

'But why was Jay here?'

'He'd heard how great it was, so thought he'd pop by for some of Mum's quiche.' Charlie was clearly enjoying my reaction.

'I was the one who told him how great it is here.' For the first time, I fully understood the term 'dazed and confused'. 'I didn't think he'd come, though.'

Charlie did a comedy eye-roll. 'He came to see *you*, you idiot.'

'Oh.' As his words sank in, I slapped my hands to my cheeks. 'But I wasn't here.'

'Your powers of observation are remarkable, Miss Bright.'

'Stop it,' said Dolly, flicking him with her cloth before shooing everyone back to work. 'He went to your house,' she said, when the staff had dispersed, chattering among themselves. 'When there was no answer, he remembered you saying you came to the café to work most days and thought he might catch you here.'

It beggared belief. I'd been in Saint-Martin, staking out the hotel, and he'd come here, looking for me. 'I thought he was filming.'

'Apparently, they started at 4 a.m. to get a sunrise shot and finished early,' said Charlie, who'd obviously had quite the chat with Jay. 'I told him we saw him on TV last night and I could tell he was dying to ask me what you'd made of it—'

'—but he asked instead if you'd meet him at the marina tonight, as arranged,' finished Dolly. She let go of a sigh. 'I know I said you'd never find anyone better than this one,' she nodded at Charlie, who took a bow, 'but I was obviously wrong.'

'Charming,' he said, good-naturedly. 'Perhaps you'd like to adopt him.' His eyes grew wide. 'Actually, please adopt him, Mum. Imagine having Max Weaver as my brother.' He began skulking around the kitchen like a vigilante killer seeking assassins, pulling open cupboard doors, and brought his fist down on a torn-off chunk of baguette. Dolly chortled her appreciation and shook her head. 'What's he like?' she said fondly. They were acting giddy and I realised it was probably always like this for Jay – that no one had a normal reaction to seeing him, apart from the people he'd known for most of his life, and it was easier than ever to understand why he craved time away from the cameras, when he could be himself. Presumably, if we became an item, the people closest to me would get used to him as Jay, and stop seeing him as Max Weaver... I sliced off my thoughts, shocked at the direction they'd taken. He might have invited me to the marina to say goodbye, for all I knew.

'Did he say anything else?' I asked, faux-casual.

'Yes,' said Charlie, passing a pile of clean trays to Stefan, who kept bobbing back into the kitchen as if suspecting Jay might have returned. 'He asked Mum to marry him.'

'Charlie!'

'I wish,' said Dolly, then winced. 'Don't tell Frank I said that.'

'I think he said he'd be at the marina at seven o'clock, and the boat is called *Moonlight*, didn't he, Mum? I was too busy wondering whether he could introduce me to Nova to really take it in.'

'You mean Susie Houlihan,' I said faintly.

'It's a yacht, not a boat.' Dolly pulled a tray of choux pastry tubes from the oven, which I knew in an hour would be oozing fresh cream and topped with chocolate fondant. 'He said he'll wait for you as long as it takes.'

'He didn't say that,' said Charlie.

'OK, he didn't,' Dolly admitted. 'But I could tell he was thinking it.'

There was a movement at the back door and Giselle came in, smelling slightly of cigarettes and chewing gum. She gave me a hard stare, before turning a sweet smile on Charlie, and the sight of it brought back the anger that had fled in the wake of Charlie's news. 'How did it go at the dentist's?'

'*Pardon?*' She paused in the act of retying her apron and gave me a querying look. A faint pinkness around her eyes gave away that she'd been crying, otherwise I might have believed I'd imagined the scene with Fleur.

'*Comment ça s'est passé chez le dentist?*' I said, hoping it passed muster.

'*Bien.*' Her smile was slightly less certain as she looked from me to Dolly and back to Charlie, before returning her attention to her apron. I noticed her hands were shaking and the sight gave me courage for what I had to say. 'You were smoking outside that day, weren't you?'

'*Quoi?*'

I wanted to stamp my foot in exasperation. 'Stop pretending,' I said. 'I know you speak English. I heard you an hour ago, talking to Fleur Dupont in Saint-Martin.'

She instantly burst into tears. 'Oh no, I am so sorry, *je ne voulais pas le faire, mais elle a dit qu'elle pourrait m'aider,* I am so bad, *je n'aime pas être trompeuse.*' Her distress was so sudden and acute, complete with hand-wringing, that I found myself shepherding her out to the courtyard and trying to calm her down. Part of me wondered whether she was deploying her acting skills, but if she was, she deserved an Oscar. Charlie and Dolly had followed us out, their faces masks of confusion – and no wonder, considering I'd reduced her to a weeping wreck.

'What's going on?' said Dolly, but before I could speak, she was summoned back inside by Stefan.

''Amish 'as widdled on ze floor,' he said, clearly tickled to have learnt a new word from Dolly. '*Pipi.*' He mimed lifting his leg like a dog.

'Go, Mum,' urged Charlie. 'We'll fill you in.' She retreated with a worried look.

'Do you want me to go too?' he said, turning to me.

'No,' I said grimly. 'I need a witness for this.'

Giselle's crying had increased to the point where she was doubled over, arms belted around her waist, and I worried she might actually be sick, but when Charlie moved to comfort her, she flung herself at him and snuffled into his shoulder. Annoyingly, she still looked stunning; her cheeks dewy rather than blotchy, her eyes great liquid pools. If I cried like that, my face took on a pumped-up appearance and my eyeballs disappeared.

'What's going on?' Charlie said. He was patting Giselle in a functional way, rather than with any passion, but I noticed her wiggle closer and felt a flash of despair.

'She knows Fleur Dupont,' I said, feeling suddenly chilled. It was almost a surprise to see that the sun was out, casting shadows across the courtyard. 'She was smoking outside the gate. She overheard our conversation about Jay and leaked it to the press. She understands English.' I was speaking in quick-fire sentences, keen to get it out. 'Then she spoke to Fleur. I don't know why. Or what was in it for her.'

Charlie let go of Giselle. 'Is that true?' He leaned back, as though keen to put some distance between them. 'Did you leak a private conversation?'

For once, there was no pretence. After dabbing beneath her eyes with the heel of her hand, she sat at the table, shoulders drooping. 'It is much more than you know.' She said it with credible sadness. 'It was a bad idea.' She shook her head. 'I never wanted to be a waitress, I want to be an actress, but it is hard.'

'Go on,' I said grimly, not seeing the connection.

'The morning that I did not come here to work,' she said, giving Charlie an apologetic half-smile, 'I was not going to dentist, I was being an extra on the film, *Maximum Force*.' She briefly met my eyes. 'I see when you jump on Jay Merino like ninja.'

I stared. 'You were there?'

She nodded. 'You talk to him for long time and then you tell Nicolas Juilliard that you know him and he will do interview for you.'

'How do you know about that?'

'You'd better tell us everything.' Charlie dropped onto the bench and it was a relief to sink beside him. My legs felt like they didn't belong to me.

Giselle's eyes flooded with fresh tears. 'Fleur is my *tante*,' she said.

I saw my shock reflected on Charlie's face. 'Your *aunt*?'

'My father, he is her brother.'

'I know what an aunt is.' I tried to make sense of this revelation and knew Charlie was trying to follow it too.

'I don't believe this,' he muttered.

'She know about you always sending the email to Nicolas Juilliard, wanting to have a job at the magazine.'

Charlie leaned across the table. 'You mean, Fleur was jealous?'

Giselle sniffed and gave a Gallic shrug. 'She started to know that Nicolas, he likes Natalie.' It was odd, hearing her say my name for the first time. 'He is...' she wrinkled her nose, '*Intrigué*.'

'Just because he had the hots for Natalie doesn't mean he was going to get rid of your aunt or anything.' Charlie sounded incredulous. 'Fleur Dupont's at the top of her game, why would she feel threatened by Natalie? No offence, Nat.'

'None taken.'

'When she hear about your call to Nicolas, that you know Jay Merino, and then you say he wants to talk to you when she has tried so long to be the exclusive, it make her go very…' she waggled her head and boggled her eyes '…very mad.' That much, I'd already guessed. 'She know about you, she look you up on the internet. She know about your job in London and was reading *les articles* you sent to Nicolas.'

'That's not creepy at all,' murmured Charlie.

'It is not uncommon to check out a rival,' said Giselle, and I was almost flattered for a moment to be considered one. 'She think you are very trashy writer.'

'Charming.' It didn't come as a surprise, but still stung.

'She's not trashy,' Charlie said hotly. 'You and your aunt should check out an article Natalie wrote about bitchy women like you. It's been trending on Twitter,' he added. 'You could learn a thing or two.'

'It's trending?' My heart bumped. 'I didn't know.'

'It's been retweeted loads,' he said keenly. 'I didn't even know you'd put it online.'

I tucked his words to the back of my mind and turned to Giselle, trying to recall if I'd seen her that day, in Saint-Martin. There'd been quite a few extras milling about, but I hadn't really paid them any attention. 'So, you saw me talking to Jay.'

'It was no big plan,' she cut in. 'At first, I do not think about it and say nothing because,' she flicked a look at Charlie, 'I was supposed to be at dentist.' She gave a quick sigh. 'Then, I was having my cigarette when you come out here with Charlie.' She threw him a hangdog look. 'I go through gate because I do not want anybody to see my smoke, then I hear you talking about…' her eyes widened in wonder. 'About *everything*,' she said, and suddenly it all made sense. 'All the things you talk with Jay about, for interview. I know who X is, because I saw you when you jump on him. I know you know him.'

I remembered the things I'd confided to Charlie and felt sick to my stomach at the thought of Giselle overhearing. 'And you went straight to your aunt and told her what you'd heard?'

'Not so simple.' Her voice was quiet.

'Oh?' I caught Charlie's eye. He made a 'what the hell is happening?' face. I shook my head. *I haven't a clue.*

'I tell her I know a way that will let her do the exclusive with Jay Merino and maybe she will get to be in charge of the magazine, but I want her to promise me something.'

I felt a stiffness in my spine, as if I was turning to stone. 'What did you want?'

'I want her to ask Jay to let me go in his next film,' she said, a defiant tilt to her jaw. 'If she could do that, then I will make your interview go away.'

'But you heard me say he was retiring.' I couldn't hide the disgust in my tone. 'There won't *be* a next film.'

'That was not good,' she said, with a downward dip of her eyes. 'But still, he could ask director for me. He knows the contacts, the right people to ask.'

'So, Fleur promised, and you anonymously leaked the conversation, giving details no one would know unless they were close to Jay.'

Charlie was shaking his head, his mouth a curl of disgust. 'How did you know he'd agree to talk to Fleur?'

'I did not,' said Giselle. 'But I know that Jay, he is very private and my *tante*, she has interviewed so many men and all of them have been a little bit in love with her, so...' another shrug. 'Why not Jay Merino?'

Why not, indeed?

'Well, your little plan worked,' I said, anger rushing from every pore. 'I didn't get my interview, your aunt did, and no doubt you'll soon be appearing in a Hollywood movie.'

Giselle's expression was pained. 'Fleur, she did not get her interview.'

'What?'

'He did not want to do it.' I let that swirl around my brain while Giselle carried on talking. 'He decided that he would talk on the news channel instead, and there would be no necessity to do the interview. He told my *tante* he always like to protect his private life and he will carry on doing that now more than ever, and he would not change his mind.'

Jay hadn't given Fleur an interview. 'Is that why you were arguing with her, earlier?'

'I know she went to meet with him yesterday. I thought she could still talk to him, or maybe his director, and she said she had tried but it was no good, he was angry.' I remembered Simon saying Jay was in a bad mood when he'd hit the bar with Fleur, but I hadn't guessed he was in a bad mood with *her*.

Giselle had started crying again. 'She said I had to grow up and do it the hard way.' She did a bad impression of Fleur's voice. '"There are no shortcuts to success".'

And yet, she'd allowed her niece to leak a private conversation to undermine me; to sow a seed of doubt about me in Jay and Nicolas's minds, uncaring of the consequences. And even if she'd got her exclusive with Jay, I doubted she'd have kept her promise to Giselle. She didn't believe in supporting women – only using them, or putting them down.

'What are you going to do?' Giselle wiped her nose on the back of her hand and gave me a miserable look. 'Will you put it in your paper, what I have done?'

My anger subsided. In spite of everything, it was impossible not to feel a little bit sorry for her. It must be hard, living in the shadow of her successful, ambitious aunt, and breaking into the acting world was almost impossible.

'We should fire you,' said Charlie. 'What you did was—'

'I'm not going to do anything.' I placed a hand on Charlie's arm to silence him. 'But I want you to do something for me.'

Chapter Twenty-Four

It was relief to find the house empty when I got back. My emotions were seesawing all over the place, and I wasn't sure I could face my parents just yet. I was wrung out by Giselle's confession, elated that Jay had come to the café and wanted us to meet, and warmed by the knowledge he hadn't given Fleur an exclusive after all. No wonder she'd been fuming.

I wondered what Nicolas had made of it; whether her failure to secure an interview would really affect her chances of filling his shoes, or whether he'd been toying with her all along, as he seemed to enjoy doing.

As if I'd somehow summoned him, my phone rang. I recognised his number now.

'Natalee,' he said, sounding full of bonhomie. 'I wanted to say, I 'ave taken your advice.'

'I didn't know I'd given you any.' I padded into the kitchen, desperate for something to drink. I was parched after all the talking, and walking back from the café where I'd left Charlie and Giselle, slipping through the gate to avoid speaking to Dolly. I'd told Charlie it was up to him whether he told her what Giselle had done, or made up something to explain our strange behaviour.

'I 'ave told Fleur she can take over running my magazine next year,' Nicolas said. 'It ees time I repaid 'er for all 'er 'ard work and I know she will do a good job.'

'Wow,' I said, filling a glass with water. 'That's quite a leap forward.'

'I know I am stubborn as a goat, but your words, they woke me up to 'ow truly special she is.' *You've no idea.* 'I wanted to zank you, Natalee.'

It was tempting to tell him just how far Fleur had been willing to go in pursuit of what she wanted, but from what I knew of Nicolas, he'd probably approve; see it as proof of her dedication to her goal. And maybe I still felt a sliver of guilt that I'd 'traded on a past connection' to secure an interview with Jay in the first place, even if it hadn't worked out for either of us in the end. 'I hope you'll both be very happy,' I said instead.

'Maybe you would like Fleur's old job?' Nicolas sounded persuasive with a hint of mischief. 'We are a very 'appy team, 'ere, Natalee. You would fit very well.'

Which showed how little Nicolas really knew.

'I don't think so, but thank you,' I said, without hesitation. 'I appreciate the offer.'

And I did, because it clarified what I *didn't* want. 'Goodbye, Nicolas.'

I stood at the sink, sipping water, letting my feelings swirl and settle until a sweep of excitement rushed through me and I ran upstairs and flung my wardrobe doors wide. What to wear for an assignation on a yacht? No, not an assignation, a *meeting*. Which sounded the same, but with a more businesslike overtone. I still didn't know the true purpose behind Jay's invitation, and could only hope that if he'd wanted to say a final goodbye, he'd have called me, instead of coming to find me – unless he wanted a face-to-face showdown over LeakGate (as I'd started to think of it). If that was the case, I was ready, and I didn't want to be in jeans and trainers this time. Unfortunately, the selection of outfits in my wardrobe hadn't magically altered, and a rummage through Mum's suitcase only confirmed we had vastly different tastes when it came to clothing. As much as I told myself appearances didn't matter, rocking up to the yacht in camouflage jeans and a fluffy cream sweater adorned with a sequinned heart was out of the question. (*Why, Mum?*) I returned to my wardrobe and dithered over a key-hole top I'd gone off since buying (it was meant to showcase my cleavage, but instead, highlighted a mole) and decided it was time to throw myself at Marie's mercy once again.

'Of course you can borrow something, Natalie. Please come in,' she said, after answering my knock right away. 'The black dress?'

'Maybe something different?'

She smiled with obvious pleasure. 'Come with me.'

As I entered the house, familiar voices carried through from the garden. 'Are my parents here?' I said, following her up the narrow staircase. It was lined with a gallery of photos of ballerinas in various poses that I'd noticed on previous visits, but hadn't ever thought to question.

'Yes, they are here.' She glanced at me over her shoulder. 'They are becoming good friends with Larry and Barbara.'

'That's nice,' I said, as she led me down the short landing to her room, which was tucked away down a couple of stairs at the end, affording her some privacy from her guests.

I paused on the threshold, feeling as if I was intruding. 'Are you sure this is OK?'

'Of course, please, do come in.' She sounded genuinely keen, her dark eyes lit with a smile as she waved me forward. I stepped into the bedroom, which was decorated in deep reds with cream and gold accents, reminding me a little of Jay's hotel suite, but on a smaller scale. The walls were hung with small oil paintings, and there was a photo over the double bed of a ballerina in a dying swan pose, her tutu ruffled around her like white feathers.

'You like ballet,' I said, stating the obvious.

She followed my gaze, a smile passing over her lips. 'One of my passions.'

'I had lessons when I was little, but my balance was awful,' I said. 'I used to fall over whenever I had to lift a leg off the ground, or spin around.'

Her laugh was somehow happy and sad at the same time. 'Your mother, she is very lucky to have you.' She crossed to the window and I joined her. My parents were sitting around the patio table with Barbara and Larry, deep in conversation. Mum broke off and looked up, perhaps sensing a movement, her face breaking into a smile. 'Come down,' she mouthed.

Marie leaned past me and pushed the window open.

'I'm going out shortly,' I called, waving to Dad, who looked the most content I'd seen him in ages, his forehead free of worry lines. 'You look like you're having fun.'

'We are, honey,' said Barbara, and Larry nodded his agreement. 'Your daddy's a hoot!'

'Everything OK?' Mum shielded her eyes, as if to get a better look at my face, no doubt wondering about my rush to get to the café earlier, when I'd asked them not to come in with me, despite Mum wanting to try a pastry and meet Charlie's mum.

'All good!' I gave a jaunty double thumbs-up to prove it. The last thing I wanted was to spoil their evening by outlining what might lay ahead for me if things didn't go the way I hoped. 'I'll see you later.'

'Be careful,' Dad called, as if I'd never been out before. 'Make sure your phone's with you at all times.'

'I will.' I rolled my eyes at Mum, who smiled and blew me a kiss, and when I turned back to the room, Marie had opened her wardrobe and laid out several outfits on the bed. 'Are you not going to join them?' I said. She'd answered the front door so swiftly, she couldn't have been outside, and I wondered why.

'I am preparing dinner.' She didn't look at me, and while it was true there were savoury aromas wafting through the house, I had the feeling it was more than that. Perhaps she was no longer comfortable with Dad, now that Mum was here. 'Your father,' she said, as if picking up my train of thought, fingering the fabric of a gorgeous pleated dress in subtle rainbow colours, 'I think he loves your mother very much.'

I felt a squeeze of emotion in my chest. 'I don't think he ever stopped,' I said gently. I wanted to capture her hand in mine because it was plain – at least to me – this wasn't what she'd hoped for. 'I'm so sorry, Marie.'

'Never be sorry for love.' She lifted her gaze and I caught a glitter of tears behind her eyes, and something else that told me this wasn't the first time she'd been disappointed; that she'd even expected it. For a fleeting moment, I was cross with Dad for getting her hopes up, for letting her think there might be more (even *I'd* thought there might be) but I knew – and sensed she accepted too – that love couldn't be manufactured, or the pieces forced into place. I'd tried too long with Matt to make us fit, and he had too for a while, but in the end, it had to come naturally to work. 'I am truly happy for them,' she said.

I couldn't help but be impressed by her generous spirit. 'You'll find someone who deserves you,' I said impulsively. 'And who'll appreciate your amazing cooking as much as we do.'

She laughed. 'I hope to find a man who will cook for *me*.'

'Quite right,' I said, flushing a little at my blatant stereotyping. 'Maybe one day a stranger will book a room here, and your eyes will meet across the doorstep and you'll know.'

'I think those things only happen in the movies,' she said firmly. 'And I am fine on my own.' Then, with an almost girlish smile, she held the dress against herself and danced an elegant twirl that made me think that she might be the woman in the ballerina photos.

'I think this will be perfect for you, Natalie,' she said, before I could form a question. 'Try it on and we will find something to cover your arms in case of a chill.'

An hour later, I barely recognised myself. True to her word, Marie had picked out a floaty cardigan that seemed to shimmer and change colour as it caught the light, and complemented the dress, which – as predicted – looked perfect in that mysterious way Marie's clothes seemed to do. The silky-soft material swayed around my calves as I climbed in the taxi I'd booked to take me Saint-Martin, and I was glad I'd thought to bring some wedge-heeled sandals from England. It was the first time I'd worn them here and the extra couple of inches was empowering.

I'd left my hair down and fixed the curls with a styling spray I'd been meaning to try for ages, so it looked shiny and swingy and less like the result of a cartoon electrocution. As I checked my face in my compact mirror (which was really getting some use), I hoped I wasn't overdressed for a trip on a yacht. Sailor pants and nautical stripes sprang to mind, but I felt good in my outfit, and if this was to be the last time I saw Jay, at least he'd remember me as the elegant woman in the rainbow dress with good hair, and not the idiot in torn jeans, crimson-faced and wheezy from running up a lighthouse.

As we drew nearer to Saint-Martin, I tried to focus on breathing deeply while gazing at the scenery, but was reminded of the night

Simon had driven me to see Jay. I was practically sipping the air by the time we arrived at the harbour, and I massively over-tipped the driver, who was delighted, insisting on helping me out as if I was a duchess.

'*Que tous vos problèmes soient des enfants et que tous vos enfants soient sans problems,*' he said with a wink, which roughly translated as *May all your troubles be little ones, and all your little ones be trouble-free* – a saying I'd heard from my grandmother a long time ago.

'It is an Irish wedding toast,' he said, proudly. 'My grandparents came from Dublin.'

I was reading too much into it, but his words felt like a good omen. Buoyed up, I strolled along the cobbled street and past parked bikes and cars, as the surrounding cafés and restaurants got busy for the evening. The atmosphere was jolly, music, chat and laughter drifting on the air, which was rich with mouth-watering smells. As I passed a table piled with crustaceans on an iced tray, my stomach grumbled with hunger, even though I wasn't keen on crabs or lobster.

I was early, but didn't linger, heading straight to the concrete jetty where the boats were moored, treading gingerly as I ascended the stone steps. The last thing I wanted was to take a tumble and end up being stretchered to hospital with a fracture.

There were several yachts of different shapes and sizes lined up, but it was easy to spot *Moonlight*, which reared above the rest, its name in sloping blue letters on the sleek white fibreglass side. I stood and admired it, trying to picture myself on board with Jay, sailing out on turquoise water to find a cove where we could drop anchor. We'd have a light supper on deck, and drink champagne while we talked, and we'd watch the sun go down, before making love in a comfortable cabin, and be lulled to sleep by the gently rocking boat.

Obviously, this cinematic scenario would depend on a couple of things: Jay turning up; his sailing skills (there were alternative versions, where the boat hit a rock and sank, or a terrible storm sprang up and one of us – probably me – dropped overboard and drowned) and whether we could put to rest the matter of who had talked to the press, which depended on someone else showing up.

I turned, looking back the way I'd come, praying she would keep her word. My phone vibrated and I pulled it out to see a message from Charlie.

Have fun tonight, hope it goes well. Give him a fist-bump from me.
PS can he introduce me to Susie Houlihan? (just kidding. Not.) X

Even as I smiled, my nerves resurfaced. I checked the time. Jay would be here soon, but I couldn't get on the yacht with him until… my head lifted. *Thank God.* She was trotting down the steps, her blonde hair flapping as a breeze sent a cloud scudding across the evening sun. I lifted a hand in greeting, but she didn't wave back. I guessed she was nervous too and felt grateful she'd come at all. I didn't have a backup plan.

'Hi Giselle,' I said, when she reached me. 'I'm glad you're here.'

'Hello.' She plucked a strand of hair from her pale lips, her wide grey gaze briefly meeting mine, and gave a little shiver. She was wearing a flimsy T-shirt with her jeans and without the sun, the air felt cool. I was glad of Marie's cardigan and drew it around me. 'You look nice,' she said, wrapping her arms around her waist. I was struck by how young she looked and how, with no Charlie to impress, she seemed less antagonistic. 'He is here?'

'Not yet,' I said, glancing across the harbour to the hotel. A dark-clad figure emerged, and my heart jumped as he began the walk that would bring him around to where we were waiting. This time, even from a distance, there was no mistaking it was Jay. 'He's on his way.'

'It is better like this,' said Giselle, a determined set to her jaw. 'I do the right thing.'

Better late than never. 'Good.'

'I read your blog,' she said, casting her gaze to her black lace-up sneakers, her hair blowing across her face. 'I'm sorry if I think you are into Charlie.'

'Even if I was,' I said, 'you shouldn't be mad at me.'

'But you have to fight for your man.'

I thought of Mum, letting Dad slip away, even though she loved him. Would she have come over if Dad hadn't called, worried about me? I had a feeling she'd have found an excuse, after I'd let slip that he was 'dating'. 'Charlie wasn't your man,' I said. 'He told you he wasn't interested in having a relationship with you.'

She looked up, pouting her lips. 'Because of you.'

I shook my head, thrusting my hair back as the breeze grew stronger and pushed it across my face. 'Because of *him*.'

Her brow puckered. 'You mean, because of me?'

'No, I don't.' I was hardly qualified to lecture on love and relationships, but felt somehow ancient and wise compared to Giselle – as though I'd lived many lives. 'You're not right for Charlie, but you will be for someone else,' I said. 'And when you meet him, you won't need to fight.'

She looked at me for a moment, her big eyes very clear, in spite of her sobbing session earlier – the sort of sobbing that would have left me practically blind for days. 'Maybe I like to fight,' she said, a ghost of a smile crossing her face. 'It can be fun.'

'As long as you don't mind losing,' I said. 'And as long as you know when to walk away.'

'I think, now, maybe I will be a better person.'

'Don't take advice from your Auntie Fleur,' I said, looking past her for Jay.

'*Auntie*,' she repeated, doing a good impression of my accent. 'I like that.'

I almost felt bad now for extracting a promise from her to meet me here this evening, to tell Jay to his face that she was the one who'd talked to the press with the intention of ruining our interview, in exchange for a favour from Fleur.

'Have you told her you're doing this?' I said.

She shook her head. 'I do not want to speak to her for now.' She looked pensive. 'I need to go away for a while. Maybe to London. I know friends who are there.'

'Did Dolly fire you?' I said.

She frowned. 'Fire?'

'Have you lost your job?'

She hugged herself tightly as goosebumps pinged up on her arms. 'Dolly, she heard our talk,' she said. 'Like I heard you and Charlie.' Her mouth twisted, as if she got the irony. 'She was not happy at all.' She shook her head. 'She said to me to go.'

'I'm sorry,' I said, because in spite of everything, I was, but Dolly was such an open and fair-minded person, I knew she wouldn't ever trust Giselle again.

Giselle gave a little shrug. 'It is best I start over,' she said. 'Be fresh.'

'A clean slate,' I said.

'I like these words, they are funny.' I'd never noticed she had a dimple when she smiled – probably because she'd never smiled at me. 'A clean slate.'

As a figure appeared at the top of the steps, my pulse rate rose. 'He's here,' I said, attempting to hold my hair down and smooth my dress at the same time. 'Ready?'

She blew out a little sigh. 'I am ready. And, Natalie...' I tore my gaze from Jay's approach, resisting the urge to run towards him. 'I am sorry,' she said.

Chapter Twenty-Five

Jay slowed as he reached us, as if suspecting an ambush, glancing from me to Giselle with a wary frown. I didn't get a chance to explain why she was there as she cleared the distance between us and started talking fast, as if she was being timed.

'I didn't understand much of that.' Jay looked to me for help when she paused for breath. 'I'm afraid my French isn't very good.'

'She's apologising,' I said, my eyes taking in every detail before settling on his face. When he smiled, my stomach did a forward roll, and it was an effort to return my gaze to Giselle. 'Say it more slowly, in English, if you can. I'll help translate if you can't.'

'I cannot believe I am talking to Jay Merino.' Her eyes were glossy with sudden, girlish excitement. 'Maybe we can do a selfie?' I gave her a hard stare. 'Sorry, that is improper of me.' She puffed out her cheeks and blew out a breath and Jay, who'd been watching me with an unreadable expression, refocused. As she began to talk again, it started raining softly. So much for styling my hair. Within seconds it would go poofy, like Monica's in *Friends* when they went to Barbados, but bigger.

'Hang on.' Jay's expression was as dark as the raincloud overhead. He held up a hand, pausing Giselle's halting explanation. 'You leaked a private conversation between Natalie and her friend about me, to get a part in a film, and Fleur Dupont is your *auntie*?'

I'd almost giggled when Giselle had said it, but for Jay – hearing the truth for the first time – it must have been galling, to say the least. 'Why did she think I'd speak to her, after I'd already talked to Natalie?' He shot me a look and I wondered queasily whether he was angry that I'd repeated our private chat to Charlie – a fact I hadn't even mentioned; I'd been so convinced the leak must have come from someone in Jay's camp.

'She has always got what she wants in the past.' Giselle seemed oblivious to the lightly pattering rain and even with her hair reduced to rat-tails, she still looked stunning – like Rachel McAdams in *The Notebook* before she kisses Ryan Gosling. 'But, I think, she did not even care, as long as Natalie did not do the interview for *Magnifique*.'

'She didn't want me getting my foot in the door,' I said. 'But it's fine, because I don't want my feet anywhere near the door now.'

Jay's expression was tense with concentration. Rain glistened on his hair and the shoulders of his shirt were damp, but if he'd noticed he didn't react. Overhead, a seagull gave a lethargic squawk, as though it couldn't really be bothered. 'What am I supposed to do with this?' he said.

'I am telling you so you know it was not her.' Giselle inclined her head in my direction and Jay's eyes followed. 'Although, if she had not talked, there would be nothing for me to hear.'

His eyebrows lowered. 'You're really passing the blame?'

'It's true,' I said wretchedly, the impact of Giselle's words hitting home. 'I shouldn't have talked to anyone, but after our meeting, I was overwhelmed and had to tell somebody. I didn't think for a moment it would go any further, Jay. I'm so, so sorry.'

He shook his head, but whether it was a rejection of my apology, or an attempt to shake raindrops from his hair was hard to tell. 'How did you find out?' he asked me.

'It was my bad habit.' Giselle took up the story again, keeping her arms folded. 'She saw me smoking my cigarette from the room above the café, and then with Fleur at the hotel in Saint-Martin.'

'I put two and two together,' I said miserably.

'Lucky, really.' Jay's face was stern as he looked at Giselle. 'We'd never have known, otherwise.'

'Lucky, yes.' Giselle seemed to have run out of steam, her shoulders dropping. The rain had stopped as suddenly as it had started and the sky began to clear. 'I will go now,' she said, looking dejected. 'Can you forgive me?'

I looked at Jay, who hesitated, then nodded. 'What you did was… it was wrong,' he said. 'And it's Natalie's forgiveness you should be asking for really, but I appreciate you telling me the truth.'

'I had to, or they talk to my *tante* and my family will find out.' She gave one of her eloquent shrugs. 'But, also, I am truly sorry.'

She looked for a moment as though she might try to hug Jay, her arms moving out from her sides, but instead she moved past him and walked quickly back the way she'd come without looking back, reminding me strongly of Fleur.

'I… don't know what to say.' Jay ran a hand over his damp hair. 'That wasn't what I was expecting when I came out.'

The rain had lifted a warm scent from the ground that filled my senses. 'I know,' I said, gripping the edges of my cardigan across my chest. 'I'm so sorry to spring it on you, but I couldn't get on that boat with you until you'd heard what had happened directly from her.'

'Just so you know, I do trust you.' He held out a hand, then let it drop to his side. 'I knew you wouldn't have talked to the press, but I did wonder how else word could have got out.'

'I really am sorry,' I said quietly. 'For not keeping my big mouth shut.'

'You've every right to talk to your best friend,' he said, emphatically. 'There's no way you could have known you were being listened to, or what she would do with the information.'

'Even so…'

'No.' He held up both hands, cutting me off. 'You've nothing to be sorry for.'

The sun pierced the clouds, spilling shafts of light onto the water behind him.

'You didn't suspect Simon?'

His head jerked. 'Definitely not,' he said, with absolute conviction.

'Maybe you should tell him.'

He gave me a short, sharp look. 'Why do you say that?'

'He called me last night,' I said. 'He told me he thought you suspected him, because you'd been asking him questions.'

Jay shook his head, and briefly closed his eyes. 'I asked if he recalled seeing anyone in the garden when you came to the hotel, that's all. I didn't for a moment think it was him.'

'Well, he's worried that you do.'

'I thought he was in a funny mood today.'

'And he's not here tonight.' I looked across the sparkling harbour, half-expecting to see him watching us through binoculars.

'He took off somewhere,' said Jay, pressing his fingertips to his forehead. 'I thought maybe he wanted to spend the evening with Susie, but now I know why. He thinks I don't trust him any more.'

'Maybe you should go and talk to him.'

Jay looked torn. 'Later,' he said finally, lowering his hand. 'I'm here because I wanted to see you, and I don't have long. I have to be at the airport at midnight.' My heart clenched at the look in his eyes, and the thought of him leaving. 'I wasn't sure you'd even come.'

I struck a silly pose. 'Well, here I am.'

His face cracked into a grin. 'You look lovely, by the way.'

'Hardly,' I said, fingering a spiral of hair. 'I don't suit the rain.'

'You do in that dress. It's like…' he drew back for a better look. 'I don't know what that colour is, but it makes me think of rainbows or mermaids, or unicorns… or something.'

I laughed. 'I'll tell Marie, she'll love that.'

'Who's Marie?'

'A friend.' I realised we had so much to say; so many things we'd yet to discover about each other, and a few precious hours together to talk, before he left for Budapest. 'So, what about this yacht?' I said, swivelling to look at its shiny hull, which glittered with raindrops in a ray of sunshine. 'I've never been on one before.'

'In that case…' Jay squared his shoulders and crooked his elbow and I slipped my arm through his. 'You're in for a treat, Mademoiselle.'

The sun deck was slippery with rain, but the interior of the yacht made me catch my breath with delight. Bathed in soft light, its cream leather sofas and velvety grey carpet exuded a quietly luxurious air, while art deco touches in black and silver added a retro feel. 'It's gorgeous,' I breathed, feeling as if I'd stepped into another world.

'I must admit, it's fancier than I expected,' said Jay, sitting on a large, deeply padded swivel chair like something from the *Starship Enterprise*. 'The charter company have obviously laid on their very best vessel in our honour.'

'In *your* honour,' I said. 'You are Jay Merino, after all.' I ran my hand over a shiny, glass-fronted drinks cabinet, then quickly wiped off the smudges with the edge of my cardigan. 'I expect Joe Bloggs would have had to make do with an old dinghy.'

'Well, there are some perks to being Jay Merino,' he acknowledged, a smile in his eyes. 'Though, I doubt there are any old dinghies on the Île de Ré.'

'Probably not,' I conceded. 'It doesn't even feel like we're on the water,' I added. I'd expected the yacht to be pitching up and down.

'That's because we're not really.' His smile was warm enough to make me forget I was cold and damp. 'Are you ready to set sail?'

I felt a throb of excitement and ignored the sight of my curls, pinging in all directions in the reflective surface of the cabinet. 'You really know how to drive this thing?'

'Come and watch, if you don't believe me,' he said. 'You do know it's motor powered, not a sailing yacht with sails and keels and rigs?'

'Of course,' I fibbed. 'Shame, though. I was looking forward to you shouting *starboard, hoist the pulley* and…' I racked my brain for sailing terms. 'Hopefully, not *abandon ship*.'

He laughed, engaging in some heavy-duty eye contact. 'I do know how to sail, but I wanted us to relax and have something to eat, if that's OK with you.'

'Absolutely not,' I joked, my heart pulsing hard in my chest. 'What is there to eat?' My eyes fixed on his lips.

'There's a fully stocked fridge, if you want to check it out,' he said, rolling up his shirt sleeves as he rose from the swivel chair. 'I'll power her up and get us out on the water.'

'Why are boats always referred to as "she"?'

'I don't know for certain, but a couple of theories are that men tend to name them after important women in their lives, or it's an ancient custom derived from Old English texts, which referred to inanimate objects as "she".'

'Not just a pretty face,' I said, impressed. I had the feeling again that, despite not having a clue about the little things, like how he took his coffee (did he even drink coffee?) or which side of the bed he preferred (I hoped it was the right), I'd known him a very long time. Watching him move towards me with a look of intent on his face, a pin-bright happiness welled up inside me and I knew I was going to savour every second of what happened next.

He looked as if he was thinking the same thing, lips shaping a sexy smile, but as he reached for me, a groan emerged from behind a glossy black door I'd assumed opened onto a cabin, containing a sizeable bed. 'What was that?'

'I don't know.' Jay's face darkened. 'Sounds like we have a stowaway.'

'But… who else has access?'

'Simon filled in the paperwork and picked up the keys earlier today, so maybe he has a spare.'

Another groan, followed by a crash, had us surging towards the door. Jay grabbed the chrome knob and pulled it, and we rushed through to see a half-naked Simon on the floor by the bed, an empty whisky bottle at his side.

The blood rushed from my head as Jay crouched at his side and put two fingers to his neck, as I'd seen paramedics do in TV dramas, and I scanned the cabinet by the bed for signs of scattered pills. There was only an empty glass and a paperback copy of *Pride and Prejudice*.

'He has a sensitive side.' Jay had caught my stunned gaze.

'Is he OK?'

Simon had begun to mumble and shake his head, as though in the grip of a nightmare.

'He's not dead, just drunk,' said Jay.

I felt a savage relief. 'Thank God for that.'

Simon shot bolt upright, his eyes bright and unfocused. It was stuffy and he was sweating like a water-sprinkler. 'Jus 'ad a lil snifter, thass all.' His beard was unkempt and his tattooed torso gave off an air of menace in the softly lit cabin – until I looked more closely and made out a pair of cherubs, the word *Mum* in curly script and a guardian angel spreading her wings.

'Like I said, a sensitive side.' Jay was apparently reading my mind. 'He doesn't feel pain, that's why he has so many tattoos.' He moved behind Simon and slid his hands under his armpits. 'Come on,' he said firmly, face clenched. 'Let's get you on the bed.'

'Wanted to have a lil shower,' Simon muttered, twirling his hand to where his T-shirt lay in a crumpled heap on the floor. 'Thought I'd try a lil drinkie first.'

'More than a little,' Jay said with a stab at jollity.

I rushed to help, relieved that Simon's lower half was clothed, but it was like trying to shift a boulder. I could just about heft up one of his tree-trunk legs and Jay wasn't having much luck at the other end. 'Christ, he weighs a ton.' His face contorted with effort as he tried again, and Simon threw back his head and began to sing, 'O Sole Mio' in a hearty baritone, emitting potent whisky fumes.

'He likes opera?' I asked, as Jay gave a mighty heave and succeeded in getting Simon's top half on the bed.

'Like I said—'

'He has a sensitive side.'

Jay manoeuvred Simon further onto the bed, so his feet were dangling off the end. 'I'm sorry about this,' he said. 'I haven't seen him this drunk since England crashed out of the World Cup.'

'Why do you think he's here?'

Jay didn't get a chance to reply as Simon rolled onto his side, shoulders heaving as he released a mighty sob. 'You thought I betrayed you,' he slurred. He suddenly lurched to his feet and I took a step back, worried he was about to grab me, but he flung one arm across his chest, like a soldier on parade. 'If you do not trust me, sir, then I must resign,' he hollered.

Oh God.

Jay gave me a helpless look as Simon thumped back down on the edge of the bed, head lolling onto his chest. 'He must have come here to hide out.'

'I feel awful.' I clenched my face in an effort not to cry. 'This is all my fault.'

'No, it's not,' said Jay. 'It was a random series of events and a misunderstanding and it was Simon's choice to get drunk, but if we're going to blame anyone, how about me?'

'What?' I stared through a haze of tears. 'How's that?'

Emotions jostled in his eyes. 'If I hadn't been so stubborn all these years, refusing to do interviews like some…' he flung out an arm, 'like some prissy little diva, it wouldn't have come to this,' he said. 'I've been a bloody idiot.'

Simon dropped onto his back and began to snore.

'No.' I shook my head. 'You haven't been an idiot,' I said, touching his arm. 'You've a right to your privacy and if you hadn't been such a *prissy little diva* as you put it, we'd never have spoken the other day, and I definitely wouldn't be here with you now.'

He looked at me as if I'd given him a fresh perspective. 'I suppose that's true,' he acknowledged, his mouth lifting at the corners. 'I've never really believed in things happening for a reason, but maybe there's something in it.'

An almost musical trumpeting sound exploded from the bed and Simon gave a satisfied grunt and rolled over. Jay closed his eyes and pinched the bridge of his nose while I collapsed into laughter.

'This is not how I imagined this evening turning out,' he said. 'I'm so sorry, Natalie.'

'Shall I make some coffee?' I said, making an effort to pull myself together. 'He could do with sobering up if you've got to get on a plane tonight.'

'Wha's she doin' here?' Simon's voice made me jump. One eye was open, aimed at me like a poison dart. 'Wha's that?' He pointed to my hair. 'Where's Jay?' His hand fumbled at his waistband, as if to pull a gun, some protective instinct pushing through his alcoholic fog. 'Where is he?'

'I'm here,' said Jay, moving to the side of the bed, reaching out a restraining hand as Simon made to stand again. 'Everything's fine.' He looked at me, face shadowed with emotion. 'I think I'd better take it from here,' he said. 'I'm sorry, Natalie.'

The smile fell away from my face as reality rushed in. 'It's fine,' I said, but it wasn't. Jay was famous; he had a bodyguard, who was also his best friend, and a film to finish shooting on the other side of the world. He had a new life planned for when it was over, and he'd known me for less than a week; a week that had nearly derailed him. He was leaving shortly for Budapest, then Hong Kong, then home for a few days, he'd said. Anything could happen during that time, the least of which was Simon's voice in his ear daily, convincing him that I was a bad idea. 'I'll go, I'm only making things worse, anyway.' My stomach convulsed with misery. 'I hope you catch your plane, and good luck with the rest of the film.'

'Natalie, wait,' he said, as I turned to leave, but there was the horrible sound of Simon retching followed by soft swearing from Jay.

'It's fine,' I said again, with forced brightness. 'I'll call you.' It was a stupid thing to say, considering he didn't have a phone, but I hurried off the yacht before he could reply, pausing only briefly for a tearful look at the canopied sundeck, knowing we'd never sit there and watch the sunset.

Chapter Twenty-Six

When I woke the following morning, it was almost a shock to not be lying in Jay's embrace, water lapping the side of the yacht, golden sunshine streaming through the porthole – which was what I'd been dreaming about. Instead, I was alone under my duvet, rain drumming the window panes as though trying to get in, while Jay was in another country.

With a crushing sadness around my heart, I sat up and checked my phone: he hadn't called. He'd be striding round some moody backstreet in Budapest on the trail of his would-be assassin, who couldn't be somewhere ordinary like… well, France.

I hoped he'd managed to catch his plane and resisted the urge to text, now I had Simon's number in my phone. I doubted he would bother passing on any messages. I was sure that, even though Jay would have told him about Giselle, and reassured him he'd never been in the frame, Simon would be relieved I was out of Jay's life and go out of his way to make sure it stayed like that.

And, really, what had I been doing, getting swept up in what amounted to a holiday romance? Not even that. Jay was an actor, I reminded myself. He may not be formally trained, and Max Weaver was hardly famous for his romantic gestures, but he probably knew how to portray the right emotions to get a girl to fall in love with him.

In love. *Was I?* I definitely wasn't Julia Roberts in *Notting Hill*, 'standing in front of a boy'. We were adults, and I needed to get a grip.

Determined not to wallow in regrets – Jay had made plans for his future, it was time that I did too – I rolled out of bed, pausing as I passed Dad's door on my way to the bathroom. There was a murmur of voices and a low laugh from Mum, and I found myself smiling in spite of everything. They'd still been at Marie's when I'd sneaked out of the taxi and into the house the night before, gusts of laughter flowing through my window. The sound had made it hard to pin down my seething thoughts, and after a bout of painful weeping, I'd drifted off to sleep, waking only once in the night to find my cheeks wet with tears.

My face in the bathroom mirror was a mess; cave-dweller hair, mascara-like clown tears down my face (I'd not had the heart to remove my make-up before bed) my eyes slitty and red. No Giselle-style dewiness; I looked like a Halloween mask.

I did my best, with the help of a steamy shower and a tube of foundation I found in Mum's make-up bag by the sink, which promised to 'magic away' all my imperfections. I had a feeling it would take more than a layer of gloop, but it made me look lightly tanned, which was an improvement. After tucking a silky blue top into jeans that felt loose after a couple of days of hardly eating, I made a mental note to drop Marie's dress and cardigan to the dry-cleaners and went downstairs, creeping like a burglar to avoid disturbing my parents. It reminded me of being a teenager, sneaking out of the house to meet Gemma, except it had been midnight, to a furtively planned picnic in the park, not early morning to the kitchen for tea and toast.

There was a packet of Warburtons' crumpets on the side, which Mum must have brought with her, knowing we couldn't buy them in France, along with Cadbury's Creme Eggs and McVitie's ginger nut biscuits. (I'd done a column about it for *Expats*, and readers had written in, reminiscing about their favourite foods.) I popped two in the toaster and while waiting for the kettle to boil, I picked up Dad's notepad and scanned his latest notes.

Hiding behind a car door to avoid a hail of bullets is never a good idea. A whole vehicle between the police and perpetrator would be advisable (a round of bullets would go through a car door like a knife through butter).
Ditto, police officers jumping their cars through ditches, across bridges, and down pavements, so people have to leap out of the way. Running red lights, chasing at speed on regular roads – maybe a field if there's proper access – anything else a certain route to death.

I smiled, and after I'd made my tea and buttered the crumpets, I pulled my laptop out of my bag where I'd left it the day before and, once I'd eaten, began to type. By the time I heard movement upstairs, I'd put together a proposal and a mini-synopsis, highlighting what would make Dad's book special, citing his thirty years with the police force and his British sense of humour, along with a chapter to demonstrate how I thought it should look, and emailed it to the agents I'd made a list of months ago. If none of them bit, I was sure Dad could get his own column somewhere. I might even contact Jackie to ask if she'd like a series of real-life stories from him. He was one of the most interesting people I knew and I had a feeling her readers would think so too. On impulse, I typed her an email before my enthusiasm drained. Although she'd contacted Jools, digging for information about Jay and me, she hadn't actually gone ahead and printed anything – at least, as far as I knew.

I quickly logged into Google and typed in 'Natalie Bright and Jay Merino' but although there were tens of thousands of results for Jay and a few for me, there was nothing linking us together. Bypassing the stuff I'd already read about Jay, I clicked on the link to my blog, which I hadn't had a chance to look at, my eyes stretching when I saw how many people had commented. Several had relayed experiences of workplace bullying by jealous females, and lots more reported being shamed as 'the other woman' when 'he was the one who'd lied about being single'. Tutting at one that complained about feminism having gone too far, I pressed the Twitter icon beneath the post and gasped when I saw how many times it had been shared. There was a direct message, too, from a freckled redhead called Verity.

I just wanted to let you know that I've followed your writing for a while! You retweeted a couple of my posts a while ago, and I wanted to let you know that one of your followers – a radio presenter in the UK – invited me to give an interview about my backpacking experience, and now I write for a travel magazine. Thank you so much, Natalie! Hope to read more of your stuff soon!

In a flash, I knew that that this was what I wanted to do – the thing I'd loved all along. Writing stories for ordinary (or extraordinary) people. They didn't have to be wild and wacky or silly and sexy, like the ones at *Chatter* – though they had their place – but stories that were compelling, that would create a discussion, maybe inform and even uplift. And I wanted to carry on writing for *Expats*, because I liked Sandy and I'd somehow built up a following of people who actually enjoyed my column – even looked forward to it. I was never going to be the next Fleur Dupont or be published in the *New Yorker*, but did

I really want to be? Well, maybe a tiny part of me did, but I'd use that ambition to drive me on and who knew what would happen?

Almost on cue, an email appeared from Jackie.

Hey, Natalie, saw Jay Merino on the news – looks like he's sticking to his 'no interview' policy! Loved your latest blog post, by the way. She read my blog? *I'm attempting to drag Gossip out of the gutter and wondered whether you'd like a regular spot in the magazine, similar to those we sometimes published at Chatter, called 'Talking Point'? Call me to discuss! Jackie x*

Grinning and tearful in equal measure, I quickly replied, telling her I'd call on Monday morning, then typed a message of congratulations to Verity, jumping when Mum and Dad came down, in dressing gowns and slippers, wearing matching smiles. Dad's hair was sticking up at the back, and Mum was clutching an empty wine bottle, which she slid into the recycling bin.

'Looks like you two had a good night,' I said archly.

She fluffed her hair with her fingers and went pink around the ears. 'Very nice, thank you, sweetheart.'

'You're up early.' Dad planted a kiss on my hair, then pursed his lips. I'd forgotten my curls were sticky with styling spray. 'I've been busy,' I said, nodding at my laptop, feeling a bit swirly-headed from all the emotion. 'Getting our writing careers off the starting blocks.'

'Sorry?' He scratched his ear.

'I've got plans for us.' I nodded pointedly at his notebook.

'Oh, that.' He looked at it with little interest. 'It's just a bit of fun really, love. I'm thinking of taking my pilot's licence when I get home. Apparently, Larry flies a plane. He was telling us about it last night—'

'Wait.' I pressed my palms on the table. 'What do you mean, when you get home?'

He swapped a look with Mum. 'I'm thinking of going back to the UK,' he said gently, sitting opposite and securing the belt of his dressing gown, a furrow of anxiety between his eyebrows. By *thinking of*, I knew he'd made up his mind, and felt a plunge of anxiety.

'I thought you liked living here,' I said. 'I know you said it's not home without Mum, but it could be, if she moves here.'

Mum sat next to me and cuddled my rigid arm, and a faint smell of roses wafted over me. Her favourite scent; the one Dad bought her every Christmas. 'I love it over here, but my home's where you grew up,' she said. 'It's where my job is, and my sister and my friends.'

'You've already made new friends,' I said, feeling like I had a few years ago, when they told me they were splitting up – which was odd, when they were apparently back together. 'What about Larry and Barbara. Marie?'

'We can keep in touch,' said Dad eagerly. 'Larry and Barbara are going to come over and visit.'

'And Marie?'

'Not Marie.' He glanced at his hands in his lap, and I could tell he was thinking of the meals we'd enjoyed next door, Marie's attempts at teaching him French and their daily chats. 'She's got her business to run,' he said quietly.

'And the house?' I'd have to dip into my savings if I wanted to stay. And I did want to stay, very much. The Île de Ré was my home now, and not just because of Dad. I had Charlie and Dolly, and Marie, and Sandy, and Jools was coming to stay in a couple of months and… I twisted my mind away from Jay, but it immediately sprang back to his cottage in Sainte-Marie. He'd return one day. *The perfect escape*, he'd said. Just like this place, and the Café Belle Vie, had been for me.

Mum took hold of my hand. 'We thought we'd keep it as a holiday home, so you can stay here as long as you like, unless…' Her eyebrows flew up. 'How did your date go, last night?'

'I'm not planning to move in with anyone,' I said, dodging the question with a little too much vigour, but her words about the house had taken root. I looked around the kitchen and saw myself cooking dinner, writing in the garden when the weather improved – it was still pouring with rain – or bobbing next door to chat to Marie and shopping in Saint-Martin with Dolly, my parents coming over whenever they could. 'That's a good idea,' I said slowly. 'Are you sure?'

They nodded in tandem, their smiles almost reaching their ears, and I knew they must have discussed how to tell me and worried about my reaction – which was clearly ridiculous when I was an adult, but I supposed that's how it was when you had children. 'I'll pay rent,' I said, holding up my hands when Dad started to shake his head. 'I insist. It's about time I started to live like a grown-up, and I should have some regular money coming in soon.'

'You can always come back with us.' Mum pulled me into a full body hug. 'You don't have to worry about seeing Matt now he's moving up north.'

'He is?' I drew back in surprise. Matt had seemed so set in his ways, wedded to the town where he'd grown up. He hadn't even wanted us to go abroad on holiday, preferring to stay at the same little Cornish campsite he'd visited throughout his childhood with his family.

'I bumped into his dad,' said Mum. 'His wife-to-be has apparently inherited a house up there and the cost of living's cheaper.'

That would appeal to Matt. He'd never been too keen on spending money. 'Sounds like they've landed on their feet,' I said, examining my feelings for a hint of envy, but there was none. My life with Matt now felt like someone else's – someone who'd had a lucky escape. 'Honestly, I think I'd like to stay.' I squeezed Mum's hand. 'I'm so happy for you both,' I said, pressing a kiss on her cheek.

'And we're so proud of you.'

Dad reached over and took my other hand and we sat for a moment in a companionable silence.

'So, you never intended to do anything with your notes,' I said after a while.

He gave me a sheepish smile. 'I was sort of doing you a favour,' he said. 'Because it was part of your plan when you came here, to help me get published.'

'Oh, Dad.' I aimed a slap at his knee. 'I still say it might come to something,' I said. 'Will you be mad if it does?'

'*Que será, será*,' he said and Mum nodded her agreement.

'*Que será, será*,' she repeated softly.

That just about summed them up, I thought. *Whatever will be, will be*. And, really, who was I to argue?

Chapter Twenty-Seven

I was washing up, mulling over Dad's bolt from the blue (though maybe him wanting to move back to England shouldn't have come as a shock) while he and Mum ambled about, planning an outing with Larry and Barbara, when my phone started ringing.

My heart bounced into my throat.

'Isn't that the music from *Maximum Force*?' said Mum, doing a dramatic dance, twirling her arms and swirling her hips, her dressing gown gaping at the front.

Dad joined in, though dancing didn't really describe his actions: patting the air with his hands and curving his spine as though dodging a kick in the stomach. 'Answer it,' he said, dangerously jutting his pelvis.

I hurriedly dried my hands and grabbed my phone. 'Hi, Charlie.'

'Sorry to disappoint,' he said, picking up on my tone.

'I don't know what you mean.' I watched my parents waltz into the living room – or rather, Dad shifting Mum through the doorway as though handling a fridge-freezer. 'I was in the middle of washing-up.'

'Why aren't you here?'

'What?'

'You come to the café every morning for breakfast.'

I knew he'd be waiting to hear how things had gone with Jay and felt a jolt of grief. 'Well, today, I felt like staying here and eating with my parents,' I said. 'Dad's moving back to England with Mum.'

There was a little silence at the end of the line. 'Are you going too?'

'Course not,' I said, melting a little. 'You can't get rid of me that easily.'

'It's not that far.' His voice was deceptively casual. 'I'd be over every weekend.' But we both knew his commitments at the café meant weekends away were few and far between. 'You know that everyone would miss you? My mum, Gérard, Madame Bisset, Stefan… Definitely Hamish.'

I laughed, a little tearfully. 'They won't have to,' I said. 'But I will be going back to visit quite often.'

'Naturally,' he said. 'I'll miss your dad.'

'They'll be here more than they realise,' I said. 'I reckon Dad's fonder of this place than he thinks. He's going back because he wants to be with Mum and her heart's over there.'

'That's kind of nice,' said Charlie. 'I wish I felt that strongly about someone.'

'You could, if you let yourself.' I wondered how we'd got here so quickly. 'Giselle's gone then?'

'It's for the best,' he said, soberly. 'I couldn't have looked at her the same way, knowing what she'd done.' We were silent for a second and I found myself hoping that whatever came next, Giselle would be OK.

'So, how did Max take it?'

My heart gave a kick. 'You really have to stop calling him Max,' I said, not sure I'd be able to bear watching the new film when it came out, knowing how close I'd got to the man who'd played him. 'He was fine, actually. Glad to know the truth, but…' I let the sentence trail off and didn't pick it up.

'And?'

My sigh spoke volumes.

'Come down right now,' Charlie ordered. 'I'll get the *pains au chocolat* ready.'

The café was in full flow when I arrived, after taking a scenic walk round the marina, sifting through my feelings. I'd tried to hold onto my earlier positivity and to not think about Jay, but without much success. I sat at a pavement table to wait for a lull when Charlie could join me, mindful that they were short-staffed now Giselle had gone.

The rain had stopped by the time I'd left the house, after wishing Mum and Dad a happy trip to Saint-Clément, and the cobbles shone brightly, reflecting the emerging sun.

A group of women strolled by in sunglasses, and people spilled from the café with drinks, or sat outside to enjoy the view. I picked a leaf off the olive tree next to the table and rubbed it between my fingers, managing to summon a smile for Stefan when he came out with my coffee and a *pain au chocolat*. 'Charlie, he says he will be here soon.' He gave a charming little bow. 'You like me to send you photo?' He pointed to my phone on the table and I realised he meant the selfie he'd taken with Jay and the rest of the staff.

'Yes, please,' I said, because that's clearly what I was supposed to say, and a couple of awkward minutes followed while we worked out the best way to transfer the picture, before Dolly rapped on the window, throwing me a wink before she vanished.

When Stefan had scurried off, I opened the photo, bracing myself to look at Jay's lovely smile. Unfortunately, Stefan had sent a photo of himself with his dog – a smiling ginger Spaniel – which reminded me about my column idea for *Expats*.

I let out a cleansing sigh and switched off my phone. I was about to get out my laptop and start working (*actual* working – I was finally done with looking at micro-pigs online) when there was a flurry of movement beside me and somebody sat down.

I looked up, about to point out a couple of vacant tables, and took a sharp breath that made me cough until my eyes burned with tears.

'Not quite the effect I was hoping for.' Jay slapped me on the back, his face concerned. The face I'd looked for just moments ago in a photo, but was *so* much better in real life.

'What… why… what are you doing here?' I spluttered, dabbing my still-tender eyes. The last thing they needed was to have more tears spurting out. 'Budapest.' My voice cracked and I tried again. 'Aren't you in Budapest?'

'I had a word with my director,' he said. 'He agreed I could get a flight tonight instead.' He was grinning, hopefully at my reaction and not because I looked an utter state (*why* hadn't I done something with my hair?). 'I reminded him that I've never shown up late, thrown a tantrum, or missed a day's filming, even when I had the flu and Make-up had to work extra hard because I looked like I'd been exhumed.'

'Was that the second film?' I recalled a scene where he was supposed to wipe out a cable-car full of baddies. 'You looked like you were stifling a sneeze when you jumped from the aeroplane onto the roof of the cable-car.'

'I was.' He nodded slowly. 'I'd already done two takes, so they kept it in.'

'And so did you?'

'Only just,' he said, wincing at the memory. 'It gave me a stonking headache.'

I had no idea why we were taking about sneezing. Jay smiled, as though having the same thought.

'I can't believe you're here,' I said, a tide of emotion sweeping in. I longed to throw myself at him, but made do with saying, 'Where's Simon?'

'In Budapest by now. Recovering from the hangover from hell.'

'Was he very sick?'

'Very.' Jay grimaced. 'And then he was very, very sorry.'

'I'm not surprised.' I shuddered. 'I hate being sick.'

'Well, he *was* sorry about that, but I meant he was very sorry he'd spoiled our evening.'

'He *was?*' I recalled his one-eyed stare from the cabin bed – as though he'd hoped to vanquish me – and realised he'd probably just felt really, really rough. 'Are you sure?'

'Positive.' Jay smiled, as if he couldn't help himself. 'He likes you.'

'He has a funny way of showing it.'

'He wants what's best for me and I know that's being with you.' His eyes and tone were so honest, I had no choice but to believe him. My heart soared, and I felt a new certainty, as if everything was happening the way it was supposed to.

Jay broke eye contact as Charlie materialised, shooting me a gleeful look.

'I thought she wasn't going to turn up,' he said to Jay, drawing up a chair and sitting down, elbows on the gingham tablecloth. 'Of all the days, she doesn't show up today.'

'What are you talking about?' I was struggling to hear my own thoughts over the pounding of my heart. 'Did you know Jay was coming?'

'He rang first thing, to check you'd be working,' he winked on the word 'working' and I narrowed my eyes. 'So, I said, yes, of course, and he said, good, because he was coming to see you.'

'And you didn't show up.' As Jay edged his chair closer, I realised no one was looking at him, even though he'd been on the news just a couple of evenings ago. Maybe it was so unlikely that Jay Merino would be here of all places, he wasn't on anyone's radar. I was the one who could barely take my eyes off him.

Charlie's words penetrated my fuzzy glow. 'You've been at the café already?' I said to Jay.

'About an hour ago.' His warm grin prompted an answering smile. 'I wanted to surprise you.'

'And, once again, I wasn't here.'

'Yup,' said Charlie. 'He said he'd wait, but when you didn't turn up, I called you.'

'Why didn't you tell me he was here?'

'I told him I'd come and meet you.' Jay widened his eyes. 'But we obviously missed each other.'

'I took the long way round,' I said, starting to laugh. It was all so ridiculous – and so completely brilliant. 'Did you go to my house?' *My house.* I liked the sound of that.

'I did,' he said. 'Your dad said you were coming to the café, so I headed back.'

'You've met my dad.' I pressed my hands to my overheated cheeks. 'What did he say?'

'That you'd gone to the café.' Jay raised a droll eyebrow.

'That's all?'

'He said if I was who he thought I was…' He shifted position and cleared his throat. 'He was very sorry about my brother.' I instinctively reached out and smoothed my hand over his. 'And that if I hurt you, I'd be answering to him.'

'Wow,' said Charlie. 'Your dad, warning off Max Weaver.'

'It's JAY,' I said.

'Sorry.' Charlie winced. 'That's what I meant.'

'He said he was on his way to Saint-Clément with your mum and some friends,' said Jay, gripping my hand like a prize he'd won. Charlie noticed and stood up.

'Can I get you anything?' he said so formally, we burst out laughing.

'Actually, I've come to borrow Natalie for the rest of the day.' Jay's words sent a depth charge through me. 'I've still got the boat,' he said to me, sending a thrill to my core.

'In that case, I'll leave you to it.' Charlie squeezed my shoulders as he passed, and when he said to Jay, 'Be good to her,' a lump the size of an orange lodged in my throat. *Dear Charlie.* The best thing about coming to France had been meeting him. Well… I looked at Jay's handsome face. Not *quite* the best thing, but close.

'So, we're definitely going sailing?' I said, as we walked hand in hand to where he'd parked his little white Citroën, marvelling at how bright and clear and beautiful everything looked. Even the scruffiest boat in the harbour had a certain rustic charm, and the seagulls sounded more musical than normal. 'There's nobody hiding in the cabin?'

'There'd better not be.' He turned, pulling me into his arms. 'The only people in that cabin today will be us.'

Us. 'You know, I'm going to miss you,' I said, sliding my hands up his chest. 'When you're in Budapest and Hong Kong.'

'Come with me.'

I pulled back a little and saw he was serious. 'But you'll be working.'

'You can work too.' He flicked the strap of my laptop bag, dangling from my shoulder. 'Writers can write anywhere,' he said, adding in a low voice, 'We'll have a suite at the Mandarin Oriental.'

Excitement built as I imagined looking out at the Hong Kong skyline from the shelter of Jay's embrace. 'Won't I be in the way?'

'Never.' He pulled me back against the warmth of his body. 'The sooner we start sharing the rest of our lives the better, as far as I'm concerned.' I tried to find an argument, but couldn't. 'In just a few weeks, we'll be back here.' His eyes were bright with emotion, inviting me in. 'Home,' he murmured, bending to kiss the space between my neck and collarbone. 'What do you say?'

I didn't have to think very long. 'I say, yes,' I whispered, desire threading its way through my body.

'Really?'

'Really.'

Jay was still smiling when I pressed my lips to his, and although I'd imagined our next kiss would happen on the yacht, with a blazing sunset turning the ocean to gold, it turned out that a car park, in front of cheering onlookers, was every bit as magical.

A Letter from Karen

I want to say a huge thank you for choosing to read *Escape to the Little French Café*. If you did enjoy it, and want to keep up-to-date with all my latest releases, just sign up at the following link. Your email address will never be shared and you can unsubscribe at any time.

www.bookouture.com/karen-clarke

When deciding on a location for my new series, the place that sprang to mind was the beautiful Île de Ré, an island on the west coast of France, not far from La Rochelle. Made up of ten picturesque villages and hamlets, it seemed like the ideal setting for a character looking to start a new life, especially with a cosy café just down the road.

I'm planning a visit to the island with my husband this year, and looking forward to climbing the lighthouse steps at Saint-Clément!

I hope you loved *Escape to the Little French Café* and if you did, I would be very grateful if you could write a review. I'd love to hear what you think, and it makes such a difference helping new readers to discover one of my books for the first time.

I love hearing from my readers – you can get in touch on my Facebook page, through Twitter, Goodreads or my website.

Thanks,
Karen

 www.writewritingwritten.blogspot.com

 karen.clarke.5682

@karenclarke123

Acknowledgements

A lot of people are involved in making a book, and my heartfelt thanks go to Oliver Rhodes and the brilliant team at Bookouture for making it happen. Thanks to Abi, the best editor a writer could wish for and a pleasure to work with, to copy-editor Jennie, proofreader Jane, and cover-designer Emma (I love the new one so much!), to the marketing wizards, and to Noelle and Kim, who work so hard to spread the word and barely seem to sleep.

As ever, I'm enormously grateful to my lovely readers, as well as the blogging community, whose reviews are a labour of love, and to Amanda Brittany for her tireless feedback and friendship, even during tough times.

And last, but never least, thank you to my family and friends for not getting fed up with me talking about my books, my children, Amy, Martin and Liam, for their unwavering support, and my husband Tim, who proudly tells everyone he meets that his wife's a writer – I couldn't do any of it without you.

CPSIA information can be obtained
at www.ICGtesting.com
Printed in the USA
LVHW021234291219
641990LV00014B/815/P